John

MW01673401

The Ferns of Great Britain

Anatiposi

John E. Sowerby

The Ferns of Great Britain

Reprint of the original.

1st Edition 2023 | ISBN: 978-3-38230-414-0

Anatiposi Verlag is an imprint of Outlook Verlagsgesellschaft mbH.

Verlag (Publisher): Outlook Verlag GmbH, Zeilweg 44, 60439 Frankfurt, Deutschland
Vertretungsberechtigt (Authorized to represent): E. Roepke, Zeilweg 44, 60439 Frankfurt, Deutschland
Druck (Print): Books on Demand GmbH, In de Tarpen 42, 22848 Norderstedt, Deutschland

THE

FERNS OF GREAT BRITAIN:

ILLUSTRATED

BY

JOHN E. SOWERBY,

PROPRIETOR OF SOWERBY'S ENGLISH BOTANY.

THE DESCRIPTIONS, SYNONYMS, &c.

BY

CHARLES JOHNSON, Esq.,

BOTANICAL LECTURER AT GUY'S HOSPITAL.

LONDON:

HENRY G. BOHN, YORK STREET, COVENT GARDEN.

MDCCCLIX.

Polypodium alpestre

TO

THE PRESIDENT AND FELLOWS

OF

THE LINNEAN SOCIETY,

THIS WORK

IS

WITH THEIR PERMISSION

MOST RESPECTFULLY DEDICATED

BY

THEIR OBLIGED AND OBEDIENT SERVANT,

THE PROPRIETOR.

THE

FERNS OF GREAT BRITAIN.

INTRODUCTION.

FERNS constitute a series of vegetable productions of considerable extent, amounting to upwards of two thousand known species, the greater proportion of which is found in tropical climates, but very unequally distributed; the general habit of the fern leading it to develop most freely under the joint influence of shelter from the sun and wind, and an atmosphere replete with moisture. Hence the open prairie, the pampa, and the steppe offer conditions most unfavourable to their growth; while the land covered with dense forests, or the mountain with its rocky clefts and caverns, affords the requirements upon which it depends, especially where such occur in association with a warm and vaporous climate. The proportion that ferns bear to the aggregate vegetation of different countries, though in some measure dependent upon such circumstances, conveys no definite idea of their real numbers: thus, when we learn that in the British Islands they compose $\frac{1}{37}$th of the conspicuous vegetation of the land, and in tropical America $\frac{1}{36}$th, we are not to conclude that the numbers in the two countries at all approximate, but that amidst the exuberant development of the torrid zone the ferns maintain an equal proportion to that which they have in our less productive region. The actual amount of species, indeed, almost constantly diminishes with the increase of latitude beyond the tropics.

In a work intended as an aid to the less scientific observers and admirers of natural productions, it is not considered desirable to enter into those minutiæ of organic composition, by which the physiologist is guided in his studies of the relative structures and affinities of the various groups composing the vegetable kingdom; but, as certain general characters appertain to that before us, and as, in describing families and species, it is convenient to employ a few conventional terms, expressive of features and conditions not belonging to other plants, a concise view of the peculiarities by which ferns are collectively distinguished, becomes a necessary introduction to their examination in detail.

With much of the aspect belonging to the higher orders of vegetation, and occasionally rivaling in port and habit the more majestic of their forms, ferns have a structure indicative of a much lower grade in organization, and may be regarded as occupying an intermediate position, or rather as representing the most complicated type of that class characterized by the absence of flowers. They are, with slight exception, perennial plants, but vary much in habit, and especially in the development of the stem; this is generally either procumbent or it extends itself below the surface of the soil, and from its root-like appearance is denominated a *rhizoma*, though some writers designate it as the *caudex*. Rarely, and almost exclusively in very warm and humid climates, ferns are arborescent, the stem growing erect like the trunk of a tree, when it is called the *stipes*, and in some species attaining a height of forty or fifty feet: it is cylindrical, of equal diameter throughout, and bears leaves only at the summit, like a palm, the necessary result of its growth being only from the termination of the axis. Occasionally a tendency to upright elongation of the rhizoma is observed in some of the larger species of the British Ferns. The leaves, usually termed *fronds*, are generally more or less divided in a wing-like manner, rarely simple or entire: when the divisions extend to the *rachis* or continuation of the leaf-stalk or its branches, the fronds are described as pinnate, bipinnate, or tripinnate (once, twice, or thrice winged), the first or primary divisions being called *pinnæ*, the subsequent ones *pinnules*; when they are only partial, the fronds are said to be *pinnatifid* or wing-cleft, and the divisions are denominated lobes or segments. The disposition of the leaves of plants in the bud, generally regarded by botanists as an important feature, is called their *vernation*, and in the ferns is *circinate* (except in one small group), the divisions as well as the entire frond being coiled inwards previous to expansion like the spring of a watch, a disposition beautifully exhibited by those of some of the larger species.

The reproductive germs of the flowerless plants are very minute, indeed generally microscopic, and, notwithstanding the gigantic size of some members of the Fern tribe, no exception occurs in this respect; their production apparently taking place under different laws to those which regulate the fructifying function in flowering plants: they are not called seeds, but *spores* or *sporules*, and are enclosed in little cases denominated *thecæ*; which, in the ferns, are mostly aggregated in small clusters of different size and shape, termed *sori*, and arise from the veins on the under surface of the frond, or from their extremities upon its margins: in some instances the thecæ, instead of forming sori, are associated in spikes or clusters called panicles, formed by the depauperation of the fructifying frond or of its lobes. The primary development of the thecæ takes place in immediate contact with the vein, and beneath the epidermis or outer covering of the leaf, which is forced up by their enlargement in the form of a whitish membrane, constituting the *indusium* or protecting cover of the sori. During the advance of the fructification towards maturity, the indusium separates partly or wholly from the surrounding epidermis, and subsequently either shrivels and becomes hidden by the bursting of the thecæ, or falls off altogether. In some instances, the opening takes place in the centre, the indusium investing the sorus like a cup, when it is styled, though erroneously, an *involucre*; while in others, the epidermis from both surfaces of the leaf extends beyond the margins, including the thecæ between them, and fulfilling the office of indusium without being regarded as such: occasionally this marginal separation and extension of the leaf-membrane takes place uninterruptedly along the whole edge, but it is often only local and about the soriferous extremities of the lateral veins. In a few genera the indusium cannot be traced, the sori appearing to be produced externally; but this, probably in all cases, arises from the very early period of growth at which the disruption takes place, as careful examination of some species of *Polypodium* readily discovers.

The application of the term *frond* to the leaf of a fern is objected to by some botanists; but the association of organs, that in other plants are simply conservative, with the reproductive function in those before us, is a feature sufficiently remarkable to justify the distinction, and it has thus become almost universally adopted.

The elegance and variety of the foliage of ferns, rendering them valuable objects in amateur cultivation, with the modes of treatment that experience has proved most successful, will be found in detail, accompanying the descriptions of the several species; but, as a previous provision of material is requisite, and a few general rules applicable in most instances, much repetition may be avoided by a short preliminary notice. No plants are better adapted than are the hardy species of ferns, for filling up shaded nooks in the garden and shrubbery, and for covering the sheltered parts of ruins, grottos, and rock-work, or the margins of ponds and fountains; shade and moisture being generally favourable to their development, as is evinced by the natural localities affected by most of the species, which flourish especially under the shelter of woods and thickets, in the crevices of rocks, and in the mouths of wells, mines, and caverns, where they have little light, and enjoy an atmosphere of almost uninterrupted humidity. But while moisture is an important agent in securing, and even enhancing, that beauty which belongs to them in the wild state, drainage is no less necessary to the preservation of the greater number, and must be so far provided as to prevent the lodgement of water in a stagnant state about the roots. The subjoined materials will be found more or less requisite to those engaging in the cultivation of this interesting tribe: viz.

As draining media.

1. Shards, or fragments of garden-pots broken to the size of an inch, or larger.

2. Fragments of sandstone, limestone, slate, &c. for forcing into the soil around the roots, in planting.

3. Charcoal, broken into pieces, from the size of a filbert to that of a walnut.

As soil.

1. Peat, or bog-earth. The best is that of a blackish or dark-brown hue, and spongy texture.

2. Decayed leaf-mould, or rich garden soil.

3. Loam. The best is of a yellowish hue, containing much vegetable fibre.

4. Sand. The white or silver sand being preferable, though not essential.

5. Mortar from old buildings.

Where the collection is large or increasing, a compost, prepared by mixing the first four in equal proportions, is desirable, as being always at hand, and capable of modification as necessity may require. The old mortar is only for occasional use, but a small quantity may generally be added with advantage. The compost should be kept slightly moist, but not wet. In potting, the shards must occupy at the least one or two inches of depth at the bottom; and it is better to place over them a thin layer of moss, to prevent the soil from falling between and interfering with the ready passage of the superfluous water. A few fragments of charcoal should be placed over the moss; and the soil being then thrown in lightly around the root of the fern, and some pieces of stone or slate forced into it vertically, the whole may be settled by watering.

Without referring to the variety of adaptations of which a fern garden is susceptible on a large scale, either as ornamental, or as affording place for the reception of species of every kind of habitat, from the river-side and the swamp to the mountain-rock and the church-tower, I will confine my suggestions as to out-door planting, within the compass attainable by those who have only a small space wherein to operate. Selecting a spot in the garden sheltered from the direct rays of the sun, but if possible not subject to the drip from trees; a bank of loose soil, or common garden-mould mixed with brick-rubbish and old mortar, may be thrown up to the height of from two to four feet above the general level; in which, when settled by the rain or copious watering, so as to avoid farther sinking, excavations of different depths may be made for the reception of those species that require the most moisture, keeping up the surrounding soil with fragments of stone or burs from the brick-kiln. In planting, it is sufficient, in a general way, to supply the compost soil to the extent of five or six inches around the ball of root, as most of the larger ferns readily spread their radicles into the looser and rougher material of the bank. Around the deeper and larger excavations for the marsh and flowering ferns, a wall of loose porous stones or old bricks, with a mixture of sandy peat and decayed mortar spread between them, will afford a congenial site for the smaller rock species, especially those of the genus *Asplenium*; and, if the wall be carried up higher than the adjoining part of the bank, so that the latter may be raised against it, the Common Polypody will be induced to overrun the slope with luxuriance and pleasing effect, its matted rhizomes being at first kept firm, by disposing here and there a few heavy pieces of chalk-flint, or other stones.

It must be understood that the chief recommendations of such a bank, are the facility with which it is constructed, and the insurance of good drainage. Of course the water readily running off the higher parts, renders it necessary that evaporation should be checked as much as possible, and in order to effect this, irregular masses of stone, and cemented brick, from the kiln or the old furnace, may be scattered upon the surface around the roots of the ferns; these will not only retain a considerable degree of moisture beneath, but afford shelter to the foliage, and, carefully selected and disposed, may be rendered more subservient to the picturesque than elaborately constructed rock-work.

Many persons, in following out fancies of the latter kind, with more of the grotesque than good taste, employ the vitrified clinkers from the potteries and glass-works; but, as the object to be obtained is less ornament than utility, I prefer the brick, on account of its porosity and the quantity of water it is capable of retaining; and that the ferns have a similar preference, is evident from the complicated masses of root-fibre and spongioles that form on the surface of the soil, and even ramify into the pores and crevices of these rude masses wherever they have remained for a few months undisturbed.

The classification of the Ferns being very arbitrary and unsettled, and our view comprising only those of a particular locality far from rich in the number of species, I have not considered it requisite to disturb the sequence of the genera by allusion to it in the body of the work. As at present constructed, the British Ferns are included in three principal groups or orders, the characters and genera of which are stated below.

I. POLYPODIACEÆ.

Thecæ collected in sori on the back or margin of the frond, pellucid, reticulated; invested by an articulated, elastic, more or less complete *annulus* or ring. Vernation circinate.

The *annulus* is a continuation of the stalk of the theca; in other words, it is the middle vein of the minute circinate leaf that forms the latter, which is torn open by its extension.

* *Annulus vertical.*

1. Polypodium.
2. Woodsia.
3. Lastrea.
4. Polystichum.
5. Cystopteris.
6. Athyrium.
7. Asplenium.
8. Scolopendrium.
9. Ceterach.
10. Blechnum.
11. Pteris.
12. Allosorus.
13. Adiantum.

** *Annulus horizontal or oblique.*

14. Trichomanes.
15. Hymenophyllum.

II. OSMUNDACEÆ.

Fructification developed upon depauperated portions of a more or less compound frond. Thecæ stalked, membranaceous, reticulated, destitute of annulus, opening vertically with two valves. Vernation circinate.

16. Osmunda.

III. OPHIOGLOSSACEÆ.

Fructification developed upon depauperated simple or compound fronds. Thecæ sessile, coriaceous, opaque, without any trace of annulus or reticulation, bivalvular. Vernation straight.

17. Botrychium.
18. Ophioglossum.

Polypodium vulgare.

Genus 1. POLYPODIUM.

Gen. Char. Sori circular, naked. Margin of the frond not reflexed.

One of the most extensive and diversified genera of the order, chiefly distributed over the tropical countries of the Western hemisphere. Of the four British species, three have been occasionally referred to other genera, on account of the supposed presence of an indusium, noticed by Roth, a celebrated German botanist, but certainly not to be detected, in any stage of development, in those specimens that have passed under my own observation, either wild or cultivated, which latter I have diligently examined at every period of their growth.

The generic name is formed from πολὺς, *many*, and ποὺς, *foot*, in allusion to the form of the branched rhizoma in the most common native species.

Polypodium vulgare. Common Polypody. Tab. I.

Fronds lanceolate, deeply pinnatifid; segments linear-lanceolate, obtuse, indistinctly serrated, approximate.

Polypodium vulgare, *Linnæus*. Ctenopteris vulgaris, *Newman, Hist. Brit. Ferns*, 41.

Very frequent about the roots and moss-grown trunks of trees, on rocks, shady hedge-banks, walls, and old thatched roofs. The rhizoma branches in all directions, the branches, when it has grown long undisturbed, crossing each other and forming a thick mat-like substance: it is at first clothed with a cuticle densely covered with yellowish-brown, membranaceous, lanceolate scales, which, falling off, or becoming obliterated during the winter, leaves the surface nearly smooth and of a yellowish hue. The young fronds begin to appear in May, rapidly attaining the full size, which varies according to situation from the length of five or six inches to that of twelve or eighteen: where much exposed, and at a distance from the ground, they have generally in maturity a drooping habit, and even become almost pendent, but in sheltered localities often retain their original erect position throughout. The rachis is smooth, grooved on the upper face, and bare about half or one-third of its length.

The lateral veins of the segments are alternate, and each divides into from three to five branches, of which the lowest, directed upwards, always terminates midway, while the others are continued nearly to the margin; all of them in the barren segments being thickened in a club-like manner at the extremity. The fructification is, in most instances, confined to the upper divisions of the frond only, but sometimes they are all fertile. The sori, of a bright yellow or orange colour, changing in maturity to brown, are destitute of indusium, and very regularly disposed in a line on each side of the mid-vein, halfway between it and the margin; a disposition resulting from their development at the extremity of the first branch of the lateral vein. In very vigorous fronds the regular dotted line of fructification thus formed is sometimes disturbed, by the production of a sorus at the extremity of one or even two of the upper branches of the same vein; indeed, the thickening of this part seems to be the first stage in the development of the sorus.

The fronds of this fern are in perfection from August to November, but are, in exposed situations, always disfigured by the first frost. Under shelter it becomes evergreen, retaining the old fronds until the appearance of the new ones. In cultivation it does not generally succeed so well as do most of our native species: Mr. Newman observes that it is somewhat parasitic, and I believe he is right, never having been able to keep it in luxuriance, until it was accommodated with a large proportion of decayed wood, moss, and straw, mingled with the compost previously employed, into the interstices of which the delicate root-fibres very soon penetrated, lining every cavity with their brown hair-like spongioles.

Several varieties are met with, distinguished chiefly by the division and serrature of the segments, viz.:

1. *bifidum*, in which each segment is divided at the extremity into two diverging lobes,—not an uncommon occurrence, indeed, in the frond itself.

2. *serratum*, characterized by the more distinct or deeper serratures.

3. *Cambricum*, Welsh Polypody, with a broader frond and the segments irregularly cleft: this is always barren. Linnæus, by whom it was first described, regarded it as a distinct species.

4. *Hibernicum*, Irish Polypody, distinguished by the broader frond being bi- or tri-pinnatifid and fertile. A very striking and beautiful variety, found by Mr. Mackay, in the Dargle, in the county of Wicklow, Ireland.

Intermediate varieties connect all of these with the normal or common form.

The rhizoma is mucilaginous and has a sweetish flavour, but by long boiling it becomes bitter. An infusion of it in a recent state is sometimes administered in the country as a mild cathartic. It was once highly esteemed by the faculty as an expectorant, and especially recommended for hooping-cough; but although still occasionally employed as a domestic remedy, it has long been excluded from the list of orthodox medicines.

Polypodium Phegopteris

Polypodium Dryopteris.

Polypodium Phegopteris. Mountain Polypody. Tab. II.

Fronds triangularly lanceolate, acuminate, subpinnate: pinnæ linear-lanceolate, acute, deeply pinnatifid, with obtuse, entire lobes; the lowest pair distant, deflexed. Sori nearly marginal.

Polypodium Phegopteris, *Linnæus*. Polystichum Phegopteris, *Roth.* Lastrea Phegopteris, *Newman.* Gymnocarpium Phegopteris, *Newm. Hist. Brit. Ferns*, 49.

Not unfrequent in the alpine and subalpine or rocky districts of the south-western and northern counties of England, and in Wales and Scotland; but apparently of rare occurrence in Ireland. Its favourite habitats are moist woods, and shady spots about mountain lakes, rills, and waterfalls. The rhizoma is of a blackish hue, slender, wiry, branching and creeping in every direction, so as often to form a network over the face of the moist rock where there is no trace of soil, striking its hair-like rootlets into every crevice. The fronds make their appearance about the same period, or rather earlier than those of the common Polypody, and are in perfection from July to September: they are of a pale green colour, hairy, and vary from five or six inches to a foot in height, of which the leafy portion occupies less than half, its general outline being triangular, but much acuminated. The pinnæ are mostly opposite, the lowest pair being rather distant from the others and directed downwards and forwards, forming a very remarkable feature by which this fern is readily recognized; they are likewise perfectly distinct, and attached to the rachis by a short stalk: the upper ones, on the contrary, point toward the apex of the frond, and, with the occasional exception of the second pair, are sessile, and attached by their entire base, so as to appear confluent, as indeed those toward the extremity usually are. The lateral veins of the lobes are alternate, mostly simple, and extend to the margin, bearing, each, near the end a small circular sorus, the whole fructification thus forming an intromarginal line of spots.

It is an elegant species under cultivation, spreading very freely, and requiring little attention in planting, except to secure the almost universal requirement of the Fern, shade. Exposure to the sun, though only for a very short time, changes the delicate green hue of the frond to brown, and soon destroys a plant naturally adapted to those moist situations in which alone it luxuriates.

Polypodium Dryopteris. Tender three-branched Polypody. Tab. III.

Fronds ternate, glabrous; branches pinnate, drooping; pinnæ pinnatifid, with obtuse crenated segments. Sori nearly marginal.

Polypodium Dryopteris, *Linnæus*. Polystichum Dryopteris, *Roth*. Lastrea Dryopteris, *Newman*. Gymnocarpium Dryopteris, *Newm. Hist. Brit. Ferns*, 57.

Not unfrequent in dry stony woods and shady rocky places in the mountainous parts of the north of England, and in Wales and Scotland; often very luxuriant about waterfalls, where it is kept constantly moistened by the spray, but rarely in this case producing fructification. The rhizoma, very slender, often almost filiform, spreads widely, forming, with its complicated branches and dark-coloured radicles, a dense turf-like mass. The fronds spring up in April, and present a remarkable form of vernation, the three branches being separately coiled, so as to resemble, as observed first by Mr. Newman, three little balls supported on slender wires. In maturity they vary from three or four inches to a foot in height, are of a pale bright green, perfectly smooth, and supported by an erect, very slender brittle stalk or rachis, clothed with a few scales at the base. A general tendency to droop is characteristic of the whole of the leafy portion of this delicate fern, affecting not only the primary branches, but giving a striking convexity to all of the segments, a circumstance well expressed in our figure. The fronds are mostly barren; the fertile ones rise higher than the others, and are farther distinguished by the comparative narrowness of their segments. The lateral veins of the segments are generally branched, and, where fertile, the sori are produced near the extremity of the uppermost branches; in luxuriant specimens their regular arrangement is often disturbed by development from some of the other branches of the vein. Fructification in June and July.

In cultivation, shade is even more essential to this species than to the preceding. Next to the delicacy of texture and graceful habit, the vivid green hue of the foliage constitutes its principal beauty, and this latter is entirely lost by exposure to direct sunlight. Abundant moisture, though recommended by many, is so far from being necessary to its flourishing condition, that, unless drainage is at the same time complete, it will soon destroy the plant by causing the decay of the rhizoma. Attention to these circumstances will ensure the fact, that one of the most elegant and beautiful of our smaller ferns is likewise one of the most free growers and most easily kept.

POLYPODIUM CALCAREUM. Rigid three-branched Polypody. TAB. IV.

Fronds triangular, subternate, erect, glandular; branches pinnate; pinnæ of the lower ones pinnatifid, with obtuse segments, those of the upper branch nearly entire. Sori marginal.

Polypodium Calcareum

Polypodium calcareum, *Smith.* Lastrea Robertiana, *Newman.* Gymnocarpium Robertianum, *Newm. Hist. Brit. Ferns*, 63.

Apparently confined in its natural growth to limestone districts. Sir J. E. Smith first noticed it as a distinct species, and it is perhaps more frequent than generally supposed. In the rocky parts of Derbyshire it is far from uncommon, occurring among grass and bushes in broken limestone and tufa; the Cheddar cliffs and Ingleborough are other stations; and the growing specimens in my garden are from the vicinity of Kenilworth, where it accompanied *P. Dryopteris*, a species with which it has often been confounded, although in habit and other respects very dissimilar. The rhizoma is thicker and less spreading than that of the latter plant; the frond less distinctly ternate or three-branched, the lower branches being shorter than the terminal or middle one; all the three are rigid, expanding upward on the same plane, and not at all drooping. The colour of the frond is of a dull green, owing to the presence of numerous minute stalked glands that give a mealy appearance to the surface, and similar glands communicate a glaucous hue to the rachis. The sori arising from the extremities of the lateral veins of the segments form a more distinct intromarginal series than those of *P. Dryopteris*, and generally become confluent when the thecæ open.

Being of less compact growth than the last species, and more rigid, it is a much less ornamental plant; but it bears exposure better. Most persons who have had it under cultivation complain of its liability to die off, but I believe this to be the effect of confinement and superabundant moisture: left to itself, few ferns are more hardy, but it likes pure air and perfect drainage. Even in the wild state it cannot be styled a "free-grower," and being a very local plant, its natural condition must be considered as much as possible in our efforts to naturalize it in the fern garden. It flourishes best on a sloping bank, planted near the surface, with an admixture of lime rubbish to the ordinary compost, the ground about it being studded with fragments of stone or burs from the brick-kiln to prevent evaporation. Under these circumstances it does not seem to be injured by daily exposure to four or five hours of the mid-day sun. If grown in pots, they should be large, and about one-third filled with draining material.

Genus 2. WOODSIA.

GEN. CHAR. Sori circular; invested by an inferior involucre, the margin of which is divided into numerous jointed, generally capillary segments.

A very small genus of alpine ferns, named in memory of Joseph

Woods, a British botanist. Chiefly remarkable on account of the singular character of the so-called involucre, which is however only a modification of an indusium, opening in the centre, and splitting more or less regularly into the conferva-like filaments accompanying the magnified sorus in our figure of *W. Ilvensis*. Its true nature is very obvious on examination of the immature sori. The two British species are among the rarest of our indigenous plants: notwithstanding a considerable difference in habit, and in the divisions of the frond, many modern botanists regard them only as varieties.

WOODSIA ILVENSIS. Oblong Woodsia. TAB. V.

Fronds lanceolate, pinnate; pinnæ oblong, deeply pinnatifid, chaffy beneath. Rachis chaffy.

Woodsia Ilvensis, *R. Brown*. Acrostichum Ilvense, *Linnæus*. Polypodium arvonicum, *Withering*. Polypodium Ilvense, *Swartz*.

Only found growing in the crevices of moist rocks about the summits of our higher mountains, and so sparingly distributed in these localities as to be regarded exceedingly rare. The recorded habitats are few, viz. Falcon Clints, Teesdale, Durham; Clogwynn-y-Garnedd, Snowdon, and Llynn-y-cwn, on Glyder Vawr, Wales; and the Clova mountains, Scotland. A careful explorer of the bleak regions over which many other rarities of our alpine flora are distributed, would however probably find reason to conclude that its extension is far less limited. This remark is not one at random; but the wanton appropriation, or it might rather be styled depredation, exercised by certain wholesale collectors, not of specimens only, but of entire plants, has rendered the true botanist, in cases like the present, averse to the promulgation of his discoveries.

The fronds grow in a tuft at the extremity of a very short rhizoma, seldom exceed two or three inches in height, and in very dry or exposed situations are sometimes not above one inch. In general outline they are lanceolate and pinnate, with mostly opposite, oblong, deeply-lobed pinnæ. The under surface is more or less covered with glossy, jointed hairs, accompanied, especially about the mid-veins, by long, attenuated scales, which, with the capillary segments of the indusium, often nearly conceal the sori. The sori are produced at or near the extremities of the lateral veins of the lobes, a crenation of the margin of the latter generally attending their development. They attain maturity in August and September.

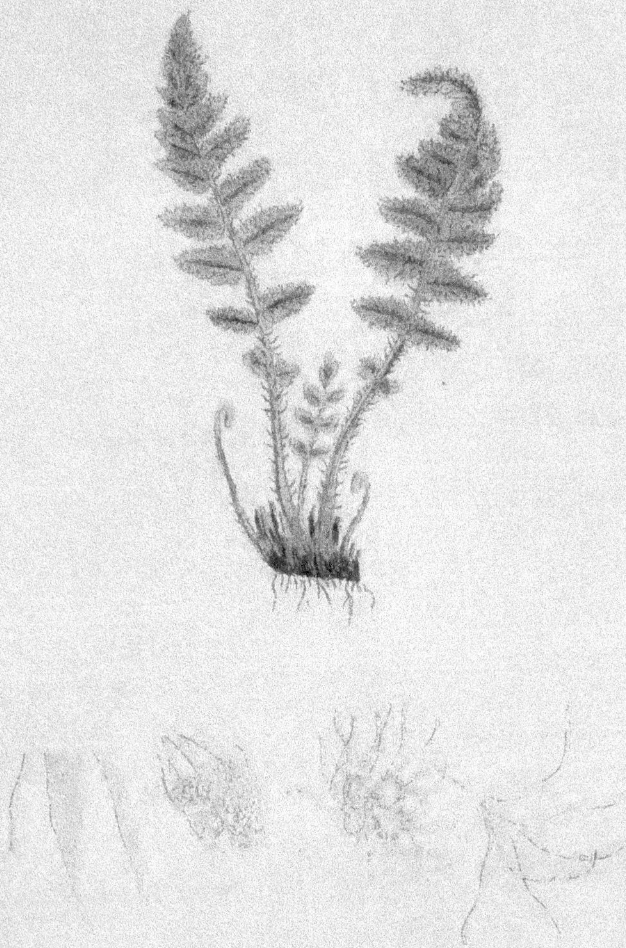

Woodsia Ilvensis

Woodsia Hyperborea.

The hairiness of the rachis, always conspicuous on the young fronds, is sometimes obliterated in their after-growth.

WOODSIA HYPERBOREA. Alpine Woodsia. TAB. VI.

Fronds linear-lanceolate, pinnate; pinnæ obtusely triangular, pinnatifid, with rounded segments.

Woodsia hyperborea, *Brown*. *E. B.* 2023. *Smith*. *Hooker and Arnott*. Woodsia alpina, *Newman*, *Hist. Brit. Ferns*, 79. Woodsia ilvensis, var., *Babington*. Acrostichum alpinum, *Bolton*.

Met with in similar situations as the preceding, but apparently of rarer occurrence. The habitats hitherto recorded are, Clogwynn-y-Garnedd, and Moel Siebog, Snowdon, in Wales; Ben Lawers, Mael-dun-Crosk, and Craig-Challiach, Perthshire; and, according to Dr. Balfour, in Glen Fiadh, Forfarshire, in Scotland. In habit it is not unlike *W. Ilvensis*, but the narrower fronds are of a thinner texture, and less hairy and chaffy; while the pinnæ, almost invariably alternate, are shorter, and nearly triangular in their general outline, and their lobes fewer and more rounded.

Our figures of these two ferns will convey the idea of specific distinction, and those of Mr. Newman, above quoted, are even more decided in this respect; but the comparison of specimens of both from different localities, and even from the same gathered in different years, renders it very doubtful whether they ought to be regarded as other than mere varieties of one species.

For successful cultivation of the *Woodsia*, shade, a moist atmosphere, and perfect drainage about the roots, are points of the utmost importance, and are especially indicated by its natural localities. Owing to their rarity as British ferns, few persons have ventured to plant them in the open air; in which, however, sheltered from the sun in summer, and from the drying easterly winds of spring, I am informed they may be grown luxuriantly. When potted, sandy peat, mingled with a small quantity of yellow loam, broken limestone and slate, affords a soil among which the black wiry roots readily extend; and if the pot be previously half filled with small fragments of stone and sand sifted among them, the plant will not be liable to suffer from the accumulation of moisture. Although a damp atmosphere is favourable during the growing season, these ferns will not bear confinement in close frames or cases; however vigorously they may grow at first, they are soon rendered feeble by the want of a free circulation of air.

Genus 3. LASTREA.

GEN. CHAR. Sori nearly circular, seated upon the back of the lateral veins; covered by a reniform indusium attached by its sinus.

The ferns included in this and the following genus, *Polystichum*, are by some botanists associated under the general name of *Aspidium*, to which genus they are referred in "English Botany." A difference in the form and attachment of the indusium has been considered a feature of sufficient importance to warrant their division. The name *Nephrodium*, originally suggested by Mr. Brown, has given way to that of *Lastrea*, bestowed upon it by Presl in honour of M. De Lastre of Chatelleraut.

LASTREA THELYPTERIS. Marsh Fern. TAB. VII.

Rhizoma creeping. Fronds lanceolate, pinnate: pinnæ linear-lanceolate, pinnatifid; lobes oblong, obtuse, the fertile ones with revolute margins. Sori submarginal.

Lastrea Thelypteris, *Presl.* Aspidium Thelypteris, *Swartz. Smith. Hooker. E. B. the fig. a mistake.* Hemestheum Thelypteris, *Newman, Hist. Brit. Ferns*, 123. Acrostichum & Polypodium, *Linn.*

A very local species, found only in a wet spongy soil, in marshes and bogs; not unfrequent in England and Wales, but rare in Scotland and Ireland. Where met with it is generally abundant, in consequence of its creeping habit, which is not unlike that of the common Brake (*Pteris aquilina*), the long, slender rhizoma growing rapidly, and branching in every direction. It is a colonizer of wet soils, as the latter fern is of dry ones. The fronds are of two kinds, barren and fertile, and spring up at short intervals, never in tufts: the barren ones make their appearance in the latter end of April or the beginning of May, and in their ultimate growth seldom attain more than a foot in height; the fertile, produced about July, are taller, not unfrequently reaching three feet or even four, the lower half or two-thirds of the rachis being devoid of pinnæ. The lateral veins divide in pairs about halfway between the mid-vein and the margin, and, in the fertile fronds, bear the sori, one on each division, forming thus an intromarginal series just within the recurvation. In maturity the sori become confluent, and all traces of the reniform indusium are obliterated.

The species is a very elegant one, and not at all difficult of cultivation; it does not seem to be injured by moderate exposure to the sun, provided the soil in which it is planted be sufficiently

Lastrea Thelypteris

Lastrea Oreopteris.

retentive of moisture to prevent the roots from becoming withered during dry weather. I have grown it for many years on the same bank with *Polypodium calcareum, vulgare,* and other rock and epiphytic species, planting it at first in a hollow less than a foot below them, and covering the rhizoma with pieces of peat turf and fragments of stone and brick. The fertile fronds under these circumstances attained a height of nearly three feet, although under the influence of the direct rays of the summer sun from eleven o'clock until two. This circumstance is referred to, because it is a common notion that in the cultivation of bog or marsh plants abundant moisture is most essential to their luxuriance, and the unlimited supply furnished in consequence too frequently occasions their destruction. The Marsh Fern will endure a more continued maceration of its roots than most others, but in lieu of forming an undrainable bed for its reception, as often recommended, it would be following nature more closely were we to permit all unabsorbed water to filter through the subsoil. My own specimens (originally brought in their native turf from Epping Forest) are grown in the black peat of Wimbledon Common, laid about four inches in depth on the common garden loam, and covered as mentioned above, for the purpose of preventing the evaporation that would take place if the soil were left bare. Their share of the general watering is all that the plants receive, and they have flourished for six years under this treatment.

Lastrea Oreopteris. Heath Fern. Mountain Fern. Tab. VIII.

Fronds tufted, lanceolate pinnate: pinnæ linear-lanceolate, pinnatifid, sprinkled with resinous glands beneath; lobes oblong, obtuse, flat. Sori marginal.

Lastrea Oreopteris, *Presl.* Aspidium Oreopteris, *Swartz. Smith. Hooker. E. B.* Polypodium montanum, *Vogler.* Lastrea montana, *Newman, Hist. Brit. Ferns,* 129. Polypodium fragrans, *Linnæus.*

A native of mountainous and upland heaths and of woods, more abundant in the north of England, and in Wales and Scotland, than in our southern counties, where, however, it is still of frequent occurrence. In Ireland it is considered rare. The fronds make their appearance about the beginning of May, springing in a circle from the apex of the short rhizoma, and attaining a medium height of two or three feet, but varying in different situations and exposures from one to four or even five feet. The general outline is lanceolate; but the pinnæ are gradually shorter from the middle downwards, until, near the base of the rachis, they often wholly lose their pinnatifid character, and assume that of small triangular leaflets with serrated margins. The under surface of the lobes is profusely sprinkled with minute, glossy, gold-coloured, glandular globules, which give a rich golden hue to the expanding fronds, that renders this beautiful fern very conspicuous when planted among others. To the secretion by these glands is probably due the peculiar odour of the fronds when bruised, which, being far from unpleasant in the open air, occasioned Linnæus to name the species *Polypodium fragrans*. The ordinary venation of the lobes, and the position of the sori, are shown in our figure; but, it may be remarked, that the latter are sometimes much more crowded, in consequence of the lateral veins dividing, as exhibited in the two lower ones, and bearing a sorus on each branch.

Many persons complain of a difficulty in rearing or establishing *L. Oreopteris*, and of its liability to dwindle and die under culture; and there seems to be a diversity of opinion respecting the soil and treatment that it requires, even among those whose experience is far from being limited. Thus, one recommends it to be planted in well-drained pots, with an admixture of turfy peat, broken charcoal and sand, and kept only moderately supplied with water; while another plants it in yellow loam, without any admixture of other soil, and keeps the pots constantly standing in water. Both methods may succeed; but the open air and free ground answer better than either. And, in regard to soil, a plant that in a state of nature grows here in the yellow loam, there in the black peat, and elsewhere in the fissure of the sand-rock, or on the side of the gravel-pit, can scarcely be much affected by the difference. A very good general rule to follow in the transplantation of the wild fern, is to carry with it a portion of the soil in which it grows; or, at least, to imitate this as nearly as possible. And I believe the reason why *L. Oreopteris* often fails, is, that this rule is not attended to; and that the plants, having their constitution adapted to the situation where their seedling growth commenced, do not readily change it under the new conditions in which they may be placed.

Some slight general resemblances between this species and *L. Thelypteris*, especially in the form and proportions of the frond and in the marginal fructification, which might mislead an inexperienced collector, render it necessary to remark upon the more obvious features by which they are distinguished. The fronds of the present species always grow in tufts; they are leafy almost to the very base of the rachis, which latter is copiously covered with pale brown scales, while in *L. Thelypteris* it is nearly smooth, and in the lower part devoid of pinnæ through about one-third of its height. The golden glands, and the perfectly flat instead of recurved margin of the fertile lobes, are characters—especially the former—that, if attended to, render it impossible to confound the plant before us with its congener.

Lastrea Filix-mas

LASTREA FILIX-MAS. Male Fern. TAB. IX.

Fronds tufted, lanceolate, bipinnate: pinnæ linear-lanceolate; pinnules oblong obtuse, serrated. Sori in a line on each side of the midvein.

Lastrea Filix-mas, *Presl.* Aspidium Filix-mas, *Swartz. Smith. Hooker. E. B.* Polypodium, *Linnæus.* Dryopteris Filix-mas, *Newman, Hist. Brit. Ferns,* 183.

The most common of our indigenous Ferns, with the exception of *Pteris aquilina,* occurring in woods, thickets, and on banks and hedge-bottoms in almost every kind of soil. The fronds spring in a circular manner from the extremity of the large scaly rhizoma, presenting vase-like tufts, hollow in the centre, a habit that renders this species highly ornamental when occupying situations sheltered from the wind; they vary according to age or exposure, from two to three or four feet in height, growing nearly erect, but with a slight determination outwards: their development commences in May, the circinate vernation, at first gradually uncoiling, being soon obliterated by the liberation of the apex, which, hanging downwards, gives the upper part of the frond a bend resembling that of a shepherd's crook, a character, however, it should be observed, not peculiar to this fern. The rachis, leafy through about two-thirds or three-fourths of its length, is more or less densely clothed with thin membranous pointed scales, of a pale, often purplish hue, especially towards the base. The lower pinnæ are much shorter than those of the middle, but never approach the diminutive size of those of *L. Oreopteris,* nor do they extend so far downwards. The pinnules, generally distinct at the lower part of the pinnæ and thus justifying the specific character, *bipinnate,* are confluent above; they are likewise liable to vary from the ordinary oblong and obtuse to the more lanceolate form, and the margin from crenate to serrate, the serratures occasionally terminating in slender spines. The sori are produced on the upper branch of the forked lateral veins a little above the furcation, and hence form a line on each side of the midvein, but seldom extending much more than half the length of the pinnule; they are covered by a very conspicuous smooth reniform indusium, of a more permanent character than that of most other British Ferns, and attached by its sinus. The fructification is usually matured in August, but the fronds retain their beauty to the close of the year, and often, in mild seasons and sheltered situations, throughout the winter.

Variations from the normal form of *L. Filix-mas* are not of unfrequent occurrence, and in a few instances they are of so striking and permanent a character as to claim a separate notice, viz.:

1. *incisa.* Frond robust, broadly lanceolate: pinnæ distant;

pinnules distinct, elongate, narrow, acuminate, deeply incised, the lobes serrated. Sori extending nearly the entire length of the pinnules. Lastrea Filix-mas, β. incisa, *Moore, Handbook Brit. Ferns*, 50. Aspidium Filix-mas, β. erosum, *Hooker and Arnott.* Dryopteris affinis, *Newman, Hist. Brit. Ferns*, 187.

2. *abbreviata.* Frond small, lanceolate, pinnate. Sori confined to the base of contracted or obsolete pinnules, forming a linear series on each side of the midvein of the pinnæ. Lastrea Filix-mas, β. abbreviata, *Babington.* Polystichum abbreviatum, *DeCandolle.*

3. *Borreri.* Frond narrow lanceolate. Rachis clothed with ruddy-golden scales and hairs. Sori few, large, two or three pairs at the base of each pinnule. Dryopteris Filix-mas, var. Borreri, *Newman, Hist. Brit. Ferns*, 189.

Of these, the variety *incisa* is far from uncommon; *abbreviata* has been found on Ingleborough, Yorkshire, on the basaltic cliffs of Teesdale, and in the Peak district, Derbyshire, everywhere apparently in dry localities; *Borreri* seems to be common, though first observed by Mr. Borrer in Devonshire, as a variety "with more copious and brighter coloured scales on the rachis, and with a bright golden-yellow tinge on the whole frond." *Brit. Flora.*

Abbreviata retains its distinguishing features in all soils and under different treatment in cultivation, and may perhaps eventually prove a separate species.

The rhizoma of this species has been employed as an anthelmintic ever since the time of Theophrastus, and it is still a favourite remedy in worm cases in many parts of the Continent. The attention of modern medical practitioners was probably first directed to it, in consequence of its being the ostensible remedy of Madame Nouffer of Switzerland, who sold her secret method of expelling the tape-worm to Louis XVI. for 18,000 francs. The inner parts of the rhizoma, carefully dried and reduced to powder, and a decoction and ethereal tincture of the same and of the unexpanded fronds or fern buds, are the preparations employed, but in this country they are now rarely resorted to, because other medicines have been found more effectual. The anthelmintic property resides in an essential oil, and is lost by keeping the powder otherwise than in well-stopped bottles, hence the fresh preparations are always preferred.

There is no difficulty in the way of cultivating the Male Fern; it will grow readily in the common soil of a garden, but is rendered more luxuriant by planting it in the compost described in our introduction, and selecting a shady and moist situation. Its compact growth, large size, and bright green hue are well adapted to contrast with the naked trunks of trees in plantations, and to break the uniformity of shrubberies and wilderness walks, but it should be so planted that its natural growth may not be disturbed

III

Lastrea Cristata.

by that of its neighbours, as much of its beauty is dependent upon the regular development of the fronds, and the erect vase-like form of them in the mass.

Lastrea cristata. Crested Fern. Tab. X.

Fronds linear-oblong, nearly bipinnate; pinnæ short triangular-oblong, deeply pinnatifid with oblong serrated lobes; the lower lobes or pinnules often almost pinnatifid. Sori chiefly confined to the upper part of the frond.

Lastrea cristata, *Presl.* Aspidium cristatum, *Swartz. Smith. Hooker. E. B.* Polypodium cristatum, *Linnæus.* Polypodium Callipteris, *Ehrhart.* Lophodium Callipteris, *Newman, Hist. Brit. Ferns,* 169.

One of our rarest English Ferns, or at least extremely local in its distribution, being confined to boggy heaths and moors, and found hitherto in only four of the counties of England. The recorded habitats are—Westleton, Suffolk; Holt Heath, Fritton, Dersingham, Edgefield, and Bawsey Heath, Norfolk; Oxton Bogs and Bulwell Marshes, Nottinghamshire; and Wybunbury Bog, Cheshire. The Suffolk station is doubtful. Several years back I searched the locality where Mr. Davy is said to have found it, without success, though guided to the alder bushes where his specimens were collected, nor could I meet with the plant anywhere in the neighbourhood. According to Mr. Newman, it does not appear to have been found there by any recent examiner.

It is remarkable that *L. Filix-mas* should have been frequently confounded with the present species, considering the striking difference in habit that exists between them; but the desire to add a rarity to his collection will occasionally lead even an accomplished botanist into a similar mistake to that by which we have a Suffolk habitat recorded for a fern that probably does not grow there.

The rhizoma is stout and strong, and, branching occasionally in different directions, frequently occupies in old plants a considerable space, sending up annually a tuft of erect fronds from the extremity of each branch or crown. The fronds attain a height of two feet or more under favourable circumstances, and are peculiarly erect, so as to render it next to impossible for a person who has once seen it growing naturally to confound it with any other native fern. Rather more than one-third of the rachis is bare of pinnæ, and more or less covered with scattered broad obtuse pale brown membranaceous scales; the pinnæ, nearly equal in length except toward the apex, are in rather distant and generally opposite pairs; their segments, often assuming the character of distinct pinnules in the lower part, are deeply serrated, and sometimes even pinnatifid, the serratures terminating sharply. The lateral veins of the lobes divide into several branches, the uppermost of which bear the sori, which thus form a line on each side the midvein about half-way between it and the margin, extending to the extremity of each lobe or pinnule. The indusium is nearly circular, very permanent, and conspicuous from the contrast of its white or pale leaden hue with the black or dark-coloured thecæ. The regular arrangement of the sori is frequently disturbed in luxuriant specimens by super-development, and they generally become confluent in maturity, a state attained in the latter end of August. The fronds remain green in mild seasons throughout the winter.

This is not at all a shy species under cultivation: it succeeds best in turfy peat, without admixture of any other soil, and, though naturally an inhabitant of boggy ground, seems to bear drought better than some of those belonging to drier situations; neither is shade so essential as to render exposure to the sun a matter of any importance: indeed I have this summer a specimen, two feet high, and in fine condition, growing on a sloping bank, and quite unshaded from sunrise to three o'clock in the afternoon.

The specific name, *cristata*, has been cavilled at by some botanists, but was evidently bestowed on it by Linnæus, in consequence of a fanciful comparison between the cluster of its peculiarly erect fronds and the aigrette of vertical feathers on the head of the peacock, *Pavo cristatus*: that of Ehrhart, *Callipteris*, literally *beautiful fern*, adopted by DeCandolle, associates ill with a species not at all remarkable among its congeners for the attribute expressed.

Lastrea rigida. Rigid Lastrea. Tab. XI.

Fronds triangular-lanceolate, bipinnate, glandular: pinnules oblong, obtuse, lobed, the segments broad, rounded, 2-5-toothed. Indusium persistent, fringed with glands.

Lastrea rigida, *Presl.* Aspidium rigidum, *Swartz. Smith. Hooker E. B.* Lophodium rigidum, *Newman, Hist. Brit. Ferns*, 175 Polypodium fragrans? *Linnæus.*

This appears to be a very local species, having hitherto been almost exclusively found in the mountainous districts of the north of England. It was first noticed as a British fern by the Rev. Mr. Bree, who met with it growing on Ingleborough, and subsequent researches have shown that it is abundantly distributed along the limestone formation of Yorkshire, Westmoreland, and Lancashire. Mr. Pinder and others have remarked upon the profusion in which it grows, at intervals, between Arnside Knot (near Silverdale, Westmoreland) and Ingleborough, springing from the deep fissures of

Lastrea rigida

the natural platform, and occasionally high in the clefts of the rocks. It is generally, he observes, much shattered by the winds, or cropped by the sheep, which seem to be fond of it. Mr. Tatham found it abundant in the fissures of limestone rocks, near Settle, in Yorkshire, at an elevation of 1550 feet; and also on White Scars, above Ingleton. A single plant, found by Mr. Vize, near Bath, and one Irish habitat furnished by Mr. Darby, who gathered it at Townley Hall, Louth, from a wall "built of clay-slate, and much overhung with trees," are scarcely to be regarded as exceptions to the fact that its natural site in this country is limited to the district above recorded, as in both of the latter instances circumstances seem to indicate that it was planted.

The fronds spring in tufts from the summit of a thick, slowly-lengthening rhizoma: they grow nearly erect, varying much in height according to situation, from six inches to two feet or more: the leafy portion occupies about two-thirds of the length, the lower part of the rachis being densely covered with reddish-brown membranaceous scales, broad at the base, but attenuated upwards and terminating very acutely. In general outline the frond varies, but is mostly of an elongated triangular form. Mr. Newman, however, remarks that this form is only met with in young or weak specimens, and that an elongate-lanceolate one prevails in older and stronger plants; he has figured both of these varieties, the latter having the lower pinnæ gradually shortening from the middle of the frond. The figure in Mr. Moore's 'Handbook of British Ferns,' page 54, accords with this, and, as far as my own observation extends, conveys a very erroneous notion of the general character of the species, a circumstance to be regretted, because it is almost the only faulty representation in one of the most valuable manuals ever published. Mr. Newman's left-hand figure is very characteristic of that which is generally regarded the normal condition of the plant. The pinnæ are alternate, linear-lanceolate, and all pinnate: the pinnules are oblong obtuse, sometimes slightly decurrent, more or less deeply lobed or pinnatifid; the segments broad and terminated with from two to five very acute, but not spinulose teeth, the number of which is determined by the branching of the lateral veins. The sori are disposed on the upper branches of the veins, which are always the result of the first bifurcation, and thus form two parallel lines, one on each side of the midvein; in maturity they become confluent. The indusium, reniform and attached to the vein by a short stalk at its sinus, is very permanent and conspicuous, and is fringed round the margin with stalked globular glands. Similar glands with shorter pedicels are found scattered over the whole surface of the frond, and to their secretions is probably due the not unpleasant odour that obtained for this plant the early specific name of *fragrans*, a name, however, which undoubtedly occasioned the frequent confounding of it with *L. Oreopteris.* Fructification chiefly confined to the upper part of the frond. Mature in August and September.

The geological relations of *L. rigida,* its occurrence only in limestone districts, and its absence, in those districts, where other rocks come above the surface, might induce the notion of the necessity of imitating as much as possible its natural conditions in cultivation; hence it has been recommended to plant it among fragments of limestone or old mortar, and to water it with lime-water,—precautions altogether unnecessary. As a rock-plant, it requires good drainage; as a fern, moisture and shade during the growing season are favourable to its development; but it will flourish in the ordinary garden soil, and seems almost indifferent of exposure to the sun. In habit and general aspect it is not at all a distinguished member of its tribe, being less ornamental than most of them, and rather valuable in grouping, from the contrast it affords to more graceful forms than for individual beauty. When grown in pots, a mixture of peat and loam with broken stone or shards below, occupying about a fourth of the depth in order to ensure the ready percolation of water, affords the best medium, and the pots should never be placed in water. Mr. Moore recommends planting it with the crown of the rhizoma a little above the surface.

LASTREA SPINULOSA. Narrow prickly-toothed Fern. TAB. XII.

Fronds erect, linear-lanceolate, bipinnate: pinnules oblong, inciso-pinnatifid, with serrate, spinose-mucronate lobes. Indusium persistent, not fringed. Scales of the rachis broad, ovate, pale.

Lastrea spinulosa, *Presl. Babington, Man. Moore, Handb.* Aspidium spinulosum, *Smith. Hooker.* Lophodium spinosum, *Newman, Hist. Brit. Ferns,* 157.

Much confusion exists in regard to this and the following species, of which it is by some regarded as a variety. Though found in various parts of the kingdom sparingly distributed, it seems to be chiefly confined to the southern and western counties of England, growing in marshy places and wet woods and thickets. The rhizoma elongates slowly, branching in old plants in every direction, so that when once established in any particular locality, the clusters of fronds are generally numerous. It is an early grower, the fronds making their appearance in April, and rapidly attaining their full development, which varies from one to two or even three feet in height: they are nearly erect, bipinnate, long and narrow in the general outline, the pinnæ being of nearly equal length throughout, except toward the acuminating apex. The leafy portion occupies

Lastrea spinulosa

J. E. S. Fecit

Lastrea dilatata

about half of the length, and is perfectly flat, never convex as in *L. dilatata*; the rachis is more or less clothed with thin, almost diaphanous, rounded or oval scales, terminating with a little point, but not at all acuminated. The pinnæ are rather distant; the pinnules more or less deeply pinnatifid, and sometimes even almost again pinnate, especially in the lower part of the large fronds. All of the segments are deeply serrated, the serratures terminating in a sharp point or mucro curving towards the apex of the pinnule. The venation is somewhat complicated, a branch of the lateral vein extending to each serrature: the sori being produced upon the uppermost branch of each lobe, are opposite to the sinuses, and form a line on each side of the midvein; in luxuriant specimens this arrangement is often disturbed by superdevelopment. Fructification is perfected on the earlier fronds in July, and on the later in September. The sori are generally small, the indusium persistent, reniform, flat, a little waved on the margin, but never ciliated with glands. As the thecæ expand, the clusters frequently become confluent, especially where the plant occupies an exposed situation.

The ordinary compost, shade, and moisture, are the only requisites for the successful cultivation of this fern. It will bear exposure, if well supplied with water; but, to obtain it in its beauty, it must be screened from the direct rays of the sun: the mottled and ever-shifting light and shade produced by the intervention ot trees, is always favourable to the growth of this beautiful tribe of plants, even of those species which in a natural state occupy the most unsheltered habitats. Compared with some others, this, like *L. rigida* and *L. cristata*, is not perhaps so remarkably ornamental that it would be included in a selection for planting with a view to effect, but its character is much improved by judicious appropriation of a site sheltered from wind and sun.

In retaining this as a species, I am by no means intending to decide that it has any positive claim to be so considered. The diversity in habit, outline, and division of the frond, and other anomalies, so frequently met with in ferns the specific identity of which cannot be questioned, forbid any such assumption; but amidst the uncertainty and difference of opinion that prevail respecting the species of this and the following genus, *Polystichum*, it seems better to retain a name that has been applied to a certain well-known form like that before us, than to discard it altogether. In appointing the limits between species and varieties, our conclusions are too frequently drawn from very partial or imperfect data.

Lastrea dilatata. Broad prickly-toothed Fern. Tab. XIII.

Fronds arched, ovato-lanceolate, bipinnate: pinnules pinnatifid or pinnate, with serrate, spinose-mucronate lobes. Indusium evanescent, fringed with stalked glands. Scales of the rachis long, lanceolate, dark in the centre.

Lastrea dilatata, *Presl. Babington, Man.* Aspidium spinulosum β, *Hooker.* Lophodium multiflorum, *Newman, Hist. Brit. Ferns,* 147.

One of the most common and most generally distributed of British ferns, growing in woods, and on sheltered hedge-banks, throughout the kingdom. Contrary to the character of that of *L. spinulosa*, the rhizoma of this species is not at all creeping, rarely branches, but forms a strong, enduring, erect, stem-like base, that, in very old specimens, not unfrequently rises from six inches to a foot above the soil. The fronds grow symmetrically in a circular or vase-like cluster, arching over in every direction so as to occupy a considerable space, attaining, in mature plants and in favourable situations, a length of five feet, with a breadth in the widest part of a foot and a half; their ordinary size is, however, considerably less, viz. from a foot and a half to two feet in length: in general outline they vary from triangular to lanceolate or ovato-lanceolate, the triangular form being characteristic of the young plant, in which state it is often completely deltoid. The rachis is clothed, especially toward the base, with long lanceolate or linear-lanceolate, acuminated scales, of a deep brown or blackish hue along the centre, and nearly diaphanous at the extremity and margins. Any particular description that might be given of the divisions of the frond, beyond that already recorded under the specific character, would be of little avail in the decision of a species so protean as the present. The pinnæ are distant, so much so in the fructifying fronds as to frequently give a peculiarly meagre aspect to the plant, especially when accompanied by that convexity of the pinnules and lobes, which is an almost inseparable feature of the most common variety in exposed situations. The venation is very similar to that of *L. spinulosa*, and the situation of the sori on the upper or anterior branches is accordant likewise. The indusium is irregularly reniform, and ciliated with stalked translucent glands; it soon disappears. The fructification is less regularly disposed, and instead of being chiefly confined to the upper end, as is the case in the preceding, is scattered over the whole under surface of the frond; it is mature in August.

Some of the forms of this fern are very elegant, when grown in shade and plentifully supplied with water; but although it bears exposure well, and will live and even flourish under the circumstance, it soon loses all pretension to beauty, and remains disfigured throughout the summer. The same treatment answers equally well for this and *L. spinulosa.*

Lastrea fœniseca.

A vast amount of labour and ingenuity has been expended on the consideration of these two ferns (*L. spinulosa* and *L. dilatata*) and their varieties, with the view of establishing decided limits between the latter, or of elevating the most marked deviations from what has been agreed upon as the normal form, to the rank of species. The result has not been at all satisfactory; that which was a point of dispute a generation or two back, still remains so; and although botanists freely discuss opinions with each other, and maintain or controvert according to present conviction, every new work, nay, every new edition proves the instability of their own; the species of one day becomes the variety of another, the variety of yesterday may be the species of the morrow, or it may be discarded altogether. This has been the case over and over again with the ferns before us. Being of wide distribution, and apparently indifferent, so far as mere capability of growth is concerned, to soil, elevation, and exposure, they assume a diversity of aspect according to circumstances: to what extent the influence of such causes may have contributed to the multiplication of supposed species in this and other genera, future observation must decide; the whole genus *Lophodium* of Newman, a well-marked group among British ferns, may be implicated.

On these grounds, added to the uncertainty of definition afforded by characters too slight and variable to be depended upon, I leave the alleged varieties of *L. dilatata* to be determined by the fancy of the observer.

Lastrea fœnisecii. Recurved prickly-toothed Fern. Hay-scented Fern. Tab. XIV.

Fronds curved, elongate-triangular, subtripinnate: pinnules pinnate or deeply pinnatifid, with serrate spinose-mucronate lobes. Indusium jagged at the edge. Scales of the rachis narrow lanceolate, laciniate, pale.

Lastrea fœnisecii, *Watson. Babington, Man. Moore, Handb.* Aspidium recurvum, *Bree.* A. dilatatum, var. concavum, *Babington.* A. spinulosum var., *Hooker and Arnott.* Lophodium fœnisecii, *Newman, Hist. Brit. Ferns*, 135 (the figure far from characteristic).

This fern, though rather widely distributed in the British islands, is generally regarded as originally a wanderer from the Azores, or other Atlantic groups; in corroboration of which opinion we find it most abundant in the south-western counties of England and Ireland, the situations toward which it would naturally be drifted by the tidal wave, or where its sporules would be wafted by the prevalent south-westerly winds. That it is among the later additions to the recent vegetation of these lands, seems farther evinced by the fact of its not having hitherto been found in the central counties of Great Britain. To speculate upon the geological epoch at which its introduction took place, would be useless; but it is highly interesting to the philosophic observer, to trace the successive distributions of a plant, which, like the present, indigenous to the islands of the North Atlantic from the Cape de Verde to the Azores, wafted by wind and wave, arrives on the coast of Sussex, Devon, and Cornwall; beyond, the same agents land it in Somersetshire, Glamorganshire, Merioneth, and Anglesea; still onward, it reaches Lancashire and Cumberland, the western islands and mainland of Scotland, and plants a colony in Orkney; lastly, the returning current lodges the later wanderers in Angus, and, southward, at Scarborough in Yorkshire: in the latter county, its most inland habitats seem at present to be attained in the vicinity of Ripon and Settle.

Few ferns are more indifferent to soil or exposure: it is met with in damp woods, and under the shelter of moist hedge-banks and thickets, attaining in such localities a height of one or two feet, and a degree of luxuriance surprising to those previously only acquainted with its smaller forms; for, although shelter and abundant moisture are favourable to its full development, it is often found growing from the clefts of sandstone and other rocks in the most exposed situations, the fronds being only from two to six inches long. The fronds spring in a circular manner from a broad crown, curving downward very gracefully in large specimens, as they extend: they are of a pale but lively green hue, and remarkable for their curled or crisped appearance, arising from the margins of the lobes and pinnules being curved upwards so as to render their upper surface concave. The leafy portion occupies about one-half of the length, and is of an elongated triangular form, in young specimens nearly deltoid; the rachis, especially at the lower part, being rather densely clothed with pale, diaphanous, long, narrow, and generally laciniated scales. In mature plants, the tripinnate character is very constant at the base of the frond and of its principal divisions; and the tertiary pinnules and lobes being all serrated, the serratures terminating in short spines, give a complexity of outline so peculiar as to render it difficult, even at the first glance, to confound this with any other species or variety, especially when combined with the concavity of surface, so strikingly opposed to the convexity of that of *L. dilatata*. Minute globular sessile glands are scattered over the whole under surface of the frond, whence the odour resembling new-made hay, from which the specific name is derived. The sori are nearly equally distributed over the frond; they are covered by roundish, reniform, generally evanescent indusia, which are irregularly cut or jagged on the margin, and occasionally fringed with a few glands similar to those mentioned above.

This is a very beautiful species under cultivation, especially when the contingencies of shade, moisture, and good drainage are properly secured. Though of supposed tropical derivation, it is one of our most hardy native ferns, and perfectly evergreen. I have now, September 4th, before me a green frond of last year, just gathered from a plant that was exposed throughout the winter in a pot laid sideways on the fern-bank in my garden. This character renders it valuable in the greenhouse, to which its moderate size, lively green hue, and elegantly crisped habit, are farther recommendations. Whether grown in the open ground or in pots, the ordinary compost will suffice.

Regarded by some botanists as a variety of *L. dilatata* or *spinulosa*, this still bears so much the impress of distinctness, that it can scarcely be other than a species. In 1821, I first noticed it in the vicinity of Dolgelley, and again in the Vale of Festiniog, and, though marking its peculiarity, supposed it in my inexperience to be a form of *Aspidium dilatatum* of Smith; it had not then received name or notice among recent botanists, though apparently referred to both by Ray and Plukenet; nor was attention directed to its very distinct character, even as a variety, until, in 1831, the Rev. W. T. Bree described it in the 'Magazine of Natural History,' under the name of *recurvum*; since which period, opinion has been divided respecting its claim to rank as a species. It is to be regretted that the name *fœnisecii*, afterwards bestowed upon it by Mr. Lowe, should have been adopted in preference to that of *recurva*, the odour differing very equivocally from that of other species of fern, while the latter name expresses a positive feature by which the plant is at once recognized.

In regard to the other recorded species of the genus *Lastrea*, viz. *Aspidium dumetorum* of Smith, and *Lophodium collinum*, *glandulosum*, and *uliginosum* of Newman, they are at present too doubtfully circumstanced between the variable forms of *spinulosa* and *dilatata* to be admitted, without farther and stricter observation than has yet been bestowed, to occupy a separate station in a series already encumbered with uncertainty. Mr. Moore, in the second edition of his valuable 'Handbook,' makes *L. spinulosa* a variety of *L. cristata*, and observes:—"I unite the following forms under one species, because, although the two extremes are apparently distinct, they are so closely connected by the intermediate form (*uliginosa*) as to be undistinguishable from one or other of the conditions which the latter assumes." My own acquaintance with *uliginosa*, confined to a single growing specimen, is too limited, perhaps, to justify an opinion, but it inclines to an opposite conclusion, namely the entire exclusion of *cristata* from the equivocal series now before us.

Genus 4. POLYSTICHUM.

Gen. Char. Sori circular, seated upon the upper branch of the lateral veins; covered by a circular peltate indusium attached by its centre.

This genus, separated from *Lastrea* in consequence of the difference of the form and attachment of the indusium, is farther characterized by the rigidity of its foliage, and of the sharp spinous processes by which all the ultimate divisions of the frond are terminated, while the upper basal lobe or pinnule is always larger than the others. The British species are very nearly allied, and present a series of varieties between the simpler and more complicated forms that renders their determination difficult. The name, not well chosen, is compounded from the Greek πολὺς, *many*, and στίχας, *series*, in allusion to the regular linear arrangement of the sori.

Polystichum Lonchitis. Holly Fern. Rough Alpine Shield-Fern. Tab. XV.

Fronds rigid, linear-lanceolate, pinnate: pinnæ spinose-serrate, auricled at the base above, oblique below.

Polystichum Lonchitis, *Roth. Babington. Moore. Newman.* Aspidium Lonchitis, *Swartz. Smith. Hooker and Arnott. E. B.* Polypodium, *Linnæus.*

Its exclusively alpine habitats have caused this beautiful fern to be generally described as among our botanical rarities: in England and Wales it seems to be confined to the mountains of Yorkshire and the Snowdon district; but, in the mountainous parts of Scotland, it is widely and abundantly distributed, and in the north and west of Ireland. It is generally found springing from the clefts of the rocks in the highest and most exposed situations; but occasionally lower down, in the glens and mountain-passes, especially in the crevices and on the ledges of their most precipitous sides. The fronds grow in a tuft from the extremity of a very slowly lengthening rhizoma, varying from a few inches to a foot and a half in height: they are generally of a rigid texture and erect growth, but in some situations thinner and spreading, or even almost pendulous; the latter character, it has been remarked, belongs almost exclusively to English and Welsh specimens. The colour is of a deep glossy green. The general outline of the frond is linear, more or less acuminated at the upper part, and simply pinnate. The pinnæ are short, arranged alternately and

Polystichum Lonchitis.

obliquely on the rachis, and extending nearly to its base, which is rather densely clothed with reddish-brown chaffy scales: they are somewhat crescent-shaped, auricled at the base on the upper side, oblique below, and so closely disposed as to overlap each other when pressed flat; the margin is deeply serrated, the serratures terminating in sharp spinous processes, which, added to the rigidity and almost leather-like character of the leafy texture, and its evergreen habit, renders the English name "Holly Fern" very appropriate. The lateral veins are alternate, generally three-branched, the upper branch bearing the sorus; on the auricle, the venation is more complex, and the production of sori indefinite. The fructification is most frequently confined to the upper part of the frond, but is sometimes irregularly scattered likewise over the lower pinnæ even to the base. The sori are disposed in a regular series on each side of the midvein, and often become confluent in maturity. The indusium is circular, opening all round, and remaining attached to the venule by a short central stalk, the distinguishing character of the genus.

The cultivation of the Holly Fern is not attended with very satisfactory results in the eastern parts of England, especially about London, where few persons have succeeded in keeping it for any length of time, unless as a potted plant, and sheltered in the greenhouse or in a cool frame; and, even under these circumstances, it is exceedingly liable to "damp off," an expression that, like "blight," is often applied to denote the action of causes we do not understand. In potting *P. Lonchitis*, or any other alpine fern, the natural condition of the plant should never be lost sight of; however moist that may be, it is always well drained; a rill may constantly lave its roots, or a cascade perpetually sprinkle its leaves, but the water never stagnates, and even the scanty soil is changing from time to time, by the addition or rather substitution of new particles, as the older are washed away to maintain the fertilization of the valley below. In order to insure drainage, the pot should be large, and at least one-fourth filled with broken stone or shards mingled with charcoal and pieces of turfy peat. The ordinary compost will suffice; but fragments of slate or sandstone placed perpendicularly around the rhizoma, though not in immediate contact with it, the soil being firmly settled between them, afford an imitation of at least one important circumstance belonging to the natural site that will be found serviceable to the possessor. In the open air I once had a small specimen of this species growing for four years, but it died during the next winter after removal; and it is a very general complaint, that although it will live and apparently flourish for a season, it rarely survives the winter and spring when exposed to their influence. The absence of the snow cover, that in their native habitats shelters the alpine plants alike from the excess of cold and drying influence of the winds, is the chief cause of their not flourishing generally under exposure in this part of England; added to which, is the frequent alternation of excessive wet, during those seasons when the vital energies of the plants are dormant: the injurious results arising from both of these circumstances may be obviated, in a degree, by covering the plants individually with an inverted garden-pot or a hand-glass at the period in question, exposing it only in mild and dry weather. This is a plan by which I have often succeeded in preserving some of the higher alpine species of flowering plants that are otherwise incapable of cultivation in the vicinity of the metropolis, and it was the protection afforded to the above-mentioned specimen of the fern before us.

In England, the distribution of *P. Lonchitis* may probably be found to be less confined than has hitherto been supposed, Mr. W. H. Hawker having discovered it in July of last year (1853) on Swarth-fell, near Ulleswater, and this year in one or two other stations in the Lake district.

Polystichum aculeatum. Prickly Shield-Fern. Tab. XVI.—XVII.

Fronds rigid, lanceolate or linear-lanceolate, bipinnate: pinnules confluent, obliquely decurrent, or attached by the point of their wedge-shaped base; the upper basal ones largest; all spinose-serrate, more or less auricled at the base.

Polystichum aculeatum, *Roth. Babington. Moore. Newman.* Aspidium aculeatum, *Swartz. Smith. Hooker and Arnott. E. B.* Polypodium, *Linnæus.*

Common on hedge-banks and on the borders of woods and thickets throughout the kingdom, and occasionally met with in more exposed situations on heaths and mountains. The rhizome is large and woody, increasing in length very slowly, so that even in old plants it is very short in comparison to its bulk. The fronds grow in a tuft, in young specimens spreading out horizontally, but in older becoming nearly erect in maturity, and attaining the height of two or three feet: during the early period of development they are usually very limp in texture, and the newly unfolded pinnæ and circinate apex are liable to hang down with their own weight, as if drooping for want of nourishment, but as growth advances they acquire the characteristic rigidity so remarkable in the foliage of this beautiful genus. The general outline varies greatly in different specimens, and even in fronds belonging to the same plant, being in some instances almost linear, in others even broadly lanceolate: the division too is equally diversified, and

Polystichum lobatum

17

Polystichum aculeatum.

though the bipinnate character is tolerably constant in full-sized plants, the pinnæ are rather lobed or pinnatifid than pinnate in those of smaller size, and this difference is often independent of age. The first upper division at the base of each pinna, whether lobe or pinnule, is always larger than the others, and, standing parallel with the main rachis, the two series thus formed present a very peculiar appearance in the general aspect of the frond, especially of the upper face. All of the principal divisions terminate in a sharp spinous process, and are more or less fringed on the margin with spiny serratures. The rachis is leafy to within a few inches of its base, and is clothed throughout with reddish-brown or rust-coloured scales, which are broad and densely crowded below, but become gradually fewer and more attenuated towards the extremity of the frond. There is nothing peculiar in the fructification, beyond the regularity of the disposition of the sori, and their occurrence almost exclusively on the upper pinnæ only; they are generally rather large in proportion, and often become confluent.

A fern liable to assume such diversity in outline and division as this, could scarcely fail of becoming a subject of contention among botanists, relative to the individual claim of its more permanent varieties to the rank of species. To enter into any minute detail of the differences presented by the so-called species of *Polystichum*, as figured or described by past writers, would be to little purpose; it will be sufficient here to remark that three apparent forms of the plant now before us have been so distinguished, and named respectively *lobatum*, *aculeatum*, and *angulare*. The first two are now universally admitted to be merely different states of the same plant, dependent on age or other circumstances; the last occupies, though somewhat equivocally, a more decided position as a separate species, in the works of the most recent botanists; that position I will leave it, but rather that its prominence may lead to farther inquiry, than from any conviction of its being other than a false one: *lobatum* and *angulare*, indeed, appear to me the extremes of a series connected by so many intermediate modifications of form and habit, that, in the absence of more important differential features than have hitherto been established, it is utterly impossible to determine the limits of either. As varieties, the three may be thus defined:—

1. *lobatum*. Frond rigid, simply pinnate: pinnæ lobed or pinnatifid. TAB. XVI.

2. *aculeatum*. Frond rigid, sub-bipinnate: pinnules more or less decurrent. TAB. XVII.

3. *angulare*. Frond lax, bipinnate: pinnules distinctly stalked.

Under all its varieties of form, *Polystichum aculeatum* is among the handsomest of the larger British ferns; it is evergreen, the foliage of a bright hue and glossy; and, its growth being scarcely suspended from the first development in April until the setting in of winter,—so that the pale yellowish-green of the young fronds contrasts very strikingly with the deep holly-like appearance of the older ones, throughout the whole of the summer and autumn,—it is more constantly ornamental in the fern-garden than most others. The cultivation is attended with no difficulty; it will grow in common garden soil, but flourishes best in a mixture of sandy loam and peat, and although not injured by moderate exposure to the sun, prefers the shelter of trees and shrubs, or a shaded bank. When grown in pot, the ordinary compost must be employed, and full drainage; and unless kept in the greenhouse or otherwise protected, the pot should be plunged in a dry border during the winter. All the varieties are well adapted for house culture, and their beauty is much enhanced by careful treatment; but they require a great deal of room, large pots, and space to extend their fine evergreen fronds, if the cultivator is desirous of witnessing their most advantageous development.

POLYSTICHUM ANGULARE. Angular or Soft prickly Shield-Fern. TAB. XVIII.

Fronds lax, drooping, lanceolate, bipinnate: pinnules distinctly stalked, with an obtusely-angled base, more or less obtuse at the apex, spinose-serrate.

Polystichum angulare, *Presl. Newman. Babington. Moore.* Aspidium angulare, *Willdenow. Smith. E. B. Hooker and Arnott.*

This is certainly less common in its distribution than the preceding, but inhabits similar situations; the differences between them are sufficiently striking where the contrast is made with the extremer forms of each: the habit of this is flexile and drooping, the leafy texture not so firm as that of *P. aculeatum*, the upper basal pinnules often scarcely larger than the lower ones, and all of them somewhat crescent-shaped, auriculate on the upper side, rounded below, and attached to the partial rachis by a very distinct, slender stalk, instead of being decurrent. Several deviations from this normal form have been noticed, and two especially seem marked varieties, and are well known in cultivation:—

1. *subtripinnatum.* Lower pinnules deeply pinnatifid, the lobes sometimes distinct.

2. *angustatum.* Pinnules all narrow, very acute.

The latter is frequently proliferous, or rather viviparous, by the production of bulbils about the bases of the lower pinnæ and pin-

Polystichum angulare

nules; this is especially the case where the plants are grown in pots in the greenhouse, or in very sheltered situations in the open fernery.

P. angulare and its varieties are less hardy than *aculeatum*, and are not so strictly evergreen, a consequence probably of the greater laxity of their tissue. They seem to require more careful drainage, a lighter soil, and complete shelter from the sun and cold winds. It might be a subject of question, whether these facts may not indicate *that* very specific distinction which previous remarks tend to set aside; but in opposition to any suggestion of this kind, it may be remarked, that division, variegation, or laxity of the foliage, constituting variety among the higher orders of plants, is almost universally accompanied by a less robust constitution than that belonging to the normal condition of the species.

Genus 5. CYSTOPTERIS.

GEN. CHAR. Sori roundish. Indusium attached by its broad hooded base beneath the sori, with a lengthened, fringed, free margin, opening towards the apex of the segment.

The British species of this genus are small, elegant ferns, of a very delicate, almost fragile texture; they are well adapted for house culture, throwing out their beautiful fronds, profusely sprinkled with fructification, in all seasons, when sheltered from the frost, the first approach of which, however, destroys them in the open air. They grow naturally on rocks and walls, chiefly in alpine and subalpine districts; and notwithstanding their delicate appearance, few of the smaller ferns are equally capable of living in a dry atmosphere, or exposed to the action of the sun.

The indusium is hollow at the base, forming a sort of hood fixed by its inner margin, that is curved beneath the sorus; the remarkable extension of the outer margin is best observed when the thecæ have recently burst through their membranaceous cover, which is then seen to be broken unequally into a fringe of narrow, often capillary segments, that becomes eventually reflected.

The generic name is a Greek compound of κύστις, *a bladder*, and πτέρις, *a fern*, in allusion to the peculiar character of the indusium.

This genus is very nearly allied to *Woodsia*, differing from it chiefly, if not solely, in the form and attachment of the indusium; which, in the latter, has its point of attachment beneath the sorus, inclosing it equally all round, and opening in the middle, when it divides into numerous capillary segments forming an involucral fringe around the thecæ. In *Cystopteris*, on the contrary, the attachment of the indusium is rather lateral than basal, and the margin is connected on the outer side with the back of the frond. In habit and general appearance our native species of *Woodsia* are at first sight very dissimilar to the species of the present genus, but *Woodsia Perriniana*, a North American species, is so like *Cystopteris fragilis*, as to be generally confounded with it by a casual observer, while the indusium is only fringed on the margin, thus leaving its involucral character the sole feature of distinction.

CYSTOPTERIS FRAGILIS. Brittle Bladder-Fern. TAB. XIX.—XX.

Fronds erect, lanceolate, bipinnate: pinnæ lanceolate: pinnules ovato-lanceolate, deeply pinnatifid, the segments ovate or lanceolate, sharply toothed or serrated.

Cystopteris fragilis, *Bernhardi. Hooker and Arnott. Babington. Moore. Newman.* Cystea fragilis, *Smith, Eng. Fl.* Cyathea fragilis, *Smith, Fl. Brit. E. B.* Polypodium, *Linnæus.*

Abundantly distributed over the mountainous and rocky districts throughout the kingdom, and occasionally on old walls and buildings in the lowland counties. It seems to prefer the moist crevices of limestone rocks in the vicinity of waterfalls, but is by no means exclusive in selecting a site, and though most flourishing and exuberant in its growth under the conditions of shade and moisture, is often met with occupying the most exposed situations. The rhizoma is creeping, but extends slowly, branching and forming new crowns around the old one, often several in number during the same summer and autumn. The fronds rise in tufts from these crowns in April, rapidly attaining maturity, and fading in succession as their place is supplied by others throughout the season, until the development is checked by frost. They vary in height, according to circumstances, from two or three inches to a foot or more, and differ much in form and division, even on the same crown: the general outline is lanceolate, more or less elongated; the pinnæ, distinct to the apex, occupy more than half the length of the slender rachis, which is smooth, and nearly destitute of scales; they are for the most part distant, especially the lower ones, not very regularly arranged, but with a tendency to alternate: the pinnules are similarly arranged, equally distinct, and sharply and deeply serrated, the lower ones being often, in fronds of larger size, deeply pinnatifid, or even pinnate. The venation, easily distinguished owing to the delicate translucency of the leafy texture, varies according to the division and serratures of the pinnules: in most instances each secondary vein bears a sorus, not at its extremity, but about half-way from its base; thus the sori form a line on each side, rather nearer to the midvein than to the margin, but

10

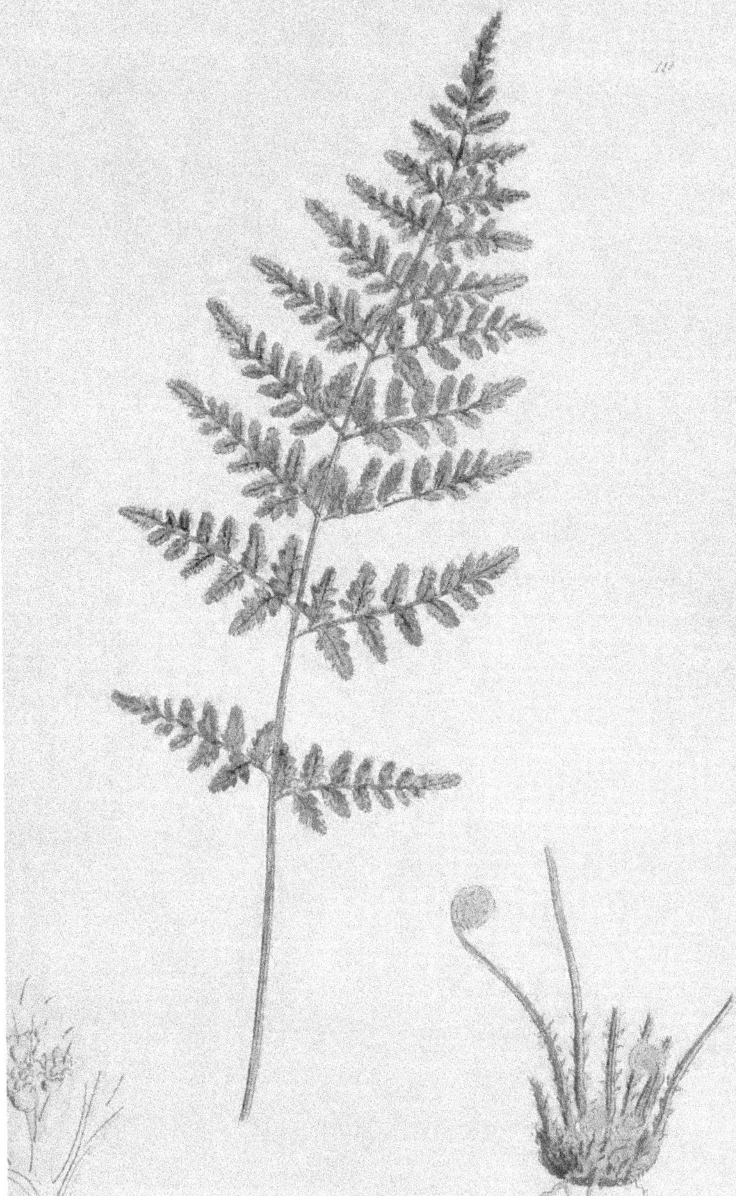

Cystopteris fragilis

Cystopteris angustata

they are generally crowded, often much confused, and in maturity, or rather on the dehiscence of the thecæ, frequently become confluent and cover the whole under surface. A tolerable notion of the position of the indusium may be obtained from the enlarged view on Tab. XIX., but it is difficult to portray its actual insertion and mode of opening; it is soon obliterated by the extension of the sorus.

So much difference of opinion exists regarding this normal species of *Cystopteris* and its kindred species or varieties, and so uncertain at present are our rules for specific distinction in this tribe of plants, that it is with some diffidence I venture to adopt even a very slight departure from the arrangement of my predecessors; but having cultivated them for nearly thirty years, and observed them at intervals in their various native habitats for a longer period, their present allotment is the result of an experience to myself satisfactory, and the more so, because in the main point, viz. the separation or rather retention of *C. dentata* as a species, my decision is not a solitary one.

In the Supplement to the 'English Botany,' Tab. 2790, a figure of a fern, under the name of *Cystopteris angustata*, was published, which, with its description, was evidently a mistake. In the second edition of 'English Botany' (1841), this figure was introduced, contrary to my expostulations regarding its incorrectness, and the description in the text quoted from that of the Supplement, with only one remark for which I am answerable—"That it (*C. angustata*) is only a variety can scarcely be questioned, but it is nearer *C. fragilis* than *C. dentata*." I am the more confirmed in that opinion from later observation, and now introduce it as a variety of the species before us:—

C. FRAGILIS, var. ANGUSTATA. TAB. XX.

Frond oblong-lanceolate, bipinnate: pinnules linear-lanceolate, more or less decurrent, acutely pinnatifid or toothed; ultimate divisions narrow-oblong or linear.

Cystopteris dentata, *β*. *Hooker, Brit. Fl.*

Found in similar situations to those in which *C. fragilis* grows, and occasionally accompanying it, especially on the loose stone fences of North Wales and Cumberland.

Few ferns are cultivated with greater facility than *C. fragilis*: although growing more luxuriantly, and assuming its more graceful aspect when planted in soil and situation corresponding to its natural habitat, the ordinary garden mould, unless very adhesive, is not ill adapted to its preservation. It may be grown in the open border, forming, when not too fully exposed to the sun, beautiful and elegant tufts that contrast well with the smaller species of herbaceous plants; requiring only the occasional removal of its rapidly maturing fronds to maintain the lively green appearance of the masses throughout the summer. The delicate feathery character of the foliage renders it a favourite species for pot culture, and in a cool greenhouse it becomes highly ornamental; but it is not well adapted for planting in closed cases, though often recommended for the purpose, the slender rachis being too rapidly extended in the damp confined atmosphere to support the lengthened frond, while the attacks of mildew and other fungoid pests, to which it is liable under confinement, often prove fatal to the other species in its vicinity.

All of the British species or varieties of *Cystopteris* are seen, under cultivation, to the greatest advantage when planted on shaded rock-work: like other rock and wall plants, they require good drainage, a condition readily effected by the admixture of about one-fourth of small fragments of old mortar with the soil or compost employed; the value of this addition is farther indicated by the natural preference they seem to evince for limestone districts.

CYSTOPTERIS DENTATA. Toothed Bladder-Fern. TAB. XXI.—XXII.

Fronds oblong-lanceolate, bipinnate: pinnules ovate-obtuse, bluntly toothed. Sori submarginal.

Cystopteris dentata, *Hooker, Brit. Fl. E.B.*, 2nd ed. Cyathea dentata, *Smith, Flora Brit.* Cystea dentata, *Smith, Eng. Flora. E.B.* 1588. Cystopteris fragilis, var. dentata, *Moore, Handb.*, ed. 2, 76.

Not unfrequent in the rocky parts of Wales, Scotland, and the North of England, though very liable to be passed over as a form of *C. fragilis*, with which most modern botanists indeed seem inclined to confound it. The present is, however, in maturity a smaller plant, differing considerably in the general outline of the frond, and in the form, division and arrangement of the pinnæ, which are so placed, that their upper faces, instead of being vertical, tend more or less towards a horizontal position; this character is difficult to express by figure, where, as in the ordinary state of the fern, the pinnæ are distant, but it will be understood by reference to Tab. XXII., representing an assumed variety, *C. Dickieana*. The pinnules vary in division according to the luxuriance of the frond, being deeply toothed, or, rarely, pinnatifid, but the teeth or segments are always remarkably obtuse, without the slightest tendency to become pointed at the extremity. The sori, produced at

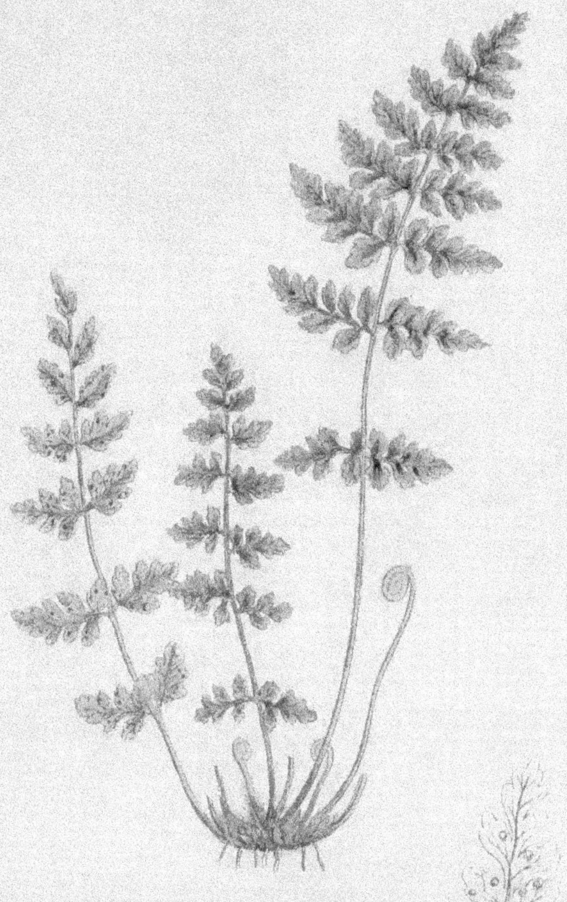

Cystopteris dentata

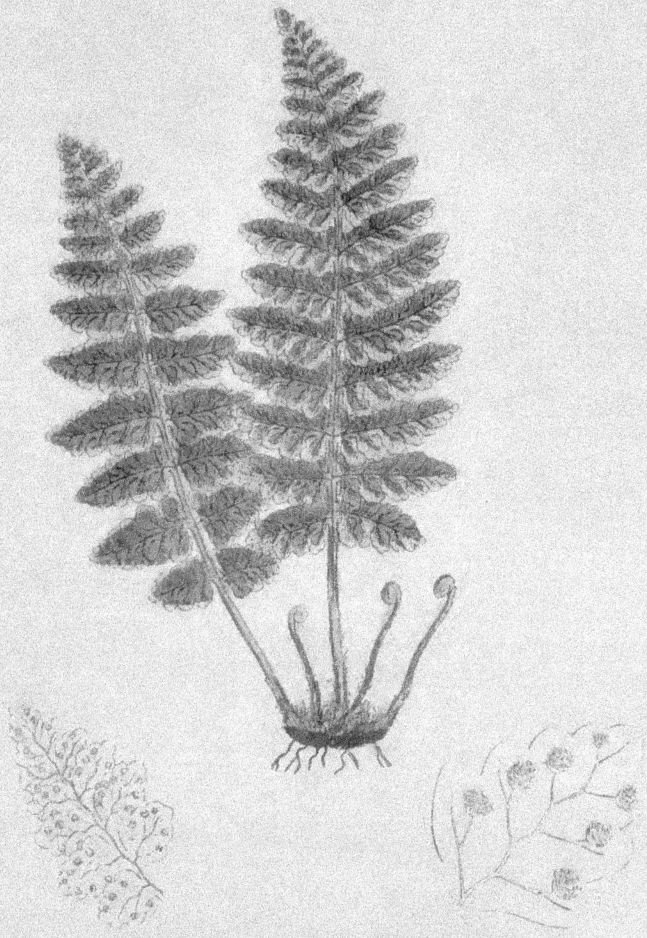

Cystopteris Dickieana

the termination of the veins, have a disposition almost marginal, and indeed, where numerous and becoming confluent, as they usually do in maturity, form a complete and striking border to the under surface of the pinnules, very different to those of *C. fragilis* and *C. angustata*. The rachis is very slender, smooth, and almost universally of a deep brownish-purple hue.

The variety *C. Dickieana*, Tab. XXII., is a very marked and peculiar one, apparently retaining its distingnishing characters under cultivation. The general outline of the frond is ovate-lanceolate, and all of its divisions are broader and more rounded than those of the normal *C. dentata*; they are likewise nearer together, and their greater breadth occasions an overlapping of each other, that, added to the more decided tendency to horizontality of the pinnæ, give it at first sight the aspect of a distinct species. A close comparison, however, with the latter plant soon dispels the illusion. The pinnæ and pinnules are often more or less confluent, instead of being quite distinct, thus departing from the bipinnate character. The sori are never confluent in maturity, but have the intromarginal position. Mr. Newman remarks, on the authority of Mr. Wollaston, that the spores of *C. fragilis* "are always echinate, those of *Dickieana* simply verrucate"; the latter is the case with those of *C. dentata*, but whether a constant character of that species I am not prepared to assert.

This remarkable variety was found by Dr. Dickie in 1846, growing in a cave by the sea near Aberdeen, and has not hitherto been met with elsewhere.

Whether the arrangement of the four allied forms of the genus here adopted or proposed be correct or otherwise is of little importance; under either circumstance the two named as species, and which I have always considered as such, will be useful as rallying-points to those who may feel inclined to discuss the subject. Mr. Moore, who has placed all the four as varieties of *C. fragilis*, remarks: "I am inclined to think *C. dentata* to be sufficiently distinct to take rank as a species, and to look upon *C. Dickieana* as an extreme form of it." Mr. Newman, on the contrary, observes: "My own judgment, improved, but by no means matured, by the observations of sixteen years, regards *dentata* as a nonentity, *angustata* as a synonym of that nonentity, and *Dickieana* as a *possible*, but by no means *established* species." Farther on, he adds: "The propriety of separating *Dickieana* from *fragilis* rests on these grounds,—it is a perfectly healthy plant, not monstrous or distorted, and produced freely from seed, becoming a perfect weed; whereas *fragilis*, under similar treatment, rarely reproduces itself. Cultivated in the same soil and in the same pot with *fragilis*, the latter becomes larger and more vigorous, *Dickieana* smaller and less vigorous: and the more care the cultivator bestows on these two plants, the more will he find they recede from each other; whereas all differences between the so-called *C. fragilis, angustata*, and *dentata*, are speedily lost in cultivation." If there be any value attaching to physiological facts of this kind, regarding the determination of species, it must depend upon their correspondence under all circumstances, and the above remarks do not agree with my own experience. Of *C. Dickieana* I know but little, indeed nothing beyond that which the examination of the plant affords as to its general characters and structure, growing specimens not having come into my possession until within the last two or three years; but of the others, cultivation from the wild state for nearly thirty years has led to very different results. The plants have retained during that period all their original features, while their spore-scattered offspring have grown up as types of the parent forms, except that *fragilis* has generally, but not uniformly, produced *angustata* instead of its own: the latter circumstance seems significant of the effect of difference of soil or situation in the production of varieties among ferns, and may account for the discrepancy of the two statements; my own specimens being chiefly grown in the open air, and never having any other protection than a cold frame or occasionally a hand-glass, while Mr. Newman's may have had the advantage of a closed case or greenhouse.

Cystopteris alpina. Alpine Bladder-Fern. Tab. XXIII.

Fronds lanceolate, sub-tripinnate: pinnæ ovate: pinnules confluent, oblong-ovate, deeply pinnatifid; the lobes broadly and shortly linear, obtuse, with two or three erect blunt teeth.

Cystopteris alpina, *Desvaux*. *Hooker and Arnott*. *Moore*. *Babington*. Cyathea regia, *Forster*. Cyathea incisa, *E. B.* 163. Cystea regia, *Smith*. Polypodium, *Linnæus*.

Though admitted by most botanical writers into the catalogue of British Ferns, this species has no other claim to be regarded as such, than the fact of its having at one time grown very plentifully on a garden wall at Low Leyton, near Walthamstow, Essex, where it was first noticed by Mr. Forster: about thirty years back, the wall needing repair and fresh pointing, it was obliterated from this habitat, or nearly so, the occasional discovery of a specimen either there or on other walls in the neighbourhood being of late years looked upon as a rarity. It has been recorded by some of the older botanists as occurring both in Wales and Scotland, but as the habitats mentioned by them have been searched in vain, it is now generally considered that dwarf and deeply-divided specimens of one or other of the preceding have been mistaken for it. It is

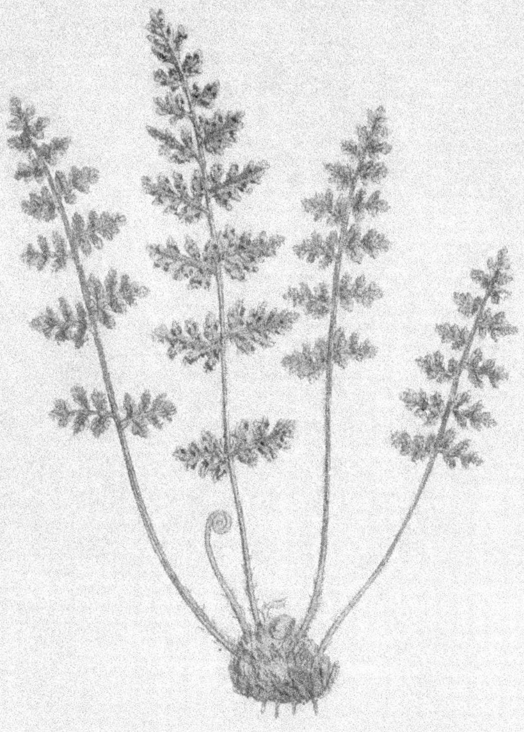

Cystopteris alpina.

23

Cystopteris montana.

very common on the Alps and Pyrenees, and most of the growing plants in our collections are of continental origin. Mr. Moore, however, observes that he has received specimens from Mr. Shepherd, of Liverpool, gathered in Derbyshire and Yorkshire, but without any particular habitat being assigned. The species is very distinct in character, when closely compared with any form of *C. fragilis* or *C. dentata*: the fronds are, strictly speaking, bipinnate, but the pinnules are so deeply lobed or pinnatifid, that, although always confluent, they give them at first sight the appearance of being again pinnate; the lobes are linear, very obtuse, and generally divided on the margin with two or three blunt teeth pointing upwards. The venation is more or less compound, according with the division and toothing of the pinnules, and the small roundish sori are submarginal. The fronds are variable in height, from two to six or eight inches in foreign plants, but I have never seen any British specimens from the wall at Low Leyton above three or four inches long.

It is not at all difficult to cultivate and multiply when once established; but is more susceptible of injury from the accumulation of moisture about the roots than *C. fragilis*; good drainage is therefore more imperative, but otherwise it may be similarly treated. A sheltered situation in the out-door fernery is better than confinement under glass.

CYSTOPTERIS MONTANA. Mountain Bladder-Fern. TAB. XXIV.

Fronds triangular bipinnate: pinnules of lower pinnæ pinnate; ultimate pinnules and lobes deeply pinnatifid, their segments toothed at the apex.

Cystopteris montana, *Link. Hooker and Arnott. Babington. Moore.* Cystopteris Myrrhidifolium, *Villars. Newman, Hist. Brit. Ferns*, 97. Polypodium montanum, *Allioni.* Aspidium montanum, *Swartz.*

First found as a British species in 1836, by Mr. W. Wilson, on Ben Lawers, one of the Breadalbane mountains, and since by others in several localities on the mountains of Perthshire and Forfarshire, but so sparingly distributed that it may be considered as one of our rarest ferns. The rhizoma is filiform, branching and creeping, like that of *Polypodium Dryopteris*, or *P. calcareum*, the latter of which, especially, this species nearly resembles in habit and general appearance. The fronds might almost correctly be regarded as ternate, the two lower pinnæ, which are opposite, being so much larger than the others as often to be nearly equal to them in the aggregate; it is in this pair only that the pinnules are pinnate, all those of the upper pinnæ being only deeply lobed: the lower inferior pinnule of the same pair is always larger than the upper corresponding one, and more divided; the disproportion gradually decreasing in each of the following, until toward the apex of the pinna the opposite pinnules are nearly equal: the upper pinnæ show very little tendency to this irregularity. The venation does not present any striking peculiarities; the lateral veins are alternate, and generally terminate in the sinus between two serratures, thus determining the arrangement of the fructification. The sori, generally numerous, are small, nearly circular, and very prominent in maturity. The indusium accords in position and attachment with that of other species of the genus; but, unless examined previous to or immediately after dehiscence, its presence will often not be recognized, so that the species might be regarded as a *Polypodium*, with certain members of which genus its habit and the form of its fronds so nearly associate.

Not having yet had living specimens of this fern in my possession, I cannot offer any remarks upon its cultivation, resulting from my own experience. From the little I have seen of it in the keeping of others, and the complaints made respecting its liability to "damp off," it seems to me probable that a treatment similar to that recommended for *Polypodium calcareum* would be likely to succeed; not indeed exposure to the sun, which all ferns are better without, and especially those of alpine localities, but fresh air and free drainage. In regard to the supply of water, there is less danger in comparative drought than in superabundance. See the remarks on *Polystichum Lonchitis*, p. 31.

Our figure is from a specimen kindly forwarded by Mr. Borrer, gathered by himself in Corrach Dh'Oufillach.

Genus 6. ATHYRIUM.

GEN. CHAR. Sori oblong-reniform or crescent-shaped. Indusium attached along the upper side of the lateral veins, opening towards the mid-vein, with a free margin fringed with capillary segments, at length reflexed.

This genus is adopted, rather to avoid the misplacement of one of the most common and at the same time most elegant of British Ferns, than under the idea of its distinctive character being other than very equivocal. *A. Filix-fœmina*, the Lady-Fern, differs so greatly in habit from all the indigenous species of the next genus, *Asplenium*, to which in point of fructification it approaches the nearest, that few amateur collectors would think of seeking among them for its description: I have therefore followed the example of most of my contemporaries, in regarding it as the type of the present.

25

Athyrium Filix-foemina.

The name, first applied by Roth, from the Greek ἄθυρος, *open*, probably refers to the turning back of the indusium.

Athyrium Filix-fœmina. Lady-Fern. Tab. XXV.

Fronds lanceolate, bipinnate: pinnæ linear-lanceolate, acuminate: pinnules oblong-lanceolate, deeply serrated or pinnatifid.

Athyrium Filix-fœmina, *Roth. Babington. Moore. Newman.* Asplenium Filix-fœmina, *Bernhardi. Hooker and Arnott.* Aspidium Filix-fœmina, *Swartz. Smith. E. B.* Polypodium, *Linnæus.*

It occurs in most parts of the kingdom, less universal in its distribution than *Lastrea Filix-mas*, but equally abundant in those localities that are adapted to its growth. Moist, shady situations are essential to its full development, and though occasionally a few stunted plants may be found on the exposed heath and hill-side, it is on the sheltered hedge-bank, and in the damp wood and ravine, that it attains the graceful and almost fragile character, which acquired for it in long past times the popular name. The fronds appear in May, springing in succession from the crown of a thick and more or less elongated rhizoma, which occasionally, in old plants, rises above the ground, in the form of a trunk or stipes, from a few inches to a foot or more in height: their early development is very similar to that described under *L. Filix-mas*, p. 19, and they not unfrequently assume the vase-like arrangement of those of the latter fern; in which case, and when of large size especially, few vegetable productions equal this in grace and beauty. In the subalpine parts of the country I have often noticed specimens so charactered, in which the central fronds had a height of between four and five feet and were nearly erect, while the outer ones drooping in every direction around them, the whole comprised the most lovely arrangement of light green feathery foliage that it is possible to conceive. I once counted thirty-seven fronds composing such a tuft. The general outline varies from a broad, almost ovate, to a linear-lanceolate, and the rachis, generally bare from about one-third to a fourth of its length, is sometimes feathered with pinnæ gradually diminishing in size almost to its base. The pinnæ are much diversified as to disposition, being either alternate or opposite, distant or close together, in different specimens. In some instances the bipinnate character is departed from, the pinnules being decurrent. The division and serrature of the pinnules are equally variable, and though the venation, owing to the delicate texture of the frond, is readily traced, it is far from presenting that regularity in its branching which would render it worthy of notice. The position of the sori is always on the upper or anterior side of the branch veins, but they are very irregular in form, being sometimes straight, and in other instances so short as to appear nearly circular, although the curved reniform or semilunar outline is the most common: in some varieties they are distant, in others so close as to become eventually confluent, even to completely covering the under surface. Such differences have afforded a wide scope for speculative botanists to indulge their fancies in the multiplication of species and varieties, and were the wishes and advice of all my kind correspondents to be attended to in regard to the latter, I might exhaust the Greek alphabet from alpha to omega in prefixes. The claim advanced on behalf of a few of the varieties to rank as species, should be very cautiously examined before its admission; those who recommend or incline to their adoption would do well to bear in mind the plasticity of vegetable nature, and the very uncertain tenure of specific distinction in the aggregate, not in this class only, but in groups far higher in grade, and in which features of more determinate character can be arraigned in evidence of supposed dissimilarity. The three principal forms, including the normal one, that are considered best entitled to the rank in question are thus characterized:—

1. *incisum.* Fronds more or less drooping, broadly lanceolate: pinnæ distant: pinnules lanceolate, distinct, flat, pinnatifid with toothed lobes. Sori distinct. A. Filix-fœmina, *Roth.*

2. *molle.* Fronds nearly erect, lax, lanceolate: pinnæ approximate: pinnules oblong, connected by the wing of the midrib, flat, toothed. Sori distinct. A. molle, *Roth.*

3. *convexum.* Fronds nearly erect, rigid, narrow-lanceolate: pinnæ distant, convex: pinnules distant, linear, toothed or pinnatifid, convex, with deflexed margins. Sori short, numerous, eventually confluent. A. rhæticum, *Roth. Moore, Handb.* 136. Aspidium irriguum? *Smith. E. B.* 2199. This is, unquestionably, the most decidedly charactered of all the forms, and less positively associated with them by intermediates.

Besides the numerous slight variations in habit, and in the outline and division of the frond, several remarkable monstrosities are met with in cultivation; of these the variety *crispum* is the most common, and its dwarf, clustered, and much-divided fronds resemble a tuft of curled parsley—a figure of one of the fronds is given by Mr. Moore, Handb. 142. It was originally found by Mr. A. Smith, on Orah Hill, Antrim, Ireland, and since by Sir W. C. Trevelyan, in Braemar, Scotland. Another Irish variety, still more peculiar, is given by Mr. Newman, Hist. Brit. Ferns, 218.

The cultivation of the Lady-Fern is not attended with any difficulty, as it will grow in almost any kind of light soil, provided the situation be not too dry or exposed to the sun. To obtain it in its beauty, however, it should be planted in a mixture of turfy peat

Asplenium fontanum.

and sand, and supplied during the growing season with abundance of water. When potted, the ordinary compost will suffice; but the pots should be large, the bottom covered with small lumps of charcoal, and placed in pans of water. In a shaded greenhouse, under these circumstances, this beautiful fern may be grown to great perfection, and it assumes a delicacy of hue and texture resembling those of tropical development. In the open air its beauty is much enhanced by planting at such a distance from others as to allow the foliage from each tuft to spread without interference, and this is a good rule to be observed in the arrangement of all the larger tufted species of the tribe; even in artificial wilderness scenery, if it be not attended to, the general effect of the masses is greatly deteriorated.

In Ireland, *A. Filix-fœmina* abounds on most of the bogs, occupying in the open parts of the country the position of the common brake on our heaths, and, like that, is employed as a packing material for fish and fruit.

Genus 7. ASPLENIUM.

Gen. Char. Sori linear-oblong, straight, attached along the upper or inner side of the veins. Indusium opening toward the mid-vein or inwardly.

The sori are in some species, as in *A. fontanum*, so short, that at first sight the generic character may appear doubtful, but the position of the indusium is more to be attended to in this genus than the outline of the masses of fructification. The mid-vein is not always present, a circumstance that has given rise to a division of the genus by some botanists, and which is here adopted in the arrangement of the species, on account of the difference of habit to which it is allied.

The name, from the Greek *a*, privative, and σπλὴν, *the spleen*, was bestowed on one of the European species, formerly in repute as a remedy in diseases supposed to originate in an enlargement of the spleen, and even considered capable of dissolving that organ if administered in excess.

* *Ultimate divisions with a distinct midvein.* Asplenium.

Asplenium fontanum. Smooth Rock Spleenwort. Tab. XXVI.

Fronds linear-lanceolate, rigid, bipinnate, glabrous: pinnæ oblong-ovate: pinnules obovate-cuneate, with a few large angular mucronate teeth. Rachis winged throughout. Sori short, oblong.

Asplenium fontanum, *Bernhardi. Smith. Hooker and Arnott. Moore, Handb.* Aspidium fontanum, *Swartz. E. B.* 2024.

Athyrium fontanum, *Presl.* *Babington, Manual.* Polypodium fontanum, *Linnæus.*

This may be considered a rarity in England; indeed most of our botanists doubt its title to admission among British species. It seems to have been first noticed here by Hudson, as growing "above Wybourn, in Westmoreland," and afterwards as being found on Agmondesham or Amersham church, Buckinghamshire, but these localities have been since searched in vain. The herbarium of the Botanical Society of London contains specimens, presented by Mr. Newnham, from Cavehill, Belfast, and others collected in 1838, on rocks in Wharncliffe Wood, Yorkshire, by Mr. Redhead: Mr. Moore mentions its having been gathered "on rocks near Stonehaven, Kincardineshire, in a spot since destroyed by the construction of a railway," and likewise at Matlock, in Derbyshire. As it is a not uncommon fern in rocky districts on the continent of Europe, it is not unlikely that the preceding habitats may be correctly stated; but it has been unfortunately circumstanced, like *Cystopteris alpina*, in being so scantily distributed as to escape the observation of succeeding inquirers, or to be obliterated by the march of improvement; the latter was the case in the only instance in which I ever met with it otherwise than under cultivation, viz. on an old wall on Tooting Common, Surrey, where the ruthless hand of repair had already commenced its destruction. The Rev. W. H. Hawker found it last year "growing in some quantity on a very old wall near Petersfield, in Hampshire."

The fronds grow in a dense tuft, varying from two or three to five or six inches in length; they are smooth, of a deep green hue and very rigid texture, are more or less erect and of a linear or narrow lanceolate outline: the rachis is slightly winged and leafy almost to the base, the lower pinnæ gradually diminishing in size and becoming more distant, the upper ones being shorter and more crowded as they approach the apex; the pinnules are often decurrent, they are of an obovate form tapering below, and deeply divided with from two to five sharp spinous teeth. The sori, two or three generally on each pinnule, are very short, sometimes approaching to circular; their disposition is far from regular, and they often become confluent.

In cultivation this pretty fern has with many a very indifferent character for endurance: in the open air it is exceedingly liable to die off during the winter, unless the situation be well sheltered and the drainage complete; indeed, I have never known it to exist beyond the second year in the vicinity of London, unless when planted on a fragment of an old and mouldering wall, under the shade of some aged trees, but at the same time so arranged as to avoid their drip. Under glass, in a close frame or shaded greenhouse, there

Asplenium lanceolatum

is no difficulty in keeping it; but it should be planted in sandy peat, and the drainage secured by filling the pot about one-fourth with pieces of old mortar and charcoal intermixed. Mr. Moore recommends elevating the caudex a little above the level of the soil between two or three pieces of soft sandstone, and I have no doubt the plan would be advantageous in securing the growth of a small specimen; though, if the arrangement below be such as to prevent any accumulation of superfluous moisture about the roots, a plant once established is not liable to damp off under ordinary care. Although a comparatively small species, I have found that it requires considerable space to extend its roots, and that it is safer to use a large than a very small pot, so that when settled it may remain undisturbed for two or three years at the least. The increase by division of the main caudex should be avoided by those who may be desirous of retaining a fine specimen, as its growth is slow, and, unless assisted by the temperature of a hothouse, liable to receive a check that the plants do not readily recover. This remark is addressed to the amateur cultivator not possessing all the appliances requisite to ensure success in propagation, and it is induced by having witnessed the destruction of two noble specimens under the infliction. It is an evergreen species, and, under cover, continues its growth throughout the year.

Asplenium lanceolatum. Lanceolate Spleenwort. Tab. XXVII.

Fronds lanceolate, bipinnate: pinnæ ovate-lanceolate: pinnules obovate, deeply and sharply toothed. Rachis not winged. Sori short, nearly marginal.

Asplenium lanceolatum, *Hudson. Smith. E. B.* 240. *Hooker and Arnott. Moore. Babington. Newman.*

A very local species in this country, where it is almost exclusively confined to the maritime counties of the south of England and of Wales. Being a native of the Atlantic Islands and of the south of Europe, it may be regarded rather as naturalized than indigenous. In the Channel Islands, Jersey especially, it is most abundant. Its favourite localities are in the crevices of rocks and old walls, and lining the sides of wells and the shafts of deserted mines. The fronds rise from a tufted base or crown, varying greatly according to situation, in size, position, form, and even texture: they are of a bright green colour, the lower part of the rachis excepted, which is purplish-black, when growing exposed to light. In shady and moist places they attain a length of twelve or eighteen inches, while on dry rocks and walls they often do not extend to more than two or three inches; sometimes they are erect in growth, sometimes drooping or even spreading horizontally. The rachis is more or less covered with bristle-like scales. The general outline of the frond varies from linear-lanceolate to a broader and more directly lanceolate form, and in some specimens it is nearly triangular: the pinnæ and pinnules are equally variable, and the former are often, and not in young plants only, lobed instead of pinnate; the ultimate divisions in either case are deeply and sharply toothed or serrated, a branch of the lateral veins extending to the extremity of each serrature. The sori are remarkable, compared with those of other species of the genus, both as to form and position; they are produced near the terminations of the branch veins, usually one to each serrature, and are at first, while yet covered by their thin white indusium, oblong or even linear, but become circular as they enlarge, and eventually often confluent, so as to form a line round the whole under-margin: their arrangement in luxuriant specimens is very irregular. When the frond approaches the triangular outline, this fern is apt to be mistaken for the following species, *A. Adiantum-nigrum*, the peculiarity of the sori constituting the most marked differential character between them.

Like other maritime species of ferns, natural importations from a warmer climate, the Lanceolate Spleenwort is not at all adapted for cultivation in the open air in the eastern parts of England; this may be understood by noticing the limited extent of its distribution here, reaching, it is true along the whole southern coast from the Land's End to Kent, and along the western as far north as Caernarvonshire; but still confined to localities influenced by the great current and swell of the Atlantic, and chiefly to those so situated as to receive their continuous flow,—the counties between the Channel and the estuary of the Severn. A treatment similar to that recommended for the last species, *A. fontanum*, I have found to succeed the best hitherto, except that it makes less root, and does not require so large a pot in proportion to the size of the plant. Another circumstance to be noted is, that it is very susceptible of injury under close confinement, and consequently not adapted for the Wardian cases. From observation of several plants placed under different conditions, I believe this injury to the fern in question to arise from the accumulation of water on the surface of the fronds: breathing a moist atmosphere, it must be admitted, is very distinct from drowning, and to the latter process the moisture-loving fern is too frequently subjected by the mismanagement of a very useful invention. In Nature, superfluous moisture is removed quickly by evaporation, and although some plants are capable of adapting their functions according to the circumstances in which they may be placed, others are less pliant, and our *Asplenium* is one to which a perpetual vapour-bath is death. Under all its forms it is ornamental, and, like most of its congeners, evergreen.

28

Asplenium Adiantum nigrum

Asplenium Adiantum-nigrum. Black Spleenwort. Tab. XXVIII.

Fronds triangular attenuated or ovate, twice or thrice pinnate: pinnæ triangular: pinnules ovate or ovate-lanceolate, inciso-pinnatifid, sharply toothed. Sori linear-elongate, approximate to the midvein.

Asplenium Adiantum-nigrum, *Linnæus*. *E. B.* 1950. Generally adopted.

One of the most generally distributed of our smaller ferns, being found in almost every part of the kingdom, growing in the crevices of rocks and old walls and on shaded hedge-banks. The fronds spring in tufts from the crowns of a slowly-branching rhizoma, and vary greatly in development in different habitats, being often on exposed walls and rocks not above two or three inches in length, while under the influence of shade and moisture they extend to one or two feet. The rachis is bare about half of its length, and this part is glossy and of a deep purple almost black. The leafy portion of the frond is mostly of an elongated triangular outline, but sometimes perfectly deltoid, the lowest pair of pinnæ being always longer than the others, unless occasionally in very small specimens when an ovate-lanceolate form prevails. The pinnæ are pinnate, obliquely triangular, and generally point upwards toward the apex of the frond; they differ much in division, but it is only in very large fronds that the tripinnate character is fully developed. The ultimate divisions are unequally toothed, the teeth being more or less attenuated or obtuse, but always terminating in a point. The venation is very distinct, and varies with the division of the frond, the fructification being always produced on the inner or upper side, near the separation of the branches from the midvein, and thus occupying the middle of the pinnules. The sori are linear, covered at their first appearance with a white indusium attached on the outer side to the vein; in maturity this is covered by the expansion of the thecæ and the sori become confluent, often spreading so as to occupy the whole under surface.

The protean character of this fern is apt to mislead the too sanguine collector in his search for novelties, and an assemblage of all its diversities of form would certainly puzzle the discriminative faculties of any one beholding them for the first time: a little farther acquaintance, however, and especially the results obtained by cultivating them under corresponding treatment, will soon dispel any illusion regarding specific distinction. A very striking difference is presented in contrasting the two extremes of form to which it is liable, the intermediate and most common one being that on which the foregoing description has been chiefly framed.

When of small size, as before remarked, the form of the frond is often less triangular, and in such case it is less divided, and the divisions are broader and more obtuse:—this not unfrequent condition, dependent on accidental circumstances, presents us with the original *Asplenium obtusum* of Willdenow, the variety *obtusum* of later authors.

A second form has acquired more importance on account of its being still regarded by some as a separate species, viz. *Asplenium acutum*, Bory (Newman, Hist. Brit. Ferns, 231). Mr. Newman's figure represents a luxuriant frond from Ireland, to which country, in the text, he confines its British habitats. I have met with the same, smaller in size, in several parts of North Wales, and have preserved specimens collected in 1821 from the walls of the Cathedral at St. Asaph, between which and those of Irish growth I am unable to trace any difference. In regard to its being a species, such claim is very doubtful, resting apparently at present solely upon a slight difference in texture, not appreciable by the aid of the microscope, and the narrow linear form of the ultimate divisions of the frond.

The Black Spleenwort was formerly employed medicinally in diseases of the chest, its real or supposed efficacy in asthma, cough, &c. being probably based upon a slight tonic quality belonging to the ferns generally, and the relief afforded by its mucilaginous juices.

All the forms are ornamental and well adapted for rock-work, but though it will live in exposed situations, the more luxuriant states are only obtainable in the shade. It will grow in any light soil, but succeeds best when planted in a mixture of sandy peat and old mortar. It is well fitted for the stove or greenhouse, but the pots should be carefully drained. In the close case, it soon becomes mouldy and decays.

Asplenium marinum. Sea Spleenwort. Tab. XXIX.

Fronds linear, pinnate: pinnæ stalked, oblong-ovate, inciso-serrate, oblique, obtuse, unequally wedge-shaped, and more or less auricled at the base. Rachis winged.

Asplenium marinum, *Linnæus. Smith. E. B.* 392. *Hooker and Arnott. Babington. Moore. Newman.*

Frequent on rocks and cliffs, and especially in caverns, near the sea; it grows likewise on old walls, castles, and churches, but very rarely in inland situations. Its principal localities are on the southern and western shores of the island, commencing with the sand cliffs of Hastings; but it is distributed at intervals around the Scottish coast, terminating on the eastern side about Scar-

Asplenium marinum.

borough in Yorkshire. On the shores of Ireland and in the Channel Islands it is most abundant. Few of our native ferns vary more in size and general aspect than this; in exposed situations the fronds being often not above an inch in length, while in warm and sheltered ones they are not unfrequently one or two feet or even more. The rhizoma is short, firmly fixed by long and very slender wiry radicles that penetrate deeply into the crevices of the rocks, which renders transplantation difficult and precarious; it forms new crowns or branches that divide very slowly, so that in plants of large size the fronds compose a dense tuft. The rachis is bare for about one-third of its length, glossy, and of a dark purplish-brown colour, passing into black at the base. The pinnæ are nearly equal in length throughout, except towards the apex, giving the frond generally a linear but slightly acuminated outline; they are of a deep green above, pale beneath, in maturity of a firm, almost leathery texture, and so placed as to point more or less obliquely forward; in form and distance on the rachis they vary according to size and exposure, the general figure being an oblong-oval, with an unequal base, more or less auricled on the upper side and truncated below; the margin is serrated, and occasionally so deeply as to become lobed. The lateral veins are alternate and forked, bearing the linear sori on the upper division.

Although so common and so widely distributed along our sea-shores, this is a troublesome fern in cultivation; it will not bear exposure at all in the vicinity of London. I have tried it several times on rock-work, and under various treatment as to soil and elevation, but have never succeeded in keeping it through the winter. In many of its native habitats it occupies caverns and narrow crevices, of such depth that the light must be almost totally excluded; in these it attains the greatest luxuriance; and in an imitation cleft, a small Devonshire specimen, planted this spring, bids fair to rival its wild associates, and, judging from present appearance and progress, to find itself quite at home. Independent of the effect of cold upon plants, we do not pay sufficient attention in cultivation to the circumstances attending their natural growth. I have previously referred to the necessity of observation in this respect, and believe the want of such observation to be a main obstacle to that success, the failure of which is so often deplored by the fern amateur. Now, in regard to the species before us, it will be found, almost universally, growing sheltered from the wind, and so disposed as to avoid the lodgement of rain upon the fronds; the latter is a point most essential to the health of an evergreen fern, and if attended to, would, as I know from experience, ensure that duration which is in many instances so equivocal. In pot-cultivation, *A. marinum* requires the same care of ensuring perfect drainage that is necessary to rock-plants generally. The soil may be a mixture of peat and sand in about equal proportions, or an additional fourth of the latter material may be added to the ordinary compost; pieces of broken slate or angular fragments of granite forced through the loose soil at the time of planting and before settling the whole by watering, assist the after-drainage, and form a medium over which the growing radicles are encouraged to extend their ramifications. The pots may be kept in a cold frame or green-house; in the latter case, it is better to cover it with a glass shade. In the hot-house it will attain a large size, and when the air is kept moist, does not require a glass. In such circumstances I have seen the fronds eighteen or twenty inches long; certainly it luxuriates in warmth.

The distribution of this species, extending from the north of Africa and the Canaries and Madeiras, along the shores of Spain and France, and its absence in other parts of Europe, apparently well authenticated, is a curious geographical phænomenon, pointing to a probability of its having taken place prior to the great disruption of the chalk and the vast deposit of alluvial matter along the eastern coast of England, especially when added to the fact of its sparing occurrence in Hampshire and Sussex, and to its non-existence throughout the former line of connexion between this country and the continent, and even beyond this northward to Flamborough Head.

The pinnæ of *A. marinum* are occasionally very narrow, and the serratures so deep as to give a totally different aspect to the plant; but no permanent or decided varieties exist deserving more than a passing notice.

Asplenium Trichomanes. Common Wall Spleenwort. Common Maiden-hair. Tab. XXX.

Fronds linear, pinnate: pinnæ opposite, roundish-oblong, obtuse, crenated, stalked, truncated and cuneate below. Rachis purple or black.

Asplenium Trichomanes, *Linnæus. Smith. E.B.* 576. *Hooker and Arnott. Babington. Moore. Newman.*

This beautiful little evergreen fern is one of very general distribution on shaded rocks, old walls and buildings, generally selecting a northern aspect, or at least a position not exposed to the sun; occasionally it is met with covering hedge-banks in a sandy soil. The fronds grow in tufts from a short, dense rhizoma, erect or spreading according to circumstances, and vary in length from two or three inches to a foot. The rachis is smooth, glossy, of a deep purple approaching to black, and leafy almost to the base. The

Asplenium Trichomanes

pinnæ, mostly opposite, vary in distance, and are of a roundish oval form, sometimes nearly rhomboidal; they are of a deep glossy green colour, slightly crenated on the margin, and attached to the rachis by a very short stalk formed by the attenuation of the wedge-shaped base. The lateral veins divide about midway into two or rarely three branches, the upper one bearing a sorus near its extremity, obliquely pointed towards the apex of the pinna.

The fronds are occasionally forked or even multifid at the apex; but this is not a character sufficiently permanent to constitute a variety. Plants having the pinnæ of a thin texture, and more or less deeply pinnatifid, are sometimes met with, and such have retained this character under cultivation, constituting the variety *incisum* of some botanists. It is generally barren.

The common Spleenwort is very easily cultivated, and is among the most elegant of the smaller ferns, and, above all, admirably adapted for the decoration of shaded rock-work. Of course we must be guided in our treatment by bearing in mind, as in regard to other species, the conditions of its natural growth. Many persons think that if they put the root of a plant into soil, and water it, they have done all that is necessary, and are surprised and disappointed when their expectations are not realized. Now, the wall and rock ferns require something more than this, or they will not grow to please us. The thin succulent extremities of the wiry roots, insinuating themselves into every crevice, and absorbing on all sides the scanty moisture retained by the coarse material upon which they vegetate, are in removal generally left behind; and yet the plant is expected to live and flourish, for the simple reason that, as it must have been half-starved upon the dry wall, and now has plenty to feed upon, it ought to do so. The decayed mortar and the mouldering brick, while they afford the potash, lime, and other mineral substances necessary to fern-structure, ensure the grand requisite of drainage, and admit no accumulation of moisture beyond that which is essential to vegetable life. Stagnant water, and especially when lodged in soil abounding in decomposing organic matter, is fatal to most of the species of this genus; and though *A. Trichomanes* will flourish under shelter in almost any kind of compost employed by the fern-grower, I have never found it succeed so well in the open air, under exposure to the alternate wet and frost of winter, as when planted in old mortar mingled with a very small proportion of sandy peat. It may be grown in pots in the green-house or in a cold frame, but does not like confinement for any length of time; and though the shelter of a bell-glass is favourable to its full development within-doors, frequent change of air will alone prevent it from eventually becoming unhealthy.

Asplenium viride. Green Spleenwort. Tab. XXXI.

Fronds linear, pinnate: pinnæ alternate, rhomboidal or roundish-ovate, crenated, stalked. Rachis green.

Asplenium viride, *Hudson*. *Smith. E. B.* 2257. *Hooker and Arnott. Babington. Moore. Newman.* A. Trichomanes ramosum, *Linnæus.*

Chiefly confined to mountainous and rocky districts, and delighting in the vicinity of rills and waterfalls, but occasionally found elsewhere. It is a local rather than a rare species, and is very liable to be passed over as a form of *A. Trichomanes*, which it nearly resembles in general appearance, though usually growing more erect than the ordinary state of that species. The whole plant is however of a paler hue, especially the rachis, which, though dark brown or purple at the base, is always light green or yellowish above. The fronds are tufted, in dry situations two or three inches long, in moist ones ten inches to a foot. About one-third of the rachis is bare: the pinnæ are usually more distant than those of the preceding fern; they are very variable in form, but most frequently tend to the rhomboidal; the margin, too, is more or less deeply crenated. The lateral veins are generally alternate and forked, and the sori are produced near the point of division, rarely at or near the extremity of the upper venule as in *A. Trichomanes*.

A tendency to divide dichotomously is more remarkable in the fronds of this fern than in those of the preceding, and originated the Linnæan specific name.

In the vicinity of London the cultivation of *A. viride* is far from being satisfactory; it does not succeed well in the open air, and is apt to damp off under confinement. Among the various kinds of treatment to which it has been subjected, I have not hitherto had reason to congratulate myself as to the result; the plants live, but cannot be said to flourish; they send out new fronds strong and well-conditioned in the early summer, and then, in whatever situation they may be placed, gradually assume an unhealthy appearance, which characterizes them during the greater part of the year. A mixture of broken freestone and sandy peat seems to succeed best as soil, and the pots should be one-third filled with draining material, the upper part of which should consist of charcoal broken into small fragments: I believe the chief value of this latter medium, as applied to fern cultivation, consists in its absorbing and antiseptic qualities, which enable it to retain moisture, and at the same time to counteract the effects of it in a stagnant condition upon the soil. The foregoing remarks are only to be considered as applicable to the metropolitan climate; in a purer air and moist

Asplenium viride

Asplenium Ruta-muraria.

J.E.S. Sc.

sheltered situation it seems almost, if not quite, as much at home as among its native alpine rocks.

** *Ultimate divisions without a midvein.* Amesium, *Newman.*

Asplenium Ruta-muraria. Wall-Rue. White Maiden-hair. Tab. XXXII.

Fronds deltoid, bipinnate: pinnules rhomboid-wedge-shaped, notched or toothed on the upper margin. Indusium jagged.

Asplenium Ruta-muraria, *Linnæus. Smith. E. B.* 150. *Hooker and Arnott. Moore. Babington.* Amesium Ruta-muraria, *Newman, Hist. Brit. Ferns,* 253.

Very common on old walls throughout the kingdom, but indigenous to the mountainous and subalpine portion of it, where it grows in the fissures of the rocks: its original migration from the latter is indicated by the fact of its occurrence being gradually less frequent as we advance from the central counties of England toward the eastern coast. Its predilection for brick walls was noticed at an early period, hence the common English name, and it may be accounted for by the preference it exhibits in the wild state for rocks of calcareous composition. In general appearance and stature it is very much diversified; in the low countries, as a wall-plant, we are familiar with it as one of small size, with fronds sparingly divided, from half an inch to two inches in length; while, in the rocky clefts of the hills of Derbyshire, Wales, and Scotland, they attain a length of six or eight inches, and a branched habit that might readily induce the casual observer to regard it as a different species. Our figures are rather to be taken as expressive of the ordinary than of the alpine form, which latter is subject to considerable deviation. The fronds grow in tufts from the extremity of a slowly extending and branching rhizoma; they are of a thick, almost leathery substance and deep green colour, but in exposed situations always covered with a glaucous secretion, whence the name White Maiden-hair. In young and starved specimens, the fronds are sometimes undivided or only simply pinnate with roundish or reniform pinnæ, but the more compound character and triangular outline above assigned prevail even in comparatively small plants. The normal arrangement of both pinnæ and pinnules is alternate, but they are not unfrequently opposite in the dwarfer forms, and the latter vary in figure from bluntly wedge-shaped to rhomboidal, more or less attenuated in both directions, so as to become in some instances almost linear; under all circumstances the upper margin is irregularly toothed or serrated, the wedge-shaped base entire. The veins diverge in a flabelliform manner from the stalk-like base of the pinnules, branching above and extending to the teeth or serratures, without any apparent mid-vein. The sori, produced on the inner side of the veins, are linear elongated and eventually become confluent, covering the whole under side of the pinnule. The indusium, only traceable in the earlier condition of the fructification, is white, and the free inner margin if examined at the time of separation is more or less jagged or uneven, a character of small importance in specific distinction, unless far more decided than will be found in this instance (see the following species).

Those who would cultivate this fern should endeavour to obtain it with the roots uninjured, which it is impossible to effect by any other means than removing the brick- or stone-work among which it grows, a process not always agreeable to the owner. When obtained from the fissures of rocks, the principal portion of the fibres is often left behind; circumstances exceedingly adverse to its after-establishment. Grown in pots, brick rubbish or old mortar with a very small admixture of sandy peat, a strict attention to drainage, free air, and little water, are the conditions on which it may be expected to live, but, like many other common plants, care kills it. Wall specimens, removed with the mortar in which their roots are imbedded, and placed between bricks or stones piled in imitation of the stone-hedges of Wales, and with a little old mortar scattered between them, will generally establish themselves readily, especially if sheltered from the sun and cold winds; for though the plant is often found naturally developed from seed in very exposed places, a certain degree of exclusion may generally be traced in its choice of a habitat.

Asplenium alternifolium. Alternate-leaved Spleenwort. Tab. XXXIII.

Fronds pinnate: pinnæ alternate, distant, wedge-shaped, ascending, bifid or trifid at the apex. Indusium entire.

Asplenium alternifolium, *Wulfen. Smith. E. B.* 2258. *Hooker and Arnott.* Asplenium germanicum, *Weiss. Babington. Moore.* Amesium germanicum, *Newman, Hist. Brit. Ferns,* 258.

As a British species this is extremely rare, and, though widely distributed, far from common on the Continent. Its localities agree with those of *A. Ruta-muraria,* which however it is not found to accompany. Three habitats have been recorded in Scotland; three miles from Dunfermline, Fifeshire; Stenton Rocks, near Dunkeld, Perthshire; rocks on the Tweed, two miles from Kelso, Roxburghshire. In England it has been met with on Kyloe Crags, Northum-

33

Asplenium alternifolium

berland; in three or four places about Borrowdale, Cumberland, growing in the clefts of the rocks; and Mr. W. Hawker writes that he met with two plants of it this summer (1854) growing with *Asplenium septentrionale*, on a precipice near Scaw-fell. In North Wales, it has been collected near Llanrwst, and in the Pass of Llanberis. The habit of this fern approaches so nearly that of the preceding, that many botanists consider them to be merely varieties of the same species; and some forms of *A. Ruta-muraria* certainly do resemble it in foliation, to a degree that appears at first sight to render the question of identity far from doubtful: the general outline of the frond, however, and its division are very different; in the present it is narrow lanceolate or linear, and never more than simply pinnate, it is likewise of thinner texture and lighter green colour. The pinnæ, though varying in form and size upon the same frond, are always distant and directed upwards; they are generally of a narrow wedge-shape rapidly attenuated downwards into a slender stalk, toothed or notched at the extremity, and, the lower ones especially, not unfrequently divided into two or three lobes; not however showing any tendency to the bipinnate character. The sori are developed like those of its near ally, but differ in the margin of the indusium being entire. The fronds are usually from two to four inches in height, but some preserved specimens from the Tyrolese mountains measure six or seven inches.

The scarcity of this fern has hitherto prevented experiment upon its growth in the open air, in which it would probably succeed as well as the preceding. It is usually kept in the house covered by a bell glass, but is liable to die off during winter, and even in the full growth of summer, without frequent attention to change of air, and avoiding the accumulation of moisture upon the fronds. In planting it is advisable to keep the crown a little elevated above the surface, and the soil may be a mixture of sand and peat, to which some add a little decayed vegetable mould; I do not consider the latter necessary, if it be not injurious, by contributing to the retention of water around the roots, the supply of which ought to be limited so as merely to prevent positive drought.

It is remarkable that the plant before us should occur both in this country and on the Continent in company with *Asplenium septentrionale*, and always very sparingly. To even hint at any probability of connection between them will perhaps horrify some of our modern manufacturers of new species, accustomed as they are to measure differences by half hair-breadths, but under the risk of being classed as an innovator against all the established laws of specific distinction among ferns, I believe this may be the case; indeed, that if the three British species of the *Amesium* series are not really varieties of the same, dependent upon circumstances influencing their primary development, the affinity of the present plant is nearer to the latter than to *A. Ruta-muraria*. The ordinary form of *A. septentrionale* is certainly very different, but under cultivation it occasionally produces branched fronds, the lateral lobes of which so nearly resemble the pinnæ of *A. alternifolium*, that the most practised eye would find it difficult to trace any difference. The character of the indusium is the same.

Asplenium septentrionale. Forked Spleenwort. Tab. XXXIV.

Fronds linear, bi- or tripartite; the segments alternate, elongate, acutely two- or three-toothed above. Margin of the indusium entire.

Asplenium septentrionale, *Hull. Smith. E. B.* 1017. *Hooker and Arnott. Babington. Moore.* Amesium septentrionale, *Newman, Hist. Brit. Ferns,* 265. Acrostichum septentrionale, *Linnæus.*

A very local species in this country, growing in the fissures of rocks and the interstices of the loose stone walls that occupy the place of hedges in the northern and western parts of the kingdom. The habitats are too numerous to record, beyond general notice of the districts in which they may be expected: it is rather a sub-alpine than mountain species, not being found at any great elevation. The extreme western and northern counties of England, the Snowdon district in Wales, the southern and central parts of Scotland, yield it in tolerable abundance, so as scarcely to warrant the epithet of rare applied to it by most writers, though it is doubtless much more so than formerly, in consequence of that insatiate spirit that too often prevails among the *petit maîtres* of natural science, so numerous and so enthusiastic at the present day. The rhizoma creeps and branches, forming when left undisturbed a compact mass of stem and root fibre of large size compared with that of the upward growth. The fronds are generally simple, of an elongated linear-lanceolate form, gradually diminishing in breadth downwards into the rachis, and are from two to four inches in length; the broad part has usually two or three lateral alternate teeth, often so deep as to become lobes, and the extremities of these as well as of the main frond are usually furcate, whence the English name: the variation to which this form is liable has been already referred to in the concluding remarks on *A. alternifolium*. The venation is dependent on the divisions of the frond, a vein or branch extending into each point or segment. The sori are usually more elongated than in the other species of the series, and become confluent in maturity.

The same plan may be pursued in the cultivation of this as recommended for *A. Ruta-muraria*, but it is less adapted for exposure

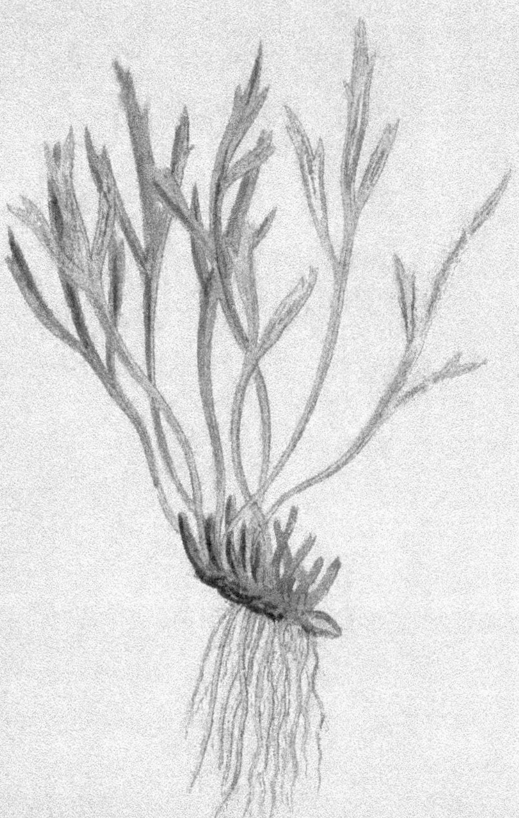

Asplenium septentrionale

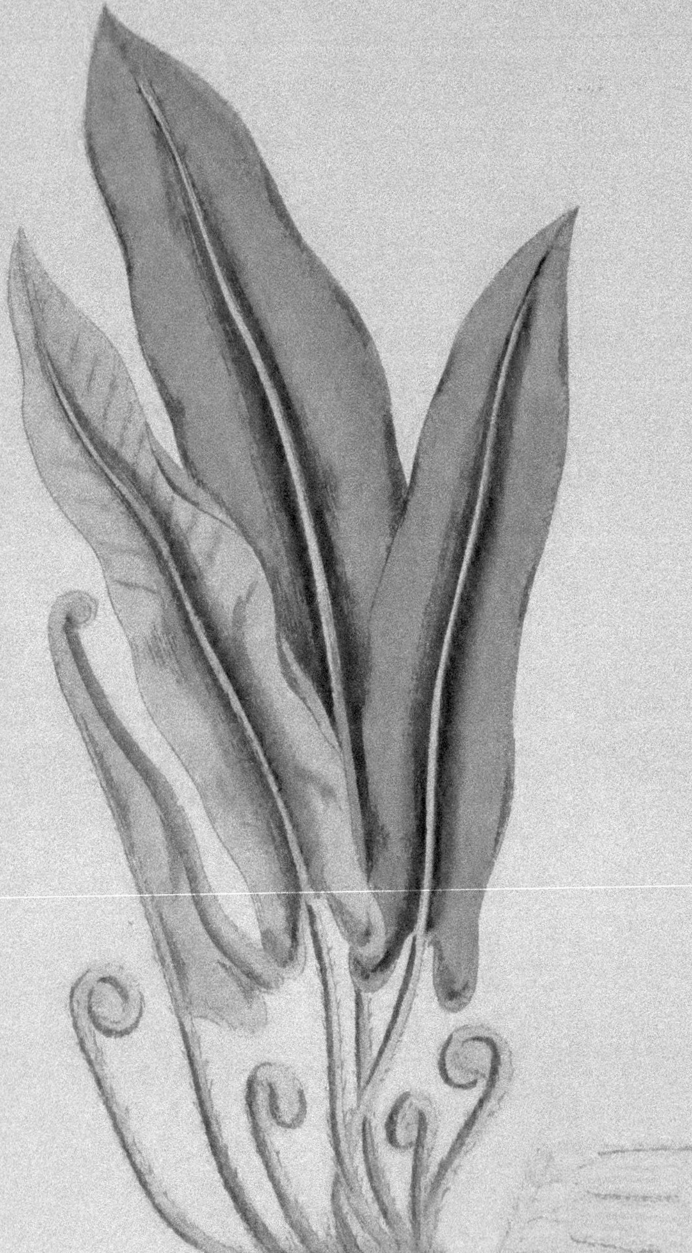

Scolopendrium vulgaris

in the open fernery, at least in the eastern parts of England, the evergreen fronds being liable to suffer from frost, and especially during the dry piercing winds of spring. It will however live and flourish when planted in a sheltered cavity better than under confinement. If potted, a cold close frame, where it may be kept with *A. marinum*, *fontanum*, &c., shaded alike from the sun and cold, will answer better than the greenhouse, bearing in mind that the absence of all superfluous moisture must be strictly attended to, and the fronds of larger ferns must not be allowed to spread over it. The crown should be elevated.

Genus 8. SCOLOPENDRIUM.

GEN. CHAR. Sori linear-elongate, straight, growing on the lateral veins, two together, approximate in one line. Indusia two, opening down the middle of the apparently simple sori.

This genus was separated from *Asplenium* on account of the very remarkable difference of its fructification. The sori are double, each pair being disposed between two parallel branches of the lateral veins, and so closely approximating as to appear as one. The two series of thecæ composing each apparent sorus, arise individually from the opposite sides of the outer branches of two principal lateral veins, each being covered at first by its appropriate indusium: the confined space thus allowed for their development occasions the two sori to become confluent, while the margins of their indusiæ, separating in opposite directions, appear like one opening down the middle. The double or compound character of the sori may be readily traced by careful examination, and will be very evident when observed in an early stage of growth.

The regularly parallel lines of fructification, disposed at equal distances on each side of the mid-vein of the long, entire frond of *S. vulgare*, bear some resemblance in arrangement to the legs of a Scolopendra or Centipede, hence the name.

SCOLOPENDRIUM VULGARE. Common Hart's-tongue. TAB. XXXV.

Fronds entire, linear or oblong-lanceolate, cordate at the base. Rachis shaggy, with narrow membranous scales.

Scolopendrium vulgare, *Symons. Smith. E. B.* 1150. *Hooker and Arnott. Babington. Moore.* Phyllitis Scolopendrium, *Newman, Hist. Brit. Ferns*, 271. Asplenium Scolopendrium, *Linnæus.* Scolopendrium officinarum, *Swartz.* S. Phyllitis, *Roth.*

One of our most common ferns, growing on moist shaded banks, in the clefts of rocks, about old buildings, and in the mouths of wells, mines, and caverns. It varies greatly in size, according to the locality: in the open vault, by the great hall in Conway Castle, I have gathered fronds upwards of three feet long and nearly four inches in breadth; but in more exposed and drier situations their ordinary length is from six inches to a foot. The rhizoma is very compact and deeply rooted; it does not elongate, but increases slowly by the formation of new crowns around the older, attaining thus, when left undisturbed, considerable bulk and an almost spherical form. The fronds grow in circular tufts, unfolding at first in an erect position, but afterwards radiating and curving outwards: when springing from the side of a rock, or in the mouth of a well, they are often pendulous: in outline they are linear-lanceolate or strap-shaped, more or less acuminated at the apex and cordate below, with an entire slightly-waved margin. The rachis is generally of a dark purple hue, especially the petiolate portion, which constitutes about a third or fourth of the length of the frond, sometimes smooth throughout, but more frequently beset with chaffy membranous pale-brown scales, that give it a shaggy appearance, and are often distributed along the under side of the midrib likewise. The parallel linear sori are usually very regular in their disposition, but liable to vary in length, and sometimes form two series, alternately longer and shorter: their peculiarity of development has been already referred to, under the generic character of *Scolopendrium*, and is illustrated, as well as the venation, in the outline figure of a portion of the frond on our plate.

So many deviations from the normal form are presented by the varieties of this fern, and so closely do they approach each other, that it is very difficult to select those deserving a separate notice. In some instances the diversity arises from the division of the rachis, in others from peculiarity in the marginal development of the leaf, and occasionally from a combination of both. Among the apparently endless and far from constant forms thus resulting, the following, well known to the fern cultivator, are the most marked and permanent:—

1. *polyschides.* Fronds narrow linear, deeply and irregularly crenato-lobate on the margin. *Moore, Handb. Brit. Ferns,* 174, fig. δ, 178. Phyllitis polyschides, *Ray.*

The narrow linear form is the distinguishing character of this, the division of the margin being often very obscure. The fronds are generally fertile.

2. *crispum.* Fronds thin, strap-shaped, the margins much undulated or curled, the base cordate-auriculate. *Moore, Handb. Brit. Ferns,* 175, fig. γ, 178.

The dilatation of the margin, which occasions the curled character, is the probable cause of this very elegant and permanent variety being almost uniformly barren.

3. *lobatum.* Fronds strap-shaped below, dilated at the upper part and divided there into two or more acute lobes. *Moore, Handb.* 175, fig. *β*, 178.

When the midrib divides only once, it is the variety *furcatum.* The lobes are generally flat, and fertile like the lower part of the frond. In some instances the primary division of the rachis occurs in that part which may be regarded as the petiole. This constitutes the variety *ramosum*, of which however a correspondent form is met with in the next.

4. *multifidum.* Fronds strap-shaped below, dilated above, repeatedly divided toward the extremity; the lobes more or less obtuse, undulated, crowded. *Moore, Handb.* 175. Phyllitis multifida, *Ray.*

This is a very beautiful variety when grown luxuriantly, but is liable to pass into the preceding form in dry seasons and situations. The lower part of the frond is fertile, the undulated terminal lobes barren.

5. *laceratum.* Fronds broad, the margins deeply and irregularly inciso-lobate, or pinnatifid. *Moore, Handb.* 175.

This remarkable variety was found by Mr. Young of Taunton, on a wall in that neighbourhood, and he has kindly favoured me with original specimens of it and of another, which he has named *endivæfolium*, obtained by sowing its spores; the latter chiefly differing in having the fronds broader, more deeply divided, and the lateral lobes lacerated and toothed at the extremity, while the broad apex is repeatedly divided like that of *multifidum*, which it resembles in having the terminal divisions barren, while the rest of the frond bears sori abundantly. The leading character in these two varieties seems to consist in the deep incision and lobing of the lateral margins, and in the greater comparative breadth of the frond, which is sometimes almost as broad as it is long. I include them under the same general denomination, because the distinguishing features of the so-called *endivæfolium* do not appear to me to be permanent; such at least was the case this year in the growing specimens at Kew, originally forwarded by Mr. Young, in which the two extreme forms and several intermediate ones were developed from the same root.

The broad bright-coloured patches formed by this fern and its varieties render it highly ornamental in contrast with our other native species in cultivation, and its evergreen habit is an especial recommendation to abundant plantation out of doors, as well as in pots among the less hardy exotics of the greenhouse. Though not absolutely requiring the same degree of shelter that is necessary to the preservation of many ferns, the Hart's-tongue may be regarded as a free-growing plant: it can only be obtained in its more luxuriant and ornamental condition by keeping it shaded from the sun and furnished with a copious supply of water during the growing season. In order to avoid the effect of drought, a larger proportion of yellow loam may be added to the ordinary compost to render it more retentive of moisture, but it will grow in almost any kind of soil that is not too stiff for its roots to penetrate.

It was formerly in repute medicinally as an astringent and vulnerary, and an ointment prepared from the bruised leaves is still used in some parts of the country as a dressing for wounds, especially burns and scalds.

Genus 9. CETERACH.

GEN. CHAR. Lateral veins alternate, irregularly branched, the branches anastomosing towards the margin. Sori oblong or linear, attached to the upper side of the anterior principal branches, except the lowest, which is on the opposite side of the lower or posterior branch. Indusium obsolete. Whole back of the frond covered with densely imbricated chaffy scales.

The apparent want of indusium and the anastomosing veins are the chief features that separate this genus from *Asplenium* or *Scolopendrium*, to both of which it has been referred. The indusium is however present in the British plant, partly covering the sorus in an early stage of development, and subsequently as a narrow nearly erect membrane attached to the back of the vein. The Arabian and Persian physicians, by whom the normal species has been long esteemed for its supposed medicinal qualities, call it *Chetherak*.

CETERACH OFFICINARUM. Scaly Spleenwort. TAB. XXXVI.

Fronds linear-lanceolate, deeply pinnatifid; segments oblong-obtuse, waved or slightly lobed on the margin.

Ceterach officinarum, *Willdenow. Hooker and Arnott. Babington. Moore.* Scolopendrium Ceterach, *Symons. Smith. E. B.* 1244. Grammitis Ceterach, *Swartz. Hooker. E. B.* ed. 2, 1408. Asplenium Ceterach, *Linnæus.* Notolepeum Ceterach, *Newman, Hist. Brit. Ferns,* 277.

The countries bordering on the basin of the Mediterranean and the islands and eastern shores of the North Atlantic appear to have been the original stations of this remarkable fern. In the British islands its distribution is too partial to admit of its being regarded as strictly indigenous, though probably naturalized here at a period little subsequent to the arrival of *Asplenium marinum*. It occurs here on limestone rocks, but more frequently on old walls and

30

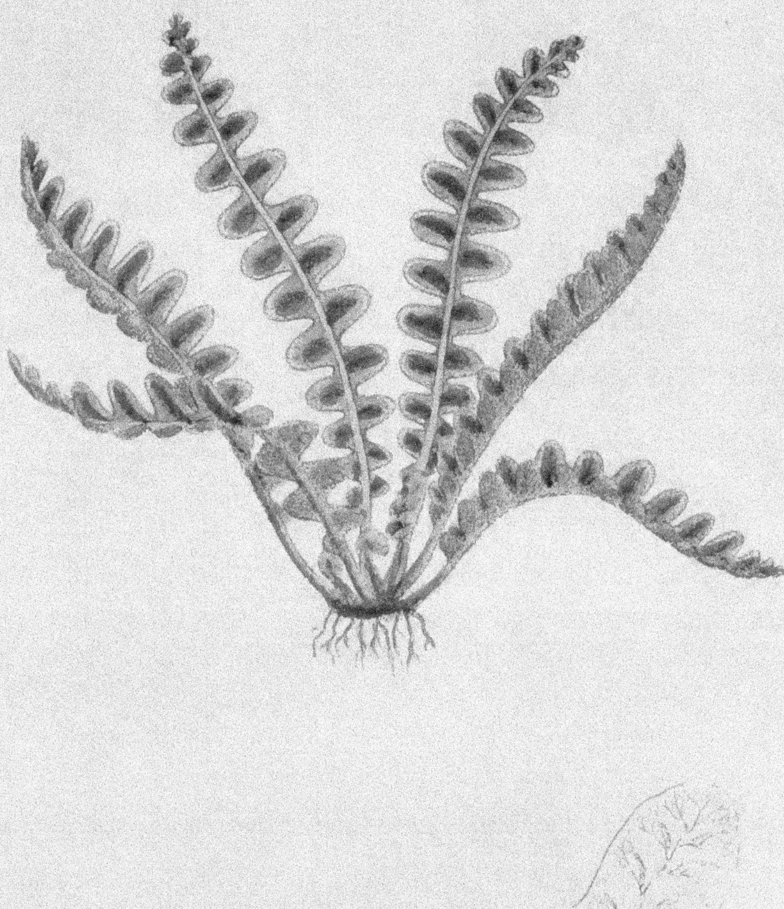

Ceterach officinarum.

ruins, rooted deeply in the decaying mortar, and often accompanying *Asplenium Ruta-muraria* and *Trichomanes*. Like other natural importations from the south, it is found most abundantly in the western maritime counties that receive the more direct flow of the tide, and has progressed slowly towards the northern and central parts of the kingdom; in Scotland it has not yet traversed beyond Perth, and is still regarded as a rare species; while in Ireland its copious distribution seems to indicate an earlier arrival. The fronds are evergreen, the new ones making their appearance in May, and at intervals throughout the summer: they vary considerably in size according to situation, and our figure may be regarded as representing the medium, from three to five inches in length, but where much exposed they are often not more than a third of this, and in very sheltered places sometimes extend to eight or ten inches. Some specimens sent from Teneriffe and Madeira measure more than a foot and a half, with a greater proportionate breadth, that induced me at first to believe them of a different species. It is, however, a fern that cannot be mistaken, and I am informed that seedling plants, raised from the spores of these giants, assumed the general aspect of those of British growth. The general outline of the frond is varied from linear to linear-lanceolate, and the alternate segments are occasionally so far separated by the extension of the rachis as to assume the character of pinnæ, especially where growing in the deeper fissures of rocks. The whole of the under surface is densely clothed with brown, pointed, imbricated scales, finely serrated on their margins, the outermost of which extend beyond the margins of the segments and often overlap them; on the unexpanded fronds these scales are white and silvery. The venation is not very readily traced unless in the young state of the frond, or by carefully removing the sori and scales from the back of an old one, when they will be found to accord with the description of them given under the generic character. The sori are oblong; their disposition has been already noticed, as well as the obscure nature of the indusium: the latter organ, if we are justified in so terming it, is rendered unnecessary as a protecting cover to the thecæ, in consequence of the disposition of the scales; which are arranged in regular series along each side of the veins and venules, pointing outwards, and conceal the sori by their broad bases, which completely overlap them in their immature condition.

The medicinal value of *Ceterach* has long been exploded by European practitioners, though still believed in among those of the East. It seems to have been the true *Asplenium* of the Greeks, mentioned by Dioscorides and others, and which, according to Vitruvius, annihilated the spleen of the Cretan swine that fed upon it.

It is not at all easy to cultivate this fern successfully: it is too impatient of confinement to live long in the greenhouse, and the cold frame, so useful for the protection of other half-hardy species, is almost certain death to this. The metropolitan cultivator is told that London air disagrees with it, and yet the only plant of it I possessed in my early career, lived in a nook of an old wall, in a back area in Hatton Garden, for several years, and may be there still, unless eradicated by repair; sun never reached it, and ancient mortar, which, constantly moist, had somewhat the consistence of paste, probably agreed with its constitution; a very necessary point to be studied in planting, as when left to its own selection, or in the wild state, it seems universally to prefer a calcareous habitat. Whether planted in the open fernery, or grown in pots, great care must be exercised as to drainage, and in the latter case especially to avoid wetting the fronds in watering.

Genus 10. BLECHNUM.

GEN. CHAR. Sori forming a continuous line on each side of the mid-vein, and parallel to it: covered with a continuous indusium opening inwardly.

Named from the Greek, *βλῆχνον*, applied to the following or some other species of fern.

The arrangement of the fructification is very peculiar in this genus, and is dependent upon an equally characteristic form of venation, which latter, however, being in most instances very obscure, I have omitted from the generic character. The lateral veins are alternate, and extend, in our British species, obliquely upward about half-way towards the margin, when, by a sudden turn, each runs parallel to the mid-vein and anastomoses with the one above it, thus forming an apparent longitudinal vein on each side of the middle one. The sori occupy the upper or inner sides of these lateral veins, from the bend to the point of contact with the next, and thus become blended into an uninterrupted line, which the continuity of their indusia renders more decided.

BLECHNUM BOREALE. Hard Fern. TAB. XXXVII.

Fronds linear-lanceolate, of two forms: fertile ones erect, pectinate-pinnate, with distant, narrow linear acute pinnæ: barren ones spreading, pinnatifid, with broadly linear blunt approximate lobes.

Blechnum boreale, *Swartz. Smith. E. B.* 1159. *Babington. Hooker and Arnott.* Blechnum spicant, *Roth. Withering. Moore, Handb. Newman, Hist. Brit. Ferns.* Osmunda spicant, *Linnæus.*

Very common in almost every part of the kingdom, on heaths

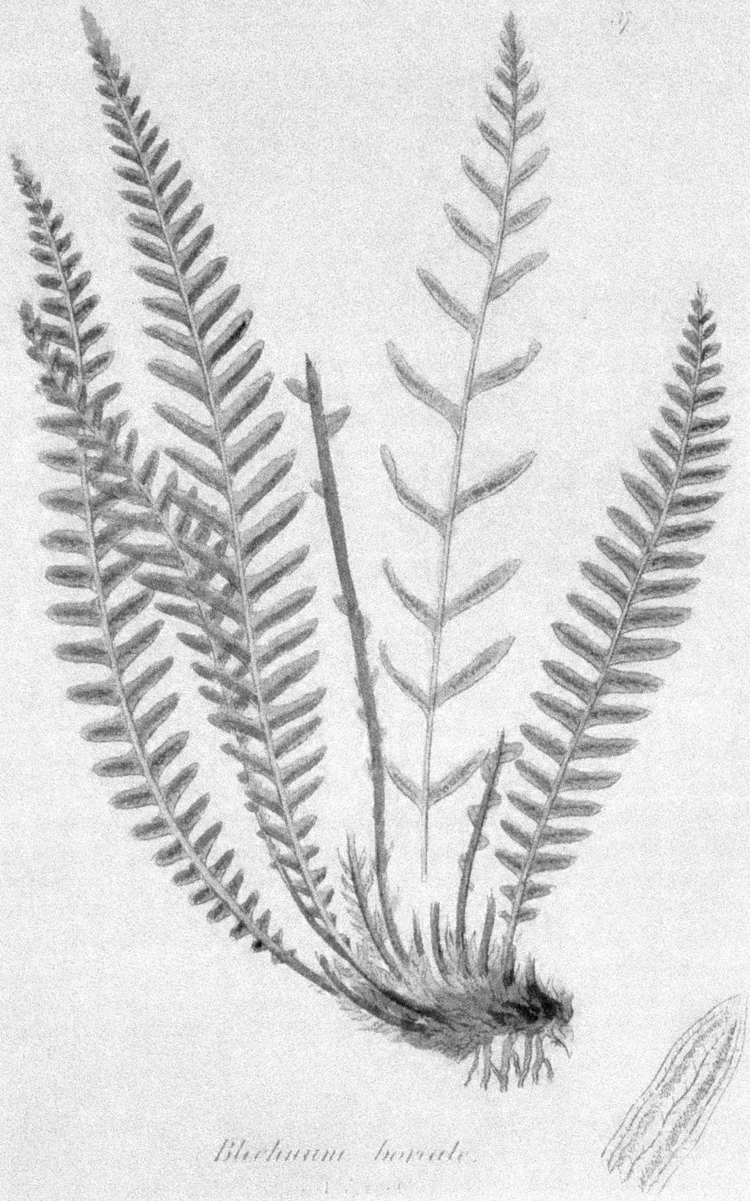

Blechnum boreale.

and uncultivated ground, in woods and thickets, and on rocky hills, especially about pools and water-courses. Its continental distribution is wide, extending from Swedish Lapland to the borders of the Mediterranean. The barren fronds, which remain throughout the winter, are always more or less spreading in their habit, and, where uninterrupted by surrounding vegetation, generally prostrate; they are pinnatifid, smooth, dark green, and leafy nearly to the base, the leafless portion of the rachis being shaggy with lanceolate membranaceous scales; the segments are linear, flat, obtuse at the extremity, more or less approximate, and remarkably regular in disposition: the ordinary length of these fronds is from six to twelve inches. The fertile fronds are always erect, from one to two feet in height, and distantly pinnated: the pinnæ are contracted, linear, generally pointed, and with the margins recurved, not above half the width of the barren segments, one to two inches in length on the upper half of the rachis, but little more than rudimentary below: the rachis is in most instances of a dark purple hue, smooth and glossy. The peculiarity in venation above described, in the remarks on the generic character, does not belong to the barren frond, the lateral veins of the lobes branching dichotomously about the middle, and their divisions extending to the margin, the main or upper branches not anastomosing. The fertile fronds may be found from May to October, but they soon wither away after the dispersion of the sporules.

Like most other ferns, this is liable to deviate from the normal character, and occasionally such deviations may under peculiar treatment become permanent in cultivation, but my own experience has not confirmed this: it is true that specimens sometimes occur in which the frond of *Blechnum boreale* is divided at the extremity, and more frequently, in which the intended fertile frond has all of its pinnæ abortive, the rachis merely developing their rudiments; but I have found the recurrence of such monstrosities too uncertain to admit of enrolling them as varieties.

It is a highly beautiful fern, well worthy of cultivation as an evergreen little liable to injury by frost, and, during the summer, presenting an elegant contrast in its varied fronds, and a habit totally dissimilar to that of all our larger species. In moving it from its natural habitat, care should be taken to bring away as much of the soil as convenience will admit; otherwise our labours will be probably disappointed, as it does not readily form new roots. From want of attention to this circumstance I used to regard it as one difficult to establish, a character quite undeserved, as few of our native species are more readily naturalized in the garden. When planted among rock-work, it must be so placed as to receive abundant moisture, and the soil employed should be more retentive than usual; a mixture of peat and stiff loam in equal proportion I have found to answer well: in the wild state it grows in almost all kinds of soil, from sand and gravel to the most retentive clay. Shade is necessary to its more luxuriant growth, but it will bear exposure better than most others, especially if well supplied with water. It may be kept in large pots, but does not like confinement.

Genus 11. PTERIS.

Gen. Char. Fructification forming a continuous marginal line, covered by the attenuated recurved margin of the frond.

The fructification in this genus is very obscure in regard to its primary development, and much difference of opinion has prevailed among pteridologists respecting the presence or absence of indusium: were it one of small extent, this would be of little importance, but the contrary is the case; and, although the local botanist can have no difficulty in recognizing our solitary indigenous species, from the above superficial character, a correct understanding of those points of structure that are generally adopted in the association or distinction of genera in this tribe of plants, is serviceable to the general student. A close examination of the fructifying frond of *Pteris aquilina* shows us that the lateral veins of the lobes divide one, two, or three times before they reach the margin, and that the extremities of the branches become anastomosed near the latter, forming an intromarginal vein; it is from this vein that the thecæ arise, the margin of the lobe recurving with them, not over them. The thecæ are not produced on the under surface, as in the true dorsiferous ferns, but on the edge of the frond, the substance of which terminates with the vein in question, while the epidermis is extended beyond it from both surfaces, and thus encloses the fructification in its earliest stage of development between two membranes, the folding of which backward with their contents has occasioned all the equivocality originally attaching to this part. Both of the membranes have their margins ciliated with jointed hairs, and under the microscope their cellular structure will be found to differ in accordance with that of the upper and under epidermis from which they are individually extensions.

Pteris, πτερις, the common Greek name for *fern*, signifying *wing* or *feather*, well accords with the appearance of the fronds of *P. aquilina*, the most common and most generally distributed of European ferns.

Pteris aquilina

Pteris aquilina. Common Brake. Braken. Eagle Fern. Tab. XXXVIII.

Fronds deltoid, with an elongated stem-like petiole, bi-tripinnate; primary pinnæ opposite; ultimate segments oblong, obtuse.

Pteris aquilina, *Linnæus. Smith. E. B.* 1679. *Hooker and Arnott. Babington. Moore.* Eupteris aquilina, *Newman, Hist. Brit. Ferns*, 23.

Abundant on heaths and moors, and on stony and sandy pastures, as well as in woods and thickets, throughout the kingdom. The rhizoma, of a dark colour and velvety exterior, extends far below the soil, branching and creeping in every direction, so as to form, where long established, a densely interwoven horizontal network at a greater or less distance below the surface, according to the character of the subsoil. It has often been observed that the plant is not found over chalk, a circumstance, however, apparently due rather to the ordinary shallowness of the soil over that rock in England, than to any prejudicial influence of the chalk itself. The repeatedly compound fronds grow upward, at intervals, to the height of from six inches to eight or nine feet, according to the fertility of the spot, or as they are more or less exposed or sheltered; in a moist wood, near Hampstead-heath, I once measured one upwards of thirteen feet long; such inordinate growth is rarely attended with the production of fruit. The stem-like portion of the rachis is light yellowish-green, passing into a purplish-brown or black at the lower part; the leafy part of the frond deep green, and smooth on the upper surface, pale and hairy beneath. The compound character varies according to size and other circumstances; the primary pinnæ, usually opposite, are generally broad, the secondary ones narrow or linear-lanceolate; the pinnules, or ultimate divisions, are sessile, always confluent towards the extremity, oblong and obtuse. Owing to the peculiar disposition of the woody tissue and its dark hue, a transverse section of the lower end of the rachis presents a fanciful image of an oak-tree, or, if cut obliquely, of the imperial or spread-eagle; in either case it is a pretty object for the microscope. The fronds appear above ground in May, but are liable to be destroyed by very slight frost before they have unfolded, and, when mature, are always among the first natural objects whose change of appearance indicates the approach of winter.

No permanent varieties occur of this most common fern, though it is liable to considerable modification in different localities. It is seldom cultivated, on account of its tendency to overrun other species, a vagrant habit that is difficult to control. Some trouble and frequent disappointment may be incurred in the endeavour to establish it, either in pots or in the garden, on account of the depth at which the growing part extends itself and the obstacles to be encountered in its removal; but, once obtained, there is little risk of loss, as it seems quite independent of difference of soil.

The Common Brake was the *Filix-fœmina*, or Female Fern of the old botanists, or those prior to the time of Linnæus, who transferred the title to another, the present *Athyrium Filix-fœmina*.

There is reason to conclude that many exotic species, so considered, belonging to different parts of the world, may not be really other than slightly varied forms of the *Pteris aquilina*, resembling it closely as they do in habit, tendency to complexity in the division of the frond, and other circumstances. Should future observation render fact that which is at present merely speculative, then might the fern before us rank as the most universally distributed of all vegetable productions, extending its dominion from west to east over both continents and islands, in a zone reaching from Northern Europe and Siberia to New Zealand, where it is represented by, and perhaps identical with, the well-known *P. esculenta*. The rhizoma of our plant, like that of the latter, is edible; and though not employed in these islands as food, powdered and mixed with a small quantity of barley-meal, it is made into a kind of gruel called *gofio*, in use among the poorer inhabitants of the Canary Islands, especially those of Palma and Gomera: its astringency, however, is so great, that it has been recommended for dressing and preparing kid- and chamois-leather, and its qualities as a vermifuge are said to equal those of *Aspidium Filix-mas*. The large fronds form a durable thatch, and are used as litter for cattle: in many parts of the country they are collected for fuel, especially for heating ovens, and sometimes even for burning limestone. The ashes contain a large proportion of alkali available in the manufacture of both soap and glass, and are often employed by country people as a substitute for the former article, for which purpose they are generally formed into balls by moistening and afterwards heating them in the fire; in this state they are well known in some districts in England by the name of ash-balls. A bed made of the fresh-gathered fronds is a provincial remedy for the *rickets*.

Genus 12. ALLOSORUS.

Gen. Char. Sori circular, near the extremities of the lateral veins, confluent in maturity; covered by the reflexed margin of the pinnules of the contracted fertile frond fulfilling the office of an indusium.

Most recent botanists place this genus next to *Polypodium*, on account of the form of the sori and the absence of a true indusium; but the eventually confluent fructification, forming an intromar-

311

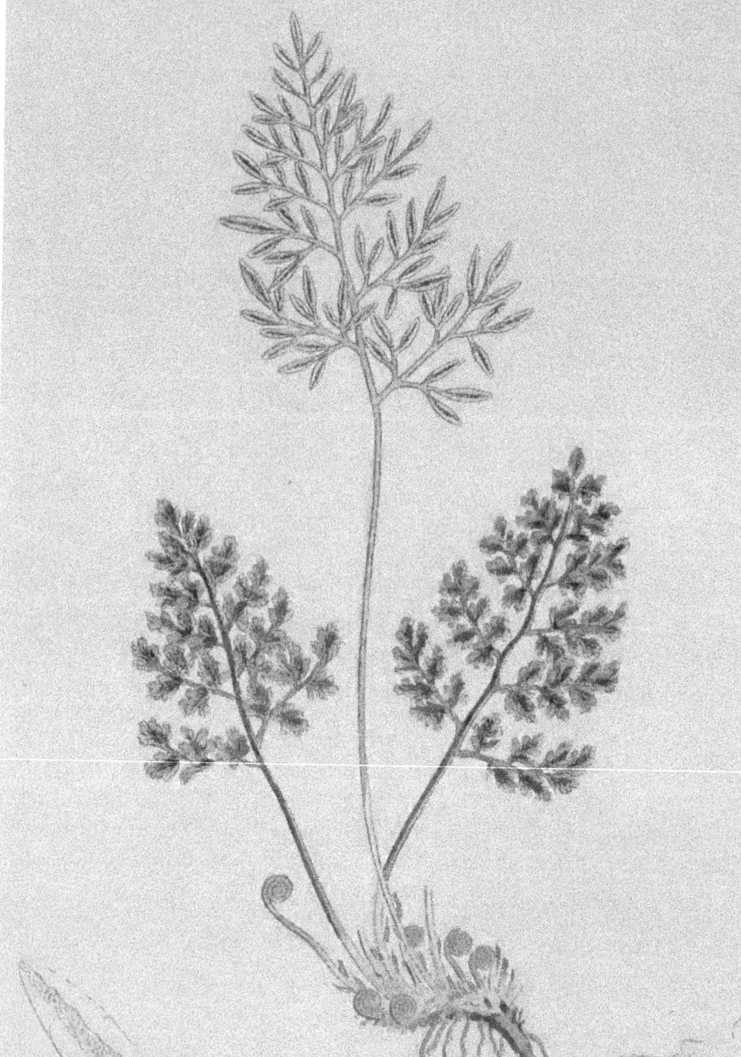

Allosurus crispus

ginal line covered by the reflexed epidermoid prolongation of the edges of the pinnules, seems to denote a nearer structural affinity to *Pteris*.

The name, from the Greek ἄλλος, implying *difference* or *change*, evidently alludes to alteration that takes place in the appearance of the sori as they become confluent.

Allosorus crispus. Parsley Fern. Curled Rock-Brakes. Tab. XXXIX.

Fronds deltoid, bi-tripinnate, of two kinds: ultimate divisions of barren fronds wedge-shaped, cut and toothed; of the fertile linear-oblong, entire.

Allosorus crispus, *Bernhardi. Babington. Moore. Newman.* Pteris crispa, *Linnæus. Smith. E.B.* 1160. Cryptogramma crispa, *Brown. Hooker and Arnott. E. B.* ed. 2, 1443. Osmunda crispa, *Linnæus, Sp. Pl.*

This elegant little fern is exclusively European, growing in the more sheltered crevices of mountain rocks, from Lapland to the Mediterranean. In this country it is generally regarded as a comparatively rare, or at least local species; the former it certainly is not, the latter only in accordance with its alpine habit. In Scotland its distribution is a wide one, though apparently less abundant than in the North of England and North Wales, where it often grows profusely on the ledges and in the narrow clefts of the slate and trap rocks. Southward it is found more sparingly, and is rapidly disappearing owing to the rapacity of collectors. In Ireland it has been rarely met with. The fronds spring in tufts from a slowly creeping and branching rhizoma, the fertile ones growing erect from six inches to a foot high, the barren ones, more numerous, being not above half that height; the latter are of a bright yellowish-green, and much resemble, at first sight and when newly expanded, the leaves of a small umbelliferous plant. The ultimate divisions of the barren frond vary in form in different specimens from wedge-shaped to oblong or oval, and in being entire or toothed and serrated: those of the fertile frond are oval, oblong, or linear, stalked, mostly entire, but in some instances forked at the extremity, and occasionally showing a tendency to become hastate below; the reflexed margins nearly meet in the middle at first, so as to completely cover the fructification. The circular form of the sori is only evident when examined at an early stage: no trace of an indusium has yet been observed.

The delicate green hue and close growth of the Parsley Fern render it one of the most beautiful among the smaller species, but its duration is very limited, the fronds appearing in May and

June and becoming disfigured by the first morning frosts of the autumn. It grows freely under cultivation, whether planted in pots or among rock-work, and I have found it succeed in several different soils, though never better than when planted on the margin of a gravel-walk, among the pebbles of which some of the finest tufts were produced. For potted specimens, light sandy peat, with a small quantity of old mortar, and fragments of slate, limestone, or granite, the first especially placed vertically throughout the soil, will be most available, when associated with a copious supply of water and as free drainage during the growing season. Exposure to the sun should be guarded against, as though not necessarily fatal to the fern, it is to the lucid green colour that constitutes its chief beauty.

Genus 13. ADIANTUM.

Gen. Char. Sori roundish, growing from the extremities of the veins on the under face of the reflexed margin of the frond, the epidermis of which is prolonged over them in the form of an indusium.

Adiantum is an extensive genus, containing about seventy known species, of which the greater number are tropical. The fronds are generally of a very delicate, almost membranaceous texture, especially those which are much divided: they have a peculiarly slender, hair-like, and elastic rachis, which, being usually of a dark-purple or blackish hue, occasions many of the species to rank among the most elegant of the fern tribe, as the thin bright-green pinnules seem to be suspended in the air. They all delight in shade and moisture, growing almost exclusively in the damp and dark crevices of rocks, among trickling streams, and in the depths of tropical forests where the atmosphere is constantly loaded with moisture. *A. pedatum* in North America, and *A. Capillus-Veneris* in Europe, are the only species met with extending naturally into cold climates. The European species was named *ἀδίαντον* by the Greeks, from *ἀδίαντος, dry,* because the foliage repels water, and is with difficulty wetted.

Adiantum Capillus-Veneris. Maiden-Hair. Tab. XL.

Fronds deltoid, lax, bi-tripinnate: pinnules stalked, rhomboidal-wedge-shaped, lobed, alternate. Fertile lobes reflexed, forming transversely oblong indusium-like folds covering several roundish sori: barren lobes serrated.

Adiantum Capillus-Veneris, *Linnæus. E. B* 1564. Generally adopted.

The common or true Maiden-hair is unquestionably a wanderer

Adiantum Capillus Veneris

here from warmer lands, being only very locally distributed in situations open to such arrivals from the Atlantic. Cornwall, Devonshire, and Glamorganshire, and the southern and western parts of Ireland, afford its principal British habitats, and it is rarely found very far from the sea; indeed chiefly in moist maritime caves and on rocks and cliffs where it is exposed to the spray, and especially where fresh water trickles down their sides. A perpendicular surface seems most favourable to its development, and hence the mouths of old wells and the deserted shafts of mines are occasionally tapestried with its beautiful foliage. Its geographical distribution over the warm and temperate parts of the globe seems, from the testimony of botanists of high repute, to be almost universal. The slender, black, scaly rhizoma creeps and branches slowly in every direction, sending up the light fronds in lax tufts from the extremities, varying in height, according to the situation, from three or four inches to a foot. The hair-like fineness of the rachis and its branches, and their glossy, black, or purplish-black hue, originated both the Latin and English names of the species, but they are not peculiar to it. The pinnules, distinct, with capillary stalks, are somewhat flabelliform in general outline, with an unequally wedge-shaped base; they are of a very thin, almost membranaceous texture, and delicate, bright, though rather glaucous green colour, and divided at the top into several unequal segments, which are either serrated or have their extremities folded backwards, bearing the sori, which thus appear to form an interrupted marginal line: their true character and position is given under the generic character, and illustrated by the right-hand enlarged figure on our plate.

This elegant fern had formerly high medicinal repute, especially as a diuretic and expectorant, but is now only remarkable in an economical point of view as giving name and a slight flavour to the well-known *Capillaire*, which is prepared by pouring boiling syrup upon the freshly-gathered fronds. It grows abundantly in the South of Europe, where, however, the North American *A. pedatum* is often employed as a substitute, being cultivated for the purpose. They are both astringent, and the syrup is esteemed useful in coughs and other pectoral ailments, but a strong decoction of the latter plant is said to act as an emetic. In the South Isles of Arran, on the coast of Galway, where the Maidenhair grows profusely in the fissures of the limestone rocks, the people use a decoction of the fronds as a substitute for tea.

The great beauty of the foliage of the *Adiantum* would render it a valuable decoration to the ruin, rock, and fountain in ornamental gardening, but, like other maritime self-naturalized species, it is liable to be destroyed by frost, unless planted in warm and sheltered situations; indeed, it is scarcely possible to preserve it alive through the winter in the open air in the eastern parts of England. The amateur grower will manage better with it as a house plant, in which case the season of dearth is that in which its delicate fronds are most attractive to the eye. It will flourish in the stove and greenhouse, but in the inhabited room requires the cover of a bell-glass, and is admirably adapted for growing in the close or Wardian case. It ought never to be exposed to the sun. In regard to soil, I have found it succeed well in the same compost as that recommended for *Asplenium marinum.*

Genus 14. TRICHOMANES.

GEN. CHAR. Sori marginal. Thecæ sessile around columnar filiform receptacles, which are extramarginal extensions of the anterior branches of the lateral veins, within open cylindrical or suburceolate involucres of the same texture as the frond.

The generic name, borrowed from *Dioscorides,* was applied by the Greeks to some species of ferns, probably *Asplenium Trichomanes,* and is not unaptly transferred to these, considering the arbitrary allotment of botanical names generally; the prefix, from θρὶξ, τρϊχὸς, a *hair* or *bristle,* bearing allusion to the hair-like receptacles of the sori, while the termination, from μανὸς, *soft, thin,* or *flexible,* accords with the character of the fronds; a convenient, though forced, interpretation, that may suffice in the absence of one more consistent.

The plants comprised under this and the following genus, *Hymenophyllum,* are remarkably different from the other ferns in the development of their fructification, in habit, and in the texture of the frond, which latter is membranaceous, and under the microscope very beautifully reticulated. They grow only in very moist and shaded places; indeed, their organization is not adapted to support those ordinary changes in the hygrometric condition of the atmosphere that do not visibly affect vegetation in the aggregate; their delicate fronds become brown, and shrivel when exposed even to a few hours' drought, and they resist all customary modes of cultivation, in consequence of the excess of light and insufficiency of moisture in the surrounding air that are their usual concomitants. The numerous species of both genera are almost all tropical, inhabiting the deep recesses of the forests of hot climates, where, in an atmosphere loaded with vapour, they flourish, as well as in similar situations to those to which they are confined in Europe.

TRICHOMANES RADICANS. European Bristle Fern. TAB. XLI.

Fronds tri-quadripinnatifid, glabrous, deltoid-ovate or lanceo-

H

Trichomanes radicans.

late; segments alternate, linear, entire or bifid, obtuse. Involucres solitary in the axils of the upper segments, shorter than the filiform receptacle

Trichomanes radicans, *Swartz. Hooker. Babington. Moore. Newman.* Trichomanes brevisetum, *Brown. Smith. E. B.* ed. 2, 1445. T. speciosum, europæum, pyxidiferum, and alatum, of authors. Hymenophyllum alatum, *Smith. E. B.* 1417.

The original locality of the Bristle Fern is doubtful, as specimens collected in several parts of the world, not essentially differing from our own, evince a wide distribution; though, being found in the West Indies and in the islands of the North Atlantic, renders its transit hither consistent with those natural causes that have enriched the catalogue of British vegetation with many other productions of warmer climates. At present this may rank as a rarity to the home botanist, not being found in any other part of the United Kingdom than in the Irish counties of Cork and Kerry, where it grows more or less abundantly on dripping rocks, about lakes and waterfalls, and depending from the walls and roofs of caverns. The rhizoma creeps and spreads like that of *Polypodium vulgare,* and in some situations attains a length of several feet, often covering the moist rocks on which it grows with a complete network; it is of a dark colour, almost black, and clothed with narrow, bristle-like, articulated scales. The fronds, developed at intervals as the rhizoma extends, are from three inches to a foot in length, and generally pendulous, in consequence of the position they occupy on the sloping or perpendicular faces of the rocks: the general outline is somewhat deltoid, but in very luxuriant plants it passes into an oblong-lanceolate form very much acuminated, constituting the variety *Andrewsii* of Mr. Newman, Hist. Brit. Ferns, 292. The rachis is winged throughout on each side, corresponding with the plane of the frond, the leafy portion of which seems to consist only of a continuation of these wings in a broader form along each side of its branches, which latter constitute the veins; this structure renders all the ultimate divisions narrow and linear. The veins, dividing alternately, are hard, woody, and wire-like, and, where barren, terminate before reaching the ends of the segments; but where fertile they extend beyond the segment, the tissue of which separates and distends in the form of a more or less elongated cup around the prolonged vein—this cup is the *involucre,* the prolonged vein the *receptacle,* referred to under the generic and specific characters. The thecæ form a small globular cluster round the receptacle at the bottom of the cup, beyond which latter organ, as they advance to maturity, the modified vein extends in the form of a bristle, varying in its exserted length from two to four or even six times that of the involucre. In the more luxuriant form of the plant, the involucral cup is very distinctly winged, in consequence of the double layer of tissue, composing the segment to which it belongs, not separating through its whole breadth; in smaller specimens the wings or margins of the modified segment are not readily distinguishable, but the cup-like cylinder is always slightly compressed to the plane of the frond, indicative of its origin as above stated. It is true that, like most other modifications of tissue attending the development of fructification, the cup changes from the bright green colour of the frond to a white or brownish hue, and loses its translucency, but the continuity of texture and similarity in other respects are readily traceable by close examination.

The growth of this rare and elegant fern is not attended with any difficulty, provided that the peculiarities of its natural habitats are studied by the cultivator; these are chiefly, an atmosphere loaded with moisture, absence of stagnant water about the roots, and exclusion of the direct rays of the sun: the first of these conditions is rarely attainable under cultivation unless with the shelter of glass. Many very successful growers have described the varying minutiæ of the several modes of treatment by which they have attained magnitude of development far exceeding that of the plant in its natural state in Ireland; but the specimens which I have hitherto seen growing in the more fanciful modifications of the closed case, and under the elaborate course of planting and after-treatment recommended in such circumstances, have always appeared to me too delicate to be consistent with health, and that they really are so, the fact, generally lamented by the amateur grower, that they never perfect fructification seems to confirm. The plant grows freely in a common pot or seed-pan; the latter is better, even commencing with a small specimen, as it affords more room for the spreading of the rhizoma; it should stand in water, and be covered with a bell-glass of sufficient size to admit of the uninterrupted extension of the fronds; the bottom should be strewn with fragments of porous stone and little lumps of charcoal intermixed, and the soil may consist of about equal parts of sand, peat, and decayed leaf-mould. In this way, sheltered from the sun, but freely exposed to the daylight, and with the occasional admission of fresh air by removing the glass for a few minutes at a time, the thecæ are not unfrequently fully formed and the filiform receptacle exserted as much as in wild specimens. Success in the treatment of small plants will readily lead to contrivances in regard to the management of larger; but those who may be desirous of emulating the more magnificent though barren state alluded to above, will find much valuable information on the subject, by reference to Mr. Ward's book 'On the Growth of Ferns in Closed Cases,' or Mr. Moore's 'Handbook,' p. 202

Hymenophyllum Tunbridgense.

et seq., of which the limits of the present work will not admit an extract.

In the durability of the fronds for several successive years, in general habit and texture, *Trichomanes* has all the characters of a tropical species, and though naturalized in our sister island, under the influence of a very moist and temperate climate, would probably not bear exposure even in corresponding localities in England, where the winters are so much more severe, and the drying effects of the easterly winds in the spring so generally prejudicial to vegetation.

Genus 15. HYMENOPHYLLUM.

GEN. CHAR. Sori marginal. Thecæ sessile on a columnar subclavate receptacle within a two-valved involucre of the same texture as the frond.

The name, from ὑμὴν, a *film* or *membrane*, and φύλλον, a *leaf*, is expressive of the pellucid filmy texture of the frond. The genus formed a part of the Linnæan *Trichomanes*, but was separated by Sir J. E. Smith, in consequence of the bivalvular involucre and short receptacle. The division is rather one of convenience than admissible on a structural foundation. The two British species carry a fragility of form and texture almost exclusively characteristic of the smaller species of tropical ferns, to the highest latitudes in which it seems capable of existing.

HYMENOPHYLLUM TUNBRIDGENSE. Tunbridge or Common Film Fern. TAB. XLII.

Fronds membranaceous, pinnate: pinnæ distichous, pinnatifid, decurrent, forming a broad wing on each side of the rachis; the segments linear, undivided or bifid, spinosely serrated. Involucre solitary, axillary, suborbicular, compressed; the valves spinosely serrated.

Hymenophyllum Tunbridgense, *Smith. E. B.* 162. *Hooker and Arnott. Babington. Moore. Newman.* Trichomanes Tunbridgense, *Linnæus.*

Abundantly distributed in the north-western and southern counties of England, in mountainous and rocky districts; in Wales; and less frequently in the Highlands of Scotland, and in Ireland; growing on shady wet rocks, and among moss on the trunks and roots of old trees, or on the ground near lakes and rivulets. The black and thread-like rhizoma spreads and branches widely, forming a kind of turf over the surface on which it grows, and from which it is in general easily separated in mat-like masses. The fronds vary from one to three or four inches in length, springing singly at short intervals from the creeping rhizoma; they are of a very thin, almost filmy texture, and composed, like those of *Trichomanes*, of the winged upper portion of the wire-like rachis and its branches. The pinnæ are alternate, connected throughout by the wing of the rachis, and deeply once or twice pinnatifid, chiefly on the anterior or upper side; the ultimate segments are linear, obtuse, and margined with sharp spiny serratures. The fructification is sessile, terminating a vein, and occupying the place of the first upper segment of each pinna, as expressed in our lower figure; the involucre being apparently formed by a modification of the segment it supplants, similar to that of the last genus. The involucre in this species is somewhat orbicular, but a little compressed, especially toward the apices of the irregularly and sharply serrated valves, and includes a short central column or receptacle bearing around it the sessile thecæ; this receptacle is, as in the previous instance, the extremity of the branch vein, but instead of being filiform, it is thickened so as to become almost club-shaped, and never extends beyond the involucre.

The figures of this beautiful little fern represent it as growing on the ground, erect; but if inverted would better display the ordinary habit, and that in which it appears to the greatest advantage; or, clothing with a tapestry of deep olive-green the shaded perpendicular faces of dripping rocks and caverns, when its filmy fronds are nearly pendulous, and the several series overlie each other at the base like the half-ruffled plumage of a bird: much of its beauty is lost when growing in a horizontal position.

It may be cultivated in the open air by imitating its natural site, and very successfully in the house under glass, on the same plan as recommended for the Bristle Fern; the chief object to be attended to being the retention of a moist atmosphere about its fronds, which, being short, do not require when grown apart from other species a glass of the same elevation as the latter; but it may be planted around other larger ferns in the closed cases, and vegetates luxuriantly under either circumstance, producing its fructification copiously at all seasons. It is little, if at all susceptible of injury from cold, a fact rather opposed to some of the recorded habitats within the tropics, which probably refer to different though perhaps nearly allied species.

HYMENOPHYLLUM UNILATERALE. Wilson's Film Fern. TAB. XLIII.

Fronds pinnate: pinnæ subunilateral, recurved, pinnatifid; the segments linear, undivided or bifid, spinosely serrated. Involucre

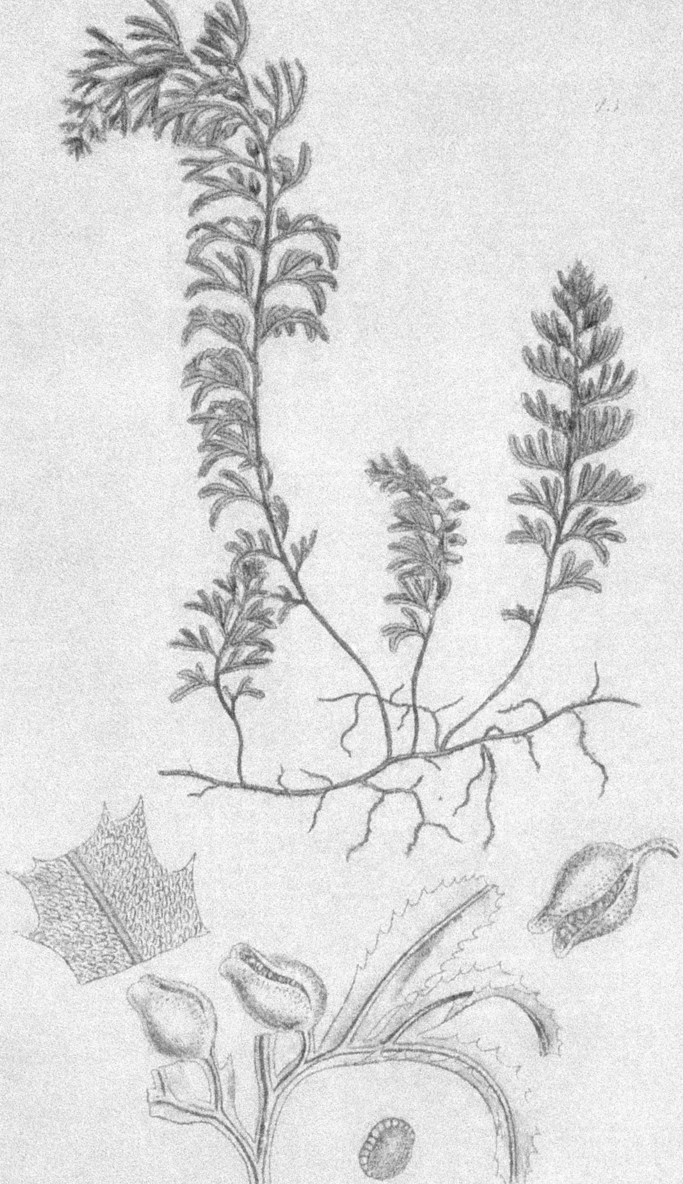

Hymenophyllum unilaterale.
J. D. C. S. Fecit

stalked, solitary, axillary, ovate, inflated; the valves entire. Main rachis very slightly winged.

Hymenophyllum unilaterale, *Willdenow. Moore. Newman.* Hymenophyllum Wilsoni, *Hooker. E. B. Supp.* 2686. *Hooker and Arnott. Babington.*

Found in similar situations to the preceding, which it frequently accompanies. Its distribution is more extended, especially in Scotland, where its extreme limit is Unst, the most northern of the Shetland Islands. In general appearance this is not very much unlike *H. Tunbridgense*, with which it was for a long time confounded; but the fronds are far less delicate in texture, and comparatively rigid. The principal characters of distinction are found in the fructification, which, occupying a similar position, is stalked instead of sessile; the involucre proportionally longer and ovate instead of rounded, with very turgid convex valves, meeting by their edges, not compressed toward the apex, and never at all serrated. The tendency of the pinnæ to assume a recurved position is not a character to be depended upon, but the darker green hue and less compact growth will generally enable the observant eye to distinguish the present at a glance from *H. Tunbridgense*, a plant of more elegant habit. The involucres are generally curved forward.

The treatment required for cultivation is the same as that already noticed for its congener, and will succeed with the exotic species of this curious family, all of which are well deserving the attention of the amateur cultivator.

Genus 16. OSMUNDA.

GEN. CHAR. Fructification naked, clustered on contracted rachiform portions of the frond, forming a (generally) terminal panicle. Thecæ stalked, subglobose, reticulated, two-valved, opening vertically.

The name is from the Saxon, *Osmund*, 'domestic peace,' but the origin of its application is unknown, though several romantic legends are connected with it.

The ferns of this genus differ greatly from those of all the preceding, not only in the peculiar disposition of the fructifying masses, which occupy, upon the veins or branches of the rachis, the place of the leafy tissue on the upper part of the fertile fronds, but likewise in the structure of the thecæ; these are exannulate, or without that prominent articulated continuation of the supporting stalk, by the ultimate extension of which those of ordinary ferns are torn open to discharge the spores; their tissue is opaque, very regularly reticulated, and the bivalvular dehiscence takes place along a striated vertical band, reaching over rather more than half of the circumference.

Osmunda regalis. Osmund Royal. Flowering Fern. Tab. XLIV.

Fronds bipinnate: pinnæ opposite: pinnules oblong, nearly entire, more or less auricled at the base. Fructification in bipinnate panicles terminating some of the fronds.

Osmunda regalis, *Linnæus. E. B.* 209. Generally adopted.

This stately fern is of common occurrence throughout the United Kingdom, in wet spongy soils about the borders of woods and thickets, and on the shaded margins of rivers, lakes, and swamps, varying much in size in different situations. The fronds grow in large tufts from a thick woody rhizoma, which sometimes extends horizontally, branching so as to occupy a large space of ground, but occasionally, and especially in much encumbered habitats, elongates in an erect position to a height of two or even three feet above the soil, assuming the character of the stipes or trunk of the tropical tree ferns. When the tufts are large and luxuriant this is by far the most magnificent of our native species of fern, the barren fronds being from six to nine feet high; I have met with them on the banks of the Dee rather exceeding the latter, and Mr. S. Murray, as quoted in the 'British Flora,' measured a tuft on those of the Clyde which was eleven feet and a half in height. The fertile fronds are shorter than the others and comparatively few in number; in both the bipinnate character is the same throughout, the primary divisions opposite, the secondary mostly alternate. The pinnules are of an elongated ovate or oblong form, approaching occasionally to lanceolate, and either entire or slightly crenated on the margin, while the base is somewhat dilated, especially on the lower side, so as frequently to become auricled. In the fruit-bearing fronds, four or five of the lower pairs of pinnæ have the leafy character, while the remainder develope clusters of thecæ in lieu of pinnules, and similar clusters displace occasionally pinnules on other parts of the frond, illustrating the true origin of the reproductive organs by modification of the leafy tissue. The clusters of thecæ are at first of a light green hue, gradually changing to a reddish-brown as they approach maturity. The fronds appear about the end of April or the beginning of May and last until November, but the fructification withers and disappears at the end of August or earlier according to the character of the season.

The rhizoma is tonic and astringent, and a decoction is esteemed in some parts of the continent as a remedy for the rickets.

Osmunda regalis.

Royal Fern

Botrychium lunaria

To thrive under cultivation, the Flowering Fern should be planted in a shady situation, either in peat or a mixture of peat and yellow loam, and be plentifully supplied with water; with these requirements it may be grown with little, if any, deterioration of its wild luxuriance, and will constitute one of the most beautiful ornaments of the fern garden, as well on account of its own stately habit, as by the contrast its foliage presents to that of the other large species. When planted near water, the outer fronds often assume an elegant curve, bending over so as to dip their extremities into the pond or rivulet, and it is in such situations that they attain their greatest length.

Genus 17. BOTRYCHIUM.

GEN. CHAR. Fructification naked, clustered on a contracted branched frond, forming a unilateral panicle. Thecæ sessile, globose, opaque, two-valved, opening vertically.

The name is from the Greek βότρυς, *a bunch of grapes*, which the branched clusters of globular thecæ somewhat resemble.

In this and the following genus, *Ophioglossum*, the venation, instead of being circinate as in ferns generally, is straight. The fructification, resembling in *Botrychium* that of *Osmunda* in disposition and origin from the branches of the rachis, differs in the coriaceous and non-reticulated texture of the thecæ. The species are few, but widely distributed, extending into Australia in the southern hemisphere. North America yields about half the number at present known, viz. five species: of these *B. Virginicum* is remarkable as being the largest of the genus, and is known there by the name of Rattle-snake Fern, probably, as Pursh observes, from its growing in places where those reptiles are generally found, and yielding them an agreeable covert, though it is stated by others to be one of the Indian remedies for the bite

BOTRYCHIUM LUNARIA. Moonwort. TAB. XLV.

Barren frond pinnate: pinnæ lunate or fan-shaped, notched or crenate on the outer margin. Fertile frond springing apparently from the common rachis.

Botrychium Lunaria, *Swartz. Hooker and Arnott. Babington. Moore. Newman.* Osmunda Lunaria, *Linnæus. E. B.* 318.

The Moonwort, though scarcely to be considered a common species, is not at all confined in its distribution, either in Great Britain or Ireland; in the former, its localities are only limited by the two extremes of the Isles of Wight and Shetland, in the latter it occurs from Cork to Antrim. Dry exposed heaths and commons, and elevated rocky pastures are the likely and frequent habitats, but it is liable to be overlooked, in consequence of the small size and frequent cropping of the fructifying frond by cattle. The habit of this plant is totally different from that of *Osmunda* and all of the soriferous ferns: it has no true rhizoma, but the growing part or caudex is very little elongated below the surface of the soil, sending out a few succulent and brittle roots that extend more or less horizontally: the upward growth is from a lengthened bud invested by the membranaceous bases of previously developed fronds. The perfect plant consists of a single pinnated barren frond, through the sheathing lower part of whose racnis rises a second, modified, and bearing the fructification. The succulency of the recent pseudo-stem thus formed, renders its positive structure obscure, and has occasioned it to be sometimes described as homogeneous, and the frond to be considered branched. The pseudo-stem is hollow; and at the base, the fronds of the following year may be traced by dissection, more or less perfectly formed, and often, the rudimentary bud of the year succeeding within the latter; the position of the barren and fertile fronds being reversed in the successional development. The pinnæ are opposite, numbering from three or four to seven pairs, of a glaucous green hue, smooth, crenated on the margin, and occasionally more or less lobed, acquiring, in the latter case, a fan-shape instead of the lunate or crescent-form which confers the specific name. The thecæ are comparatively large, and, though at first sight apparently crowded, are really disposed in two regular series upon the divisions of the panicle-like rachis, and directed towards the upper or inner face of the modified frond; their texture is more dense than in *Osmunda*, and presents no trace of the regular cellular reticulations which character the membranaceous ones of that genus: dehiscence takes place along an elevated vertical line formed by the junction of the margins of the valves. The fertile frond, which is the taller of the two, rises to the height of five or six inches, and is in perfection about the time of the hay-harvest; soon after which the plant begins to decay.

Specimens are occasionally met with bearing more than one barren or fertile frond; others with the pinnæ-bearing thecæ on their margins; and sometimes the pinnæ are so much divided as to render the frond almost bipinnate. Certain variations of the latter form may have induced some botanists to consider one or other of the continental species, *B. rutaceum*, or *B. matricarioides*, to belong to Britain, a circumstance not at all unlikely, but requiring surer evidence than we at present possess.

The only mode of ensuring the growth of the Moonwort in the fern garden, is by removing the turf containing it without dis-

Ophioglossum vulgatum.

J.E. fecit.

turbing the roots, and afterwards keeping the grass around well trimmed to prevent overgrowth. The plants removed, with a small portion of soil only, at the period of fructification seldom live beyond the following year. The turf should be planted in an exposed situation and where water cannot become stagnant around it.

Genus 18. OPHIOGLOSSUM.

GEN. CHAR. Fructification arranged on the margins of a contracted simple frond, forming a flattened stalked spike. Thecæ sessile, connate in two rows, opaque, opening transversely with two valves.

The aspect of the European species warrants the generic name, from *ὄφις, a serpent,* and *γλῶσσα, a tongue.*

The species, few in number as at present known, are chiefly natives of warm climates.

OPHIOGLOSSUM VULGATUM. Common Adder's-tongue. TAB. XLVI.

Barren frond ovate, obtuse, spathe-like. Fertile frond club-shaped, springing apparently from the common rachis.

Ophioglossum vulgatum, *Linnæus. E. B.* 108. Generally adopted.

Though local in its distribution, and more frequent in England than in other parts of the kingdom, the Adder's-tongue is generally abundant in those meadows and pastures in which it has once settled, sometimes even prevailing to such an extent as to become injurious to the grass. The situations it prefers are rarely those which foster the Moonwort, the latter requiring a dry, while the present plant flourishes best in a moist soil. The whole plant is succulent and much resembles *Botrychium* in habit, and in the development of its double frond, but differs in the production of the new plant externally instead of within the base of the old one, a circumstance illustrated in our figure. The height varies according to the luxuriance of the surrounding vegetation from two or three inches to a foot. The barren frond, of a pale yellowish-green, invests the rachis of the fertile one as the spathe of the Arum does its fructification; its form is ovate varying to ovate-lanceolate, more or less obtuse: the venation is more complicated than is usual in the fern family, anastomosing and forming an irregular network. The thecæ are imbedded in two parallel series on the margins of the club-like termination of the inner frond, to which, as they open to discharge the spores, they give the appearance of being serrated. The fructification is perfected toward the end of June, soon after which the fronds begin to die off, one or more buds being previously formed at the base, which remain dormant to the following spring.

The barren frond is often forked at the extremity, occasionally deeply lobed, and in very luxuriant specimens two or three spikes of fructification are developed instead of one. An ointment is sometimes prepared from the green fronds to use as a vulnerary. Removal of the containing turf is by far the preferable mode of introduction to the fernery, as, like the Moonwort, it is rather impatient of cultivation.

Ophioglossum lusitanicum. Lesser Adder's-tongue. Tab. XLVII.

Barren frond linear or linear-lanceolate. Fertile frond clavate.

Ophioglossum lusitanicum, *Linnæus*. *Newman, Hist. Brit. Ferns*, 331. *Lindley, Veg. Kingd.* 77.

This small species has been long known and described as a native of the south of Europe and the Atlantic Islands. For its discovery in the Channel Islands we are indebted to Mr. George Wolsey, who found it among short herbage, "on the summit of rocks, not far from Petit Bot Bay on the south coast of the Island of Guernsey," growing with *Trichonema Columnæ* and *Scilla autumnalis*. It is far from improbable that it may be found upon the southern coast of Devonshire and Cornwall; indeed, I have received a specimen said to have been collected in the latter county, but as the habitat has been, perhaps wisely, withheld, merely mention the circumstance as an inducement to farther research. The specimens from which our figures have been taken, were kindly forwarded by the Rev. Henry Hawkes, from whose correspondence it appears that the greediness of collectors has almost exhausted it in the original locality, but that it is fortunately to be met with in others not yet published. The student of nature is from the example of his tutor liberal; it is to be regretted that those who affect only to be his fellows, should by their insatiate grasping tend to render him miserly as themselves, and to desire to conceal discoveries that he would share with pleasure, merely to avoid the total loss to his country of a rare or beautiful object.

The fronds are in perfection in Guernsey in February or even earlier.

17

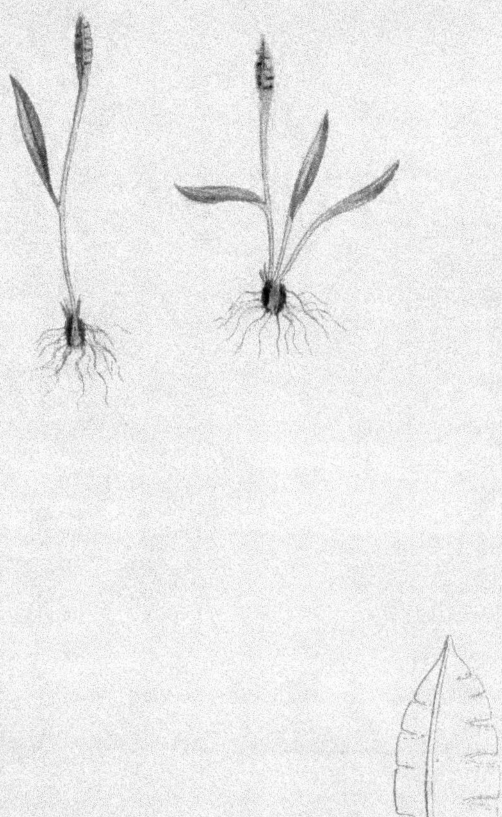

Ophioglossum lusitanicum.

J. E. S. fecit

Gymnogramma leptophylla.

J. E. S. Fecit.

Specimens of the two following ferns were not obtained sufficiently early to be introduced in their proper order. The genus *Gymnogramma* ought to follow *Polypodium*.

Genus GYMNOGRAMMA.

Gen. Char. Sori linear, naked, forked, eventually confluent.

Named from the Greek γυμνὸς, *naked*, and γράμμα, *a line* or *letter*; the situation of the sori, without indusium, upon the forked veins of the frond, presenting some resemblance to letters, or otherwise from their linear form.

Gymnogramma leptophylla. Tab. XLVIII.

Fronds ovate, sub-deltoid, bipinnate, fragile: pinnæ roundish wedge-shaped, three-lobed, the lobes cut and toothed, obtuse.

A native of the south of Europe and of the Atlantic Islands, this has no farther claim to a place among British species than from its occurrence in Jersey, where it is not very local in its distribution, being found in several parts of the island growing in shaded moist places among mosses and *Marchantia*, especially on hedge-banks and near springs, in a light sandy loam. It is a biennial plant, so far as that it appears to develope from the spores late in the summer, not sending up the longer fructifying fronds until the following year. The early fronds are small, very little divided, spreading over the ground, and usually barren; the later rise to the height of three or four inches, are generally few in number, and varying in division, according to their luxuriance being bi- or tripinnate, and the pinnæ and pinnules opposite or alternate: the ultimate pinnules are bluntly wedge-shaped, or rounded, about three-lobed, and the lobes terminate with two blunt teeth. The linear sori depend upon the termination of the vein on which they develope; this is sometimes simple, but more generally forked, each branch as it diverges bearing its portion of the thecæ, so that the sorus, commencing on the principal vein, becomes forked likewise: in maturity they are confluent and often cover the whole under-surface of the pinnules.

The chief requisites for this species in cultivation are a light friable soil and a moist atmosphere: it appears to grow with equal luxuriance in sandy loam or a mixture of peat and sand. In the hothouse it springs up spontaneously after the first introduction.

Polypodium alpestre. Alpine Polypody. Tab. XLIX.

Fronds lanceolate, bipinnate: pinnules linear-lanceolate, pinnatifid with obtuse sharply serrated lobes.

Polypodium alpestre, *Koch. Sprengel. Moore, Handb.* 50. Pseudathyrium alpestre, *Newman, Hist. Brit. Ferns*, 199.

This fern, a native of most parts of northern and central Europe, does not seem to have been recognized as a British species, until after its discovery in the Highlands of Scotland in July 1841, by Mr. Watson; having been previously overlooked as an alpine variety of *Athyrium Filix-fœmina*, which, though of less elegant habit, it somewhat resembles at first sight. Its mountain habitats render it one of local occurrence, but it appears from the observations of recent botanists to be far from sparing in its distribution in North Britain. The rhizoma has a tendency to spread and branch in a decumbent position, and the description to the contrary, given by some botanists, has probably originated from their acquaintance with its habit being confined to plants growing in situations not admitting of its natural development, or otherwise to young specimens. The fronds are produced in circular tufts from each crown, and vary in height from six inches to three feet, according to age or luxuriance. The rachis is leafy almost to the base, which is more or less thickly covered with broad pointed brown scales. The small circular sori generally spring from the lower anterior branch of the lateral veins of the pinnules, near the sinuses between the lobes, but occasionally are more numerous, and in such case become confluent in maturity.

I am only familiar with this fern, so far as its cultivation is concerned, as a continental species, and have not had an opportunity of examining many specimens of British growth; but traces of an indusium are undoubtedly present occasionally, a circumstance that probably led several European botanists to place it in the genus *Aspidium*.

The Alpine Polypody succeeds well under the same treatment as the Lady Fern.

Pseudathyrium flexile, Newman, Hist. Brit. Ferns, 203, may be, as has been suggested, only a variety of *alpestre*, but if so it is a very elegant one. The question of distinction as a separate species must depend upon subsequent observation, but there is reason for considering it such.

INDEX.

Syonyms and names incidentally mentioned are printed in Italics.

	Page	Tab.
Acrostichum alpinum	15	6
Ilvense	14	5
septentrionale	58	34
Thelypteris	16	7
Adder's-tongue, Common	81	46
Lesser	82	47
Adiantum Capillus-Veneris	70	40
pedatum	71	
Allosorus crispus	69	39
Amesium Germanicum	56	33
Ruta-muraria	55	32
septentrionale	58	34
Aspidium aculeatum	32	17
angulare	34	18
concavum	27	14
cristatum	21	10
dumetorum	29	
erosum	20	
Filix-fœmina	43	25
Filix-mas	19	9
fontanum	45	26
Lonchitis	30	15
montanum	41	24
Oreopteris	17	8
recurvum	27	14
rigidum	22	11
spinulosum	24	12
spinulosum β	26	13
spinulosum var	27	14
Thelypteris	16	7
Asplenium *acutum*	50	
Adiantum-nigrum	49	28
alternifolium	56	33
Ceterach	62	36
Filix fœmina	43	25
fontanum	45	26
Germanicum	56	33
lanceolatum	47	27
marinum	50	29
obtusum	50	
Asplenium Ruta-muraria	55	32
Scolopendrium	59	35
septentrionale	58	34
Trichomanes	52	30
Trichom. ramosum	54	31
viride	54	31
Athyrium Filix-fœmina	43	25
fontanum	46	26
Bladder Fern, Alpine	40	23
Brittle	36	19
Mountain	41	24
Toothed	38	21
Blechnum boreale	64	37
spicant	64	37
Botrychium Lunaria	79	45
matricarioides	80	
rutaceum	80	
Virginicum	79	
Brake, Braken	67	38
Bristle Fern	72	41
Capillaire	71	
Ceterach officinarum	62	36
Chetherak	62	36
Crested Fern	21	10
Cryptogramma crispa	69	39
Ctenopteris vulgaris	8	1
Cyathea dentata	38	21
fragilis	36	19
incisa	40	23
regia	40	23
Cystea dentata	38	21
fragilis	36	19
regia	40	23
Cystopteris alpina	40	23
angustata	37	20
dentata	38	21
dentata β	37	20
Dickieana	38	22
fragilis	36	19
montana	41	24

	Page	Tab.
Cystopteris *Myrrhidifolium*	41	24
Dryopteris affinis	20	
Borreri	20	
Filix-mas	19	9
Eagle Fern	67	38
Eupteris aquilina	67	38
Filmy Fern, Common	75	42
Tunbridge	75	42
Wilson's	76	43
Flowering Fern	78	44
Fragrant Fern	23	11
Gofio	68	
Grammitis Ceterach	62	36
Gymnocarpium Dryopteris	12	3
Phegopteris	11	2
Robertianum	13	4
Gymnogramma leptophylla	83	48
Hard Fern	64	37
Hart's Tongue	59	35
Hay-scented Fern	27	14
Heath Fern	17	8
Hemestheum Thelypteris	16	7
Holly Fern	30	15
Hymenophyllum *alatum*	73	41
Tunbridgense	75	42
unilaterale	76	43
Wilsoni	77	43
Lady Fern	43	25
Lastrea abbreviata	20	
Borreri	20	
cristata	21	10
dilatata	25	13
Dryopteris	12	3
Filix-mas	19	9
fœnisecii	27	14
montana	17	8
Oreopteris	17	8
Phegopteris	11	2
rigida	22	11
Robertiana	13	4
spinulosa	24	12
Thelypteris	16	7
uliginosa	29	
Lophodium Callipteris	21	10
collinum	29	
fœnisecii	27	14
glandulosum	29	
multiflorum	26	13
rigidum	22	11
spinulosum	24	12
uliginosum	29	
Maiden-Hair, Common	52	30
True	70	40
White	55	32
Male Fern	19	9
Marsh Fern	16	7

	Page	Tab.
Moonwort	79	45
Mountain Fern	17	8
Nephrodium	16	
Notolepeum Ceterach	62	36
Ophioglossum lusitanicum	82	47
vulgatum	81	46
Osmunda *crispa*	69	39
Lunaria	79	45
regalis	78	44
spicant	64	37
Osmund, Royal	78	44
Parsley Fern	69	39
Phyllitis multifida	61	
polyschides	60	
Scolopendrium	59	35
Polypodium *aculeatum*	32	17
alpestre	84	49
arvonicum	14	5
calcareum	12	4
Callipteris	21	10
Cambricum	10	
cristatum	21	10
Dryopteris	11	3
Filix-fœmina	43	25
Filix-mas	19	9
fontanum	46	26
fragilis	36	19
fragrans	17	8
fragrans	22	11
Hibernicum	10	
Ilvense	14	5
Lonchitis	30	15
montanum	17	8
montanum	41	24
Phegopteris	11	2
Thelypteris	16	7
vulgare	9	1
Polypody, Alpine	84	49
Common	9	1
Irish	10	
Mountain	11	2
Rigid 3-branched	12	4
Tender 3-branched	11	3
Welsh	10	
Polystichum *abbreviatum*	20	
aculeatum	32	17
angulare	33	
angulare	34	18
Dryopteris	12	3
lobatum	33	16
Lonchitis	30	15
Phegopteris	11	2
Prickly-toothed Fern, Broad	25	13
Narrow	24	12
Recurved	27	14
Pseudathyrium alpestre	84	49

	Page	Tab.
Pseudathyrium flexile	84	
Pteris aquilina	67	38
crispa	68	39
esculenta	68	
Rattlesnake Fern	79	
Rigid Fern	22	11
Rock Brakes, Curled	69	39
Rock Spleenwort, Smooth	45	26
Scolopendrium *Ceterach*	62	36
crispum	60	
endivæfolium	61	
laceratum	61	
lobatum	61	
multifidum	61	
officinarum	59	35
Phyllitis	59	35
polyschides	60	
ramosum	61	
vulgare	59	35
Shield Fern, Angular Prickly	34	18
Prickly	32	17
Rough Alpine	30	15
Soft Prickly	34	18
Spleenwort, Alternate-leaved	56	33
Black	49	28
Common	53	30
Forked	58	34
Green	54	31
Lanceolate	47	27
Scaly	62	36
Sea	50	28
Wall	52	30
Trichomanes *alatum*	73	41
Andrewsii	73	
brevisetum	73	41
Europæum	73	41
pyxidiferum	73	41
radicans	72	41
speciosum	73	41
Tunbridgense	75	42
Wall Rue	55	32
Woodsia *alpina*	15	6
hyperborea	15	6
Ilvensis	14	5
Perriniana	36	

REFERENCES TO ENGLISH BOTANY OMITTED.

---

1. Polypodium vulgare 1149
2. —— Phegopteris 2224
3. —— Dryopteris.......... 616
4. —— calcareum 1525
5. Woodsia Ilvensis ...... S. 2616
7. Lastrea Thelypteris 1018
8. —— Oreopteris.......... 1019
9. —— Filix-mas 1458
10. —— cristata 2125
11. —— rigida .... S. 2724
12. —— spinulosa 1460
13. Lastrea dilatata 1461
14. —— fœnisecii .... (not figured)
15. Polystichum Lonchitis 797
16., 17. —— aculeatum 1562
18. —— angulare .... S. 2776
19., 20. Cystopteris angustata .... S. 2790
24. —— montana .... (not figured)
25. Athyrium Filix-fœmina.... 1459

THE FERN ALLIES:

A SUPPLEMENT TO THE

FERNS OF GREAT BRITAIN.

ILLUSTRATED BY

JOHN E. SOWERBY,

PROPRIETOR OF SOWERBY'S ENGLISH BOTANY.

THE DESCRIPTIONS, SYNONYMS, &c.

BY

CHARLES JOHNSON, Esq.,

BOTANICAL LECTURER AT GUY'S HOSPITAL.

LONDON:

HENRY G. BOHN, YORK STREET, COVENT GARDEN.

MDCCCLIX.

FERN ALLIES.

From the earliest period of botanical arrangement certain vegetable forms, corresponding throughout a greater or lesser number of individuals, have afforded the means of constructing groups styled *genera*, and of associating these genera into larger and, for the most part, equally definite assemblages, that are now, not unaptly in many instances, denominated *natural orders*. The classification of these orders upon similar principles is a desideratum yet so imperfectly attained, that few naturalists agree in their arrangement of them; this is the case even among the higher and most elaborately organized of the phanerogamous plants, in which distinctive and associative points of structure are most readily traceable, in consequence of the greater number of features afforded by the diversified structure and disposition of the parts constituting their flower, fruit, and seed; but the difficulties are greatly enhanced in the cryptogamous or flowerless series, owing not only to the proportional paucity of characters they present for our examination, but to the minuteness and frequently indefinite nature of the organs of fructification or reproduction. Thus, while the structural resemblances between an Elm-tree and a Nettle are universally acknowledged by botanists, and even the gradations of development between these and the Rose, the Thistle, and the Magnolia are capable of demonstration, so far as to justify their arrangement in the same grand division or class of flowering plants—the association of the Fern, the Moss and the Lichen rests entirely upon the assumed absence of flowers, that is, of stamens and pistil, in all three; in other respects, so great are the differences between them, that they appear to constitute groups as widely separated as is the class in which they are placed, from the rest of the vegetable kingdom.

Certain small families among these flowerless groups, similarly segregated by general aspect and structure as are those above named, have been occasionally classed together under the collective name of "*Fern Allies*," a title for which there is really no foundation, the differences in their mutual organization, whether of growth or reproduction, being equally palpable, as it is opposed to that of the order with which caprice or misconception of the laws of physiological affinity has connected them.

These plants are highly interesting in many points of view, often elegant, and, with slight exception, easily cultivated: and, as two of the principal forms contrast harmoniously with those of the Ferns in plantations of that beautiful tribe, figures and descriptions of the British species have been considered necessary as a supplement to our illustrations of the latter; although, in a structural sense, the so-called alliance is at the best a forced—an unnatural one—and only admissible in a work of the present form for convenience sake, or in compliance with popular arrangement.

The British genera belong to four orders:—

EQUISETACEÆ.

1. Equisetum.

MARSILEACEÆ.

2. Pilularia.

LYCOPODIACEÆ.

3. Isoëtes. 4. Lycopodium.

CHARACEÆ.

5. Chara. 6. Nitella.

EQUISETACEÆ.

Leafless plants, with branched, striated, fistular, jointed stems; the articulations separable, surrounded at the base by a membranaceous toothed sheath. Fructification in terminal cones or spikes, consisting of stalked peltate polygonal scales bearing thecæ on the under surface. Sporules ovate or subglobose, spirally encompassed by elastic, hygrometrical, club-shaped filaments. The order consists of a single genus.

EQUISETUM. Horse-tail.

Gen. Char. The same as that of the order.

The species of this remarkable and most isolated of all the vegetable forms at present extant are few, probably not more than from ten to fifteen, certainly under twenty; but they are widely distributed, growing in moist ground and on the borders of lakes, ditches, and rivers in various parts of the world, from Lapland and Siberia to the countries within the tropics. Their habit is herbaceous, the stems being annually renewed from a creeping rhizoma, although in some instances they retain their vitality for indefinite periods after the cessation of growth. The largest of the European species has a height of five or six feet, but within the tropics one, at least, attains that of fifteen or sixteen. In some instances the rhizoma extends so widely and rapidly beneath the soil as to render them troublesome weeds. The true stems are rigid, rough to the touch, longitudinally striated, and tubular; the principal or central cavity being often surrounded by many smaller ones, and interrupted at intervals by the separable joints. Although destitute of true leaves, each articulation is invested at its base by a toothed membranaceous sheath, apparently formed by the union of several rudimentary verticillate ones; from beneath which, in the greater number of the species, spring whorls of branches, jointed like the stem, similar to it in general structure, and corresponding in number to the teeth of its sheaths and the striæ upon its surface.

The fructification of these plants is occasionally developed on separate stems, which make their appearance previously to those of general growth, and are, ordinarily, unbranched, succulent, and so different in aspect from the others, that the uninitiated observer would find a difficulty in recognizing the species to which it appertains. Under all circumstances the structure of the cones is peculiar, and so nearly alike that the description of one will suffice for those of the whole genus: the surface, at first smooth or indistinctly reticulated, eventually splits into numerous, generally octagonal, spirally arranged, brownish facets, which, when separated from the rachis, are found to be stalked, and to bear on the under side four or eight pendent sac-like bodies of a whitish hue—these are the thecæ, which open on the inside by a longitudinal slit for the discharge of the sporules—in general form the whole might be fancifully compared to a miniature lady's work-table with several bags. The sporules with their curious club-shaped filamentary appendages have occasioned much speculation regarding their actual nature; the former having been regarded as ovaries or as naked seeds; while the latter, attached to them like stamens around the base of a pistil, have had an office assigned to them analogous to that of those organs in flowering plants, between which and the flowerless the Equisetaceæ have been sometimes regarded as a transitional group. Our space does not admit the discussion of a subject upon which at present opinions are more problematical than plausible. The filaments are attached to one extremity of the sporule, and are rolled spirally around it while moist, but rapidly uncoiling as they become dry, cause the sporule to leap about as though it were alive; these movements, simply hygrometrical, are admirably adapted to aid the dissemination of the plants.

The rigidity of the stems and branches in this interesting tribe is due to the abundance of silica contained in the cuticle, which has been ascertained to amount in some species to as much as thirteen or fourteen per cent.; the ashes of the entire plant yield an average of more than half their weight of that earth, which is disposed in a crystalline form over the whole surface. It is to these crystals that the peculiar roughness is owing, which has acquired for the most common of our indigenous Equiseta, *E. arvense*, the name of Shave-grass, as well as the striated character belonging to the genus generally; which latter is due to their regular arrangement in parallel longitudinal series. In some instances they are so closely set, that the whole of the vegetable fabric may be removed by careful maceration without destroying the form of the part or disturbing their arrangement: the prepared stem of *E. hyemale* furnishes beautiful microscopic objects, especially under the influence of the polarizing apparatus.

The immediate economical value of these plants is trifling: as herbage, they contain little nutritive matter, hence are rarely eaten by cattle unless compelled by hunger or a deficiency of more grateful food. In a medical point of view they are slightly astringent and stimulating, and were formerly esteemed as possessing diuretic qualities, but have long been out of use. The roughness of their crystalline stems renders them useful for several mechanical purposes, as for scouring utensils of wood and metal, and for smooth-

Equisetum arvense

ing the work of the cabinet-maker, turner, and whitesmith previous to the process of polishing; but their employment by the manufacturer declined on the introduction of glass-papers and other contrivances of the kind, more easy of adaptation than these natural files. In their place in the vegetable world, they are important as colonists and contributors to the progressive elevation and fertilization of the soil.

The British species are all amenable to cultivation, and, when once established, easily kept and less liable to suffer from casualties than are many of the Ferns. The admirers of the latter will not fail to appreciate the beautiful contrasts of form which they afford, when carefully grouped among their more familiar and more highly prized, because better known, favourites.

The English name, Horse-tail, and the Latin generic, from *equus*, a horse, and *seta*, a bristle, are characteristic of the general appearance of the branched species.

* *Stems of two kinds: fertile ones simple, succulent, of a brownish hue, appearing in the spring before the sterile ones and soon dying away: sterile ones with whorled branches, harsh, green, remaining throughout the summer.*

EQUISETUM ARVENSE. Corn Horse-tail. Field Horse-tail. TAB. I.

Fertile stems unbranched; their sheaths distant, loose. Sterile stems slightly scabrous, with twelve or fourteen furrows and striæ; teeth of the sheaths lanceolato-subulate; branches simple, erecto-patent. General outline attenuated upwards.

Equisetum arvense, *Linnæus*. *E. B.* 2020. Generally adopted.

The most common British species. Frequent in corn-fields and pastures as well as on road-sides, chiefly, but not exclusively, in low moist ground, and especially where water accumulates during the winter. The fertile stems appear about the end of March, and are from seven to nine inches high, erect, smooth, succulent, of a pale brownish hue, with from three to five distant, furrowed, brown-toothed, somewhat inflated sheaths. Cone about an inch in length, encircled at the base by the membranaceous rudiment of a sheath. The barren stems are either procumbent or ascending, very rarely erect, and vary greatly in length in different soils and exposures, from a few inches to one or two feet; with numerous whorls of slender, generally simple branches, that become gradually shorter upwards, while several of the uppermost joints of the stem being bare, the whole has a somewhat attenuated lanceolate outline; the sheaths of the stem are many-toothed, those of the branches three- or four-toothed only, each tooth long and acute with a rib extending to its point.

The rhizoma of this species extends itself very rapidly beneath the soil at a considerable depth below the surface, and branching in all directions, like that of the Common Brake, *Pteris aquilina*, is very difficult to eradicate; hence it is one of the most troublesome weeds in arable land that the farmer has to contend with. When growing in pastures it is said to be injurious to cows, probably in consequence of the abrasion produced by its siliceous surface; they seem, however, never to eat it unless in the young state, and where the herbage is scanty when they are first turned out in the spring.

The Field Horse-tail is not a very desirable plant to introduce into the Fern Garden or among rock-work, on account of its spreading undergrowth, which is liable to interfere greatly with that of others, and even to destroy them; but as it will grow in almost any kind of soil, and is indifferent to exposure, it may be advantageously employed to cover the sunny side of a bank, or planted about the root of a tree, always taking care that the situation is sufficiently isolated not to admit of its doing mischief. Making all due allowance for its natural habits, which place it in the catalogue of vegetable moles, equally insidious as are the Common Bindweed and the Colts-foot, the rich green hue of its young sterile shoots and the singular parasitic aspect of the earlier fertile ones, render it more worthy of a place in our home collections than many of those exotics that are cherished with equal inconvenience and far inferior claim to notice.

EQUISETUM UMBROSUM. Blunt-topped Horsetail. TAB. II.

Fertile stems unbranched; their sheaths approximate, appressed. Sterile stems scabrous (especially upwards) with prominent points, with about twenty striæ; teeth of the sheaths subulate, appressed; branches erecto-patent, simple. General outline obtuse upwards.

Equisetum umbrosum, *Willdenow. Babington. Moore.* E. Drummondii, *Hooker, E. B. Supp.* 2777.

This species is either very rare in these islands, or otherwise it has been overlooked in consequence of the resemblance of its sterile stems to those of *E. arvense*, the fertile ones, which are very strikingly different to those of the latter plant, being usually scantily produced, and at a period of the year too early to encourage the researches of any but the more enthusiastic botanists in those localities where it is most likely to be found. We are indebted to Mr. T. Drummond for its earliest recognition as a native of Britain; he met with it growing on the banks of the Isla and Esk in Forfarshire, Scotland, "extending up the valleys almost to the sources of those rivers." Though a local plant, it has since been collected in

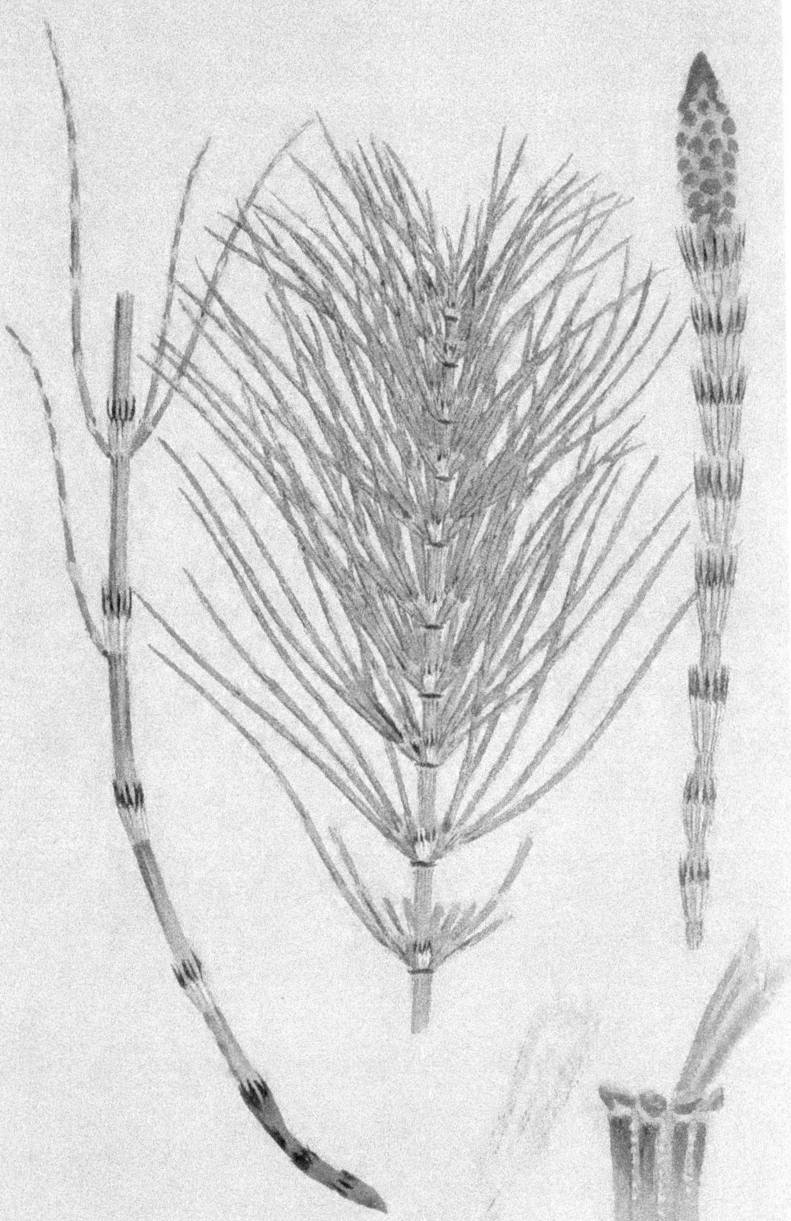

Equisetum umbrosum

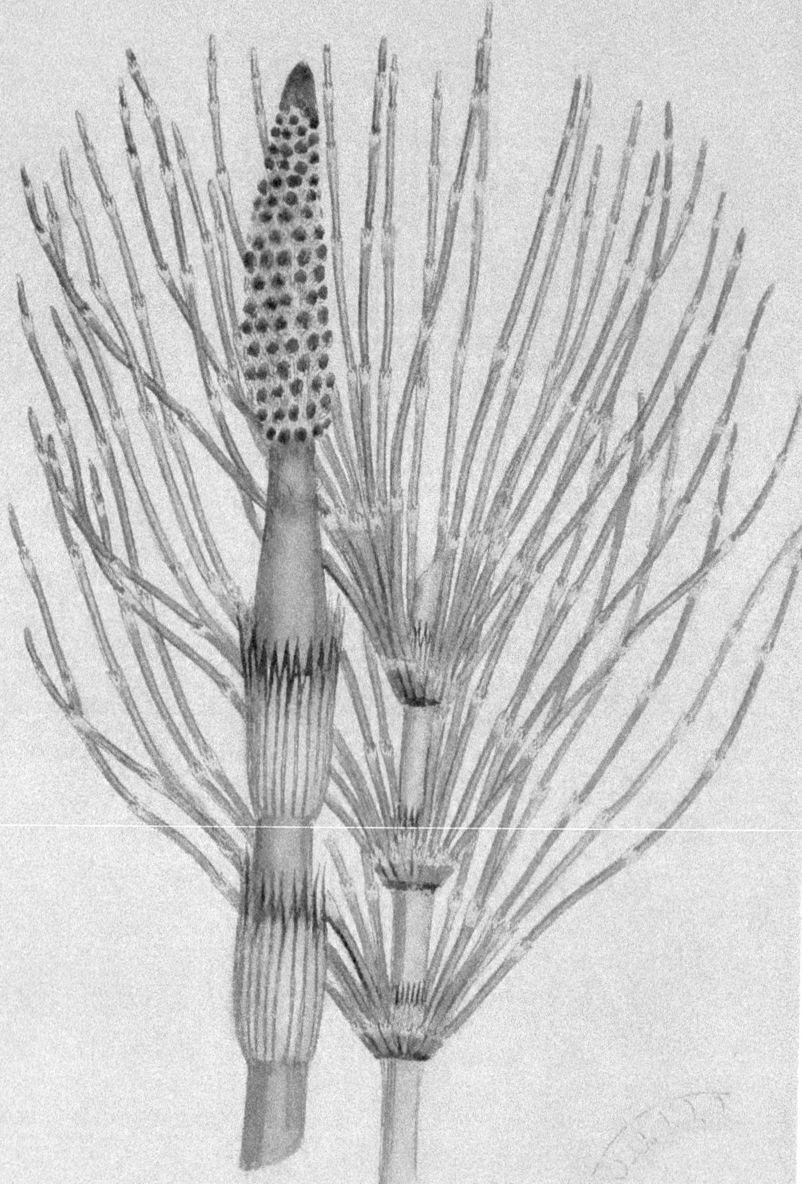

Equisetum Telmateia

several other parts of the island, and may prove not less common than some other partially distributed species. I have seen specimens of its barren stems collected this summer in Kent, Sussex, and Berkshire.

The rhizoma creeps under the soil like that of *E. arvense*, sending up at intervals three forms of stems. Of these, the earliest, which make their appearance in March or April, are fertile, five or six inches in height, unbranched, and nearly covered with numerous striated, very pale green or whitish sheaths; which are less inflated than those of the preceding, and terminate in from twelve to twenty long subulate, chocolate-coloured teeth: the cone is pale brown, and about an inch in length. As these, which may be regarded as the normal fructifying stems, mature and decay, the others make their appearance, and, occasionally, one or more of those first developed present a form intermediate between the strictly fertile and sterile states; bearing several whorls of from four to six short branches, and terminating in a small and usually abortive cone. The sterile stems attain a height or length of one or two feet, and are very rough, in consequence of the prominence of the siliceous crystals on their ridges: the sheaths are small and distant, but resemble those of the fertile stems in hue, and four or five of the lower ones are without branches, the remainder, to the summit, having whorls of from twelve to sixteen long slender ones, usually simple, and more or less ascending, so as to render the general outline obtuse; the joints of the branches, eight or ten in number, have the sheaths elongated and terminating in three or rarely four blunt or very short teeth, in which the rib terminates below the apex.

Moist woods and shady spots near water seem to be the favourite habitats of this species. I have not had it under cultivation, but the same objection exists to its introduction among other plants as in the case of *E. arvense*, viz. its tendency to spread underground, a habit which the soil usually required in the Fern Garden would in all probability encourage: setting this circumstance aside, it is a much more ornamental plant.

Equisetum telmateia. Great Horsetail. Tab. III.

Fertile stems unbranched; their sheaths crowded, ample, loose, with numerous slender subulate teeth. Sterile stems nearly smooth, with about thirty striæ, and many whorls of slender, suberect, simple branches; their sheaths close.

Equisetum Telmateia, *Ehrhart. Babington. Moore, Newman, Hist. Brit. Ferns,* &c. ed. 2. 67. E. fluviatile, *Linnæus*? *Withering. Smith. E. B.* 2022. *Hooker.*

Far from unfrequent in marshes and bogs, in watery places in woods, and about the banks of rivers and ponds, growing among the taller species of Cyperaceous plants, reed grass and rushes; often in exposed situations and drier ground, especially where the soil is stiff loam or clay, on which water lies during the winter. It is the largest of our indigenous *Equiseta*, its barren stems frequently attaining the height of six or seven feet, while its whorls of slender branches, from twelve to fifteen inches in length, present a truly magnificent appearance, and give an almost tropical aspect to the vegetation among which it occurs.

The rhizoma creeps widely in a moist loose soil, sending up its fertile stems about the end of March: they vary considerably in height according as the situation is more or less exposed, from four or five inches to a foot or more; they are thick and succulent, and of a pale brown hue, nearly covered with their large, loose, deeply-toothed sheaths, which are pale, sometimes almost white, at the lower part, while the teeth, from thirty to forty in number, are much darker and occasionally even black. The cone is between two and three inches long. The sterile stems are of a pale bright green, often more than an inch in diameter below, and varying from a few inches to the height above mentioned; they are almost smooth, but marked with from thirty to forty striæ, and, in luxuriant specimens, about the same number of slender quadrangular, deeply grooved, scabrous branches, in a whorl at each joint, which are at first nearly erect, but eventually spread out and at length become pendulous or arched: the sheaths of these stems are appressed, surrounded at the top with a well-defined blackish-brown band, the teeth being of a lighter hue and smaller and narrower than those of the fertile ones; the sheaths of the branches are four-toothed, each tooth with two denticulated ribs. Occasionally, as in *E. umbrosum*, the earlier barren stems terminate in a small imperfect cone.

According to Haller, the lower classes in ancient Rome used this species as food, and it is said, that in some parts of the continent of Europe the peasants mingle it with the food of cows, under the impression that it increases the quantity of their milk. Cattle, however, when left to their own choice, seem to leave it untouched; though Mr. H. C. Watson observes, "it is a notion among the rustics of Cheshire, that horses get 'bogged' by their endeavours to graze on this plant in the muddy pools of that county." It is more probable that such catastrophes result from their desire to escape the annoyance of the fly, than owing to their fondness for a plant, of which most writers who have mentioned the subject concur in affirming their dislike.

The highly ornamental character of the Great Horsetail renders it one of the most desirable of its tribe in cultivation, and no collec-

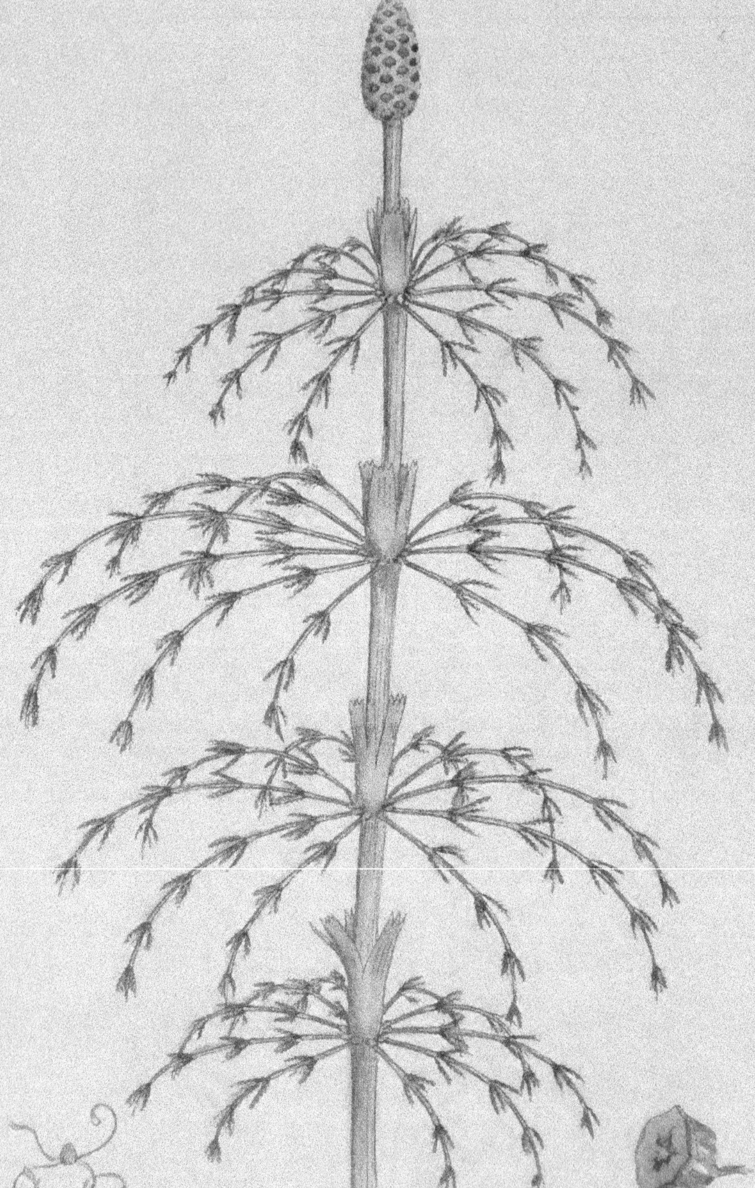

Equisetum sylvaticum.

tion should be without it in which room can be afforded for its admission. To ensure success in planting, some of the horizontal branches of the rhizoma should be taken up, as although the lower part of the upright shoots or stems will generally vegetate, the growth is slow and dwarf. The situation ought to be shaded, and the soil a mixture of about one part of peat to two of strong yellow loam, the more adhesive the better. If this soil be placed above a thick layer of crumbled brick or shards, and surrounded after planting by four or five inches of the same material, well trodden down, the encroachment of this splendid plant upon the surrounding larger species of Ferns will be in a great measure prevented, and the contrast between its graceful feathery outline and their breadth of foliage obtained in the greatest beauty. Like many other semiaquatics, it is capable of existing, and indeed of flourishing, in any situation sufficiently retentive of moisture to prevent its roots becoming dry, but its more frequent habitats, and the size attained by it where shade and moisture are the concurrents of luxuriant growth, will point out to the cultivator the circumstances under which that desirable state may be secured. The change of name, which is now adopted by most English writers, is so far valuable as it expresses a situation in which it is often met with, namely "growing in swamps," while *fluviatile* ill accords with a plant that rarely grows actually in water; but the contradictory accounts of recent collectors regarding its favourite localities, may be compared with those of the three travellers in the fable concerning the hues of the chamæleon, and are about as near to the truth; so indifferent is the species before us to superficial moisture or dryness, when once established in its habitat.

** *Fertile stems similar to the sterile ones, whether simple or branched, and appearing at the same time.*

EQUISETUM SYLVATICUM. Wood Horsetail. TAB. IV.

Stems with about twelve striæ, and several whorls of slender, spreading or deflexed, compound branches. Sheaths loose, terminating in three or four blunt-toothed lobes.

Equisetum sylvaticum, *Linnæus. E. B.* Generally adopted.

The most elegant species of the genus. A native of moist woods, thickets, hedge-banks, and other shaded situations throughout the kingdom, but more frequent in mountainous and subalpine or rocky districts. The stems vary from a few inches to a foot or even a foot and a half in height, those bearing fructification being generally shorter than the others, and occasionally, in the earlier part of the season, destitute of branches; in the latter case they wither and disappear after the dispersion of the sporules, resembling in this respect, and in their more succulent habit, those of the preceding section. The number of the striæ varies with the luxuriance of the plant from ten to sixteen, but the crystalline ridges are so little elevated that the stems are nearly smooth to the touch. The sheaths are more loose than in any other indigenous species, and split about half way down into from three to six blunt and usually toothed lobes; they are of a bright tawny-brown colour above, passing gradually below into the pale green hue that characterizes the stem. The fertile stems have occasionally six or eight, but seldom more than three or four, whorls of branches; which, being of nearly equal length throughout, occasions them to present a peculiarly abrupt termination after the decay and obliteration of the cone; this latter is of a pale brown colour, about an inch long, and is perfected about the end of April or the beginning of May. The sterile stems are pyramidal in their general outline, the whorls of branches in luxuriant specimens often fifteen to twenty in number, gradually diminishing toward the apex, which generally droops gracefully on one side, being too slender to support its own weight. The branches, ten to twenty or more in a whorl, sometimes numerous, are compound, very slender, long, and drooping.

This is less objectionable to cattle than most of the species, and is generally eaten down by them when it grows within reach. In some parts of Sweden it is collected for winter fodder, especially for horses.

The surpassing beauty of form, and the lively green hue of its long feathery branches, render the Wood Horsetail worthy of an introduction into every shaded garden and shrubbery, while in the Fernery its presence should never be dispensed with, where space can be spared for its reception. The tendency of the rhizoma to creep, and the copious moisture necessary to maintain it in a luxuriant condition, are circumstances easily obviated and provided for, by planting in a large pot, closed at the bottom and sunk in the soil over the rim, a contrivance well adapted for growing these plants generally.

EQUISETUM LIMOSUM. Smooth Horsetail. TAB. V.

Stems smooth, slightly but copiously striated; often simple. Branches few, simple, suberect. Sheaths close, with many rigid sharp-pointed teeth.

Equisetum fluviatile? *Linnæus.* E. limosum, *Linnæus.* *E. B.* 929. Generally adopted.

Common on the shallow sides of rivers, in ponds, ditches, and watery places generally. The rhizoma spreads widely, branching and rooting in all directions, so as to form a densely matted mass, that contributes to the solidification of the mud in which it vegetates,

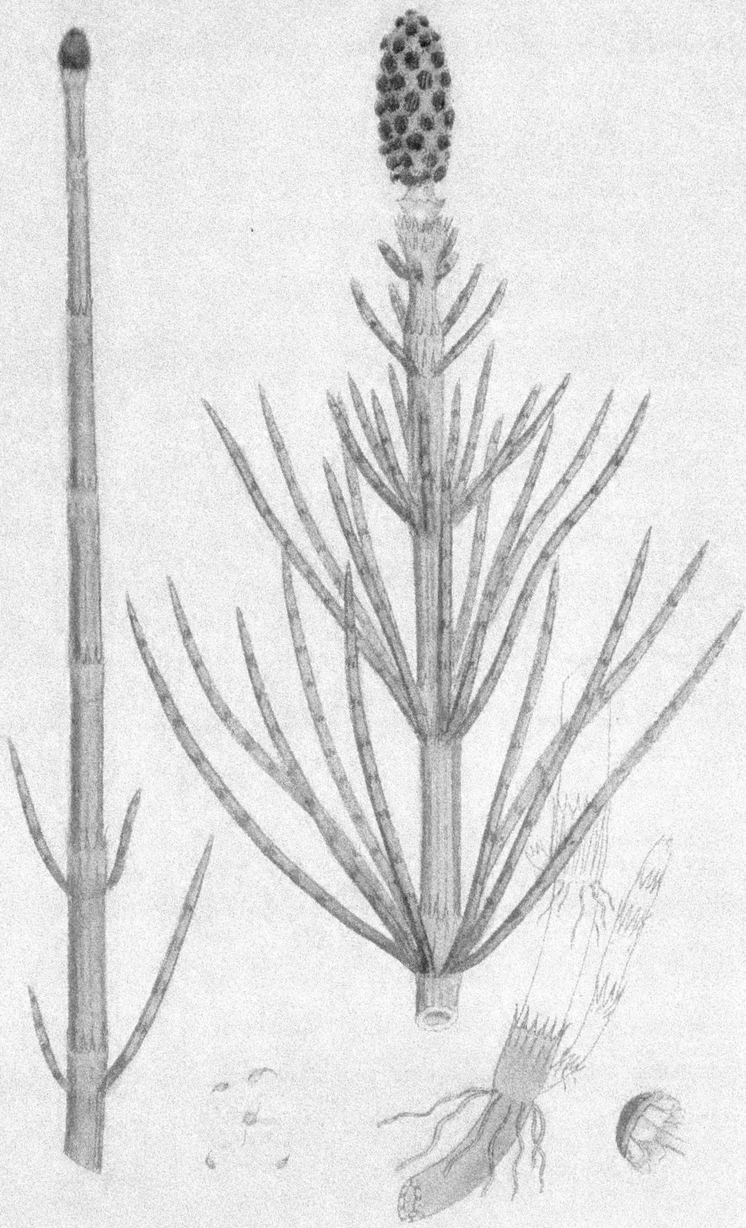

Equisetum limosum

and at the same time to the gradual contraction of the water limit; hence it is an active agent in the conversion of pools into swamps or morasses, which it abandons as the soil becomes elevated so as not to admit of the retention of water on the surface. The plant presents, in different situations, a variety of aspects, being sometimes so entirely destitute of branches as to resemble rushes, while at others, the branches, though usually few, are so abundantly developed, that a person not acquainted with its protean character might readily regard it as a distinct species. Such variations in habit are not constant in any particular localities, but their extremes will occasionally occur on the same spot in two successive years. The stems vary from one to three feet or more in height, and are almost universally submersed at the lower part, the difference of length being dependent for the most part upon the depth of the water in which they grow. They are smooth to the touch, but distinctly striated, the numerous ridges being so little elevated as to be distinguishable rather by the slight difference of their hue than by their roughness and projection. The branches are of variable length and number in each whorl, simple, and directed upwards, forming an acute angle with the stem. The sheaths are comparatively short, closely fitting to the stem, and of a similar green hue, but terminating in from sixteen to twenty sharply pointed dark-brown or blackish teeth. The cone is ovate, about an inch long, and usually invested at its base by the terminal sheath; it is perfected about the commencement of July, and, decaying soon afterwards, falls off, leaving the fructifying stems blunt-topped.

Much uncertainty exists respecting the association of this species by the older authors with *E. fluviatile*, *E. Telmateia* of recent botanists. That it is the plant recorded under the former name by Linnæus appears probable, as *E. Telmateia* is not a native of Sweden; but our limits preclude the discussion of a question of no present importance. From *E. palustre*, the following species, to which in its branched condition it approaches most nearly in general aspect, its thicker, smooth, not furrowed stems, and close green sheaths, at once distinguish it.

Cattle will frequently devour the Smooth Horsetail, when it grows within their reach, especially when the season is dry and the pasture over-stocked.

It is not a plant of sufficient beauty to render it worthy of attention in confined cultivation, but may be easily kept in a tub or shallow tank, partly filled with common garden soil, with a few inches of water over the surface: under such circumstances, however, it admits of no rivalry, soon overpowering most other plants that may be introduced to its companionship, or dying away itself if the natural colonizing propensity is restricted for their preservation.

Equisetum palustre. Marsh Horsetail. Tab. VI. & VII.

Stems rough, deeply furrowed, with six or eight broad, prominent ridges. Branches simple, suberect. Sheaths loose, with acute wedge-shaped teeth.

Equisetum palustre, *Linnæus.* *E. B.* 2021. Generally adopted.

Very frequent in marshes and watery places about the banks of rivers and ponds, especially in a black boggy soil; often accompanying *E. limosum.* The stems, from a foot to eighteen inches high, are somewhat rough, and generally branched throughout, the whorls gradually diminishing towards the apex. The branches have a similar upward direction to those of the preceding species, are uniformly simple, and the number in each whorl varies from six to ten, being frequently less, and very rarely more than that of the ridges. The sheaths are pale-coloured, loose, often somewhat inflated, terminating in acute wedge-shaped dark-brown teeth, with pale membranaceous edges, equalling in number the ridges of the stem. The cone is narrower than that of the last, being elongated oblong instead of ovate, and matures rather earlier in situations where they grow together.

The earlier European botanists seem often to have confounded this species with *E. arvense,* with which, at first sight, an inexperienced collector might consider it as having some resemblance, as well as with the more copiously branched specimens of *E. limosum.* Attention to the striking difference in habit, and to the features noted in description, will render any mistake as to their individual distinction scarcely possible.

Two, or perhaps three varieties of this common plant have been described, viz.—

1. *Polystachion,* in which the branches of one or two of the uppermost whorls terminate in small cones; the terminal one being often abortive, or of the reduced size of the others, very rarely presenting the character of full development. Tab. VII.

This variety has been noticed by most of our earlier botanists, and is far from being uncommon; sometimes growing apart, but frequently accompanying the usual form. The difference was supposed at first to be occasioned by the extremity of the primary stem having been bitten off or injured; but this, of course, cannot be the case where the terminal cone is produced, an occurrence quite as frequent as is its absence. The London collector may meet with the "many-spiked Horsetail" plentifully distributed in several localities along the banks of the Surrey Canal, between Camberwell and Rotherhithe; and this summer I found the specimen figured on the side of an enclosed portion of the old Croydon Canal, near Annerley.

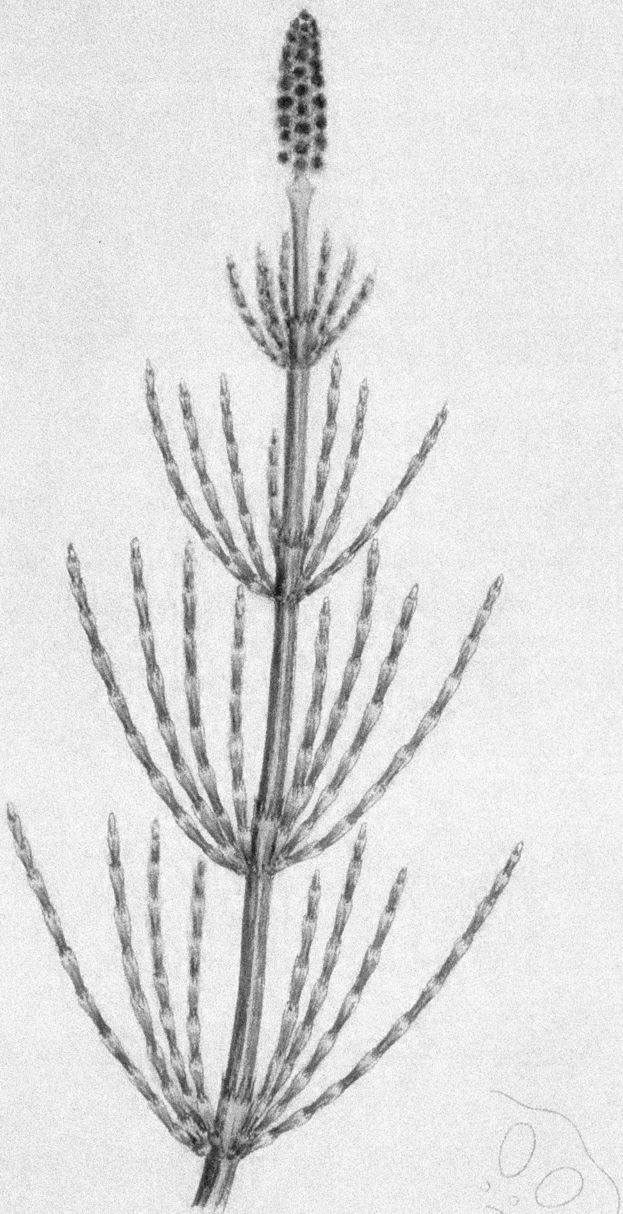

Equisetum palustre

J. E. S. Fecit

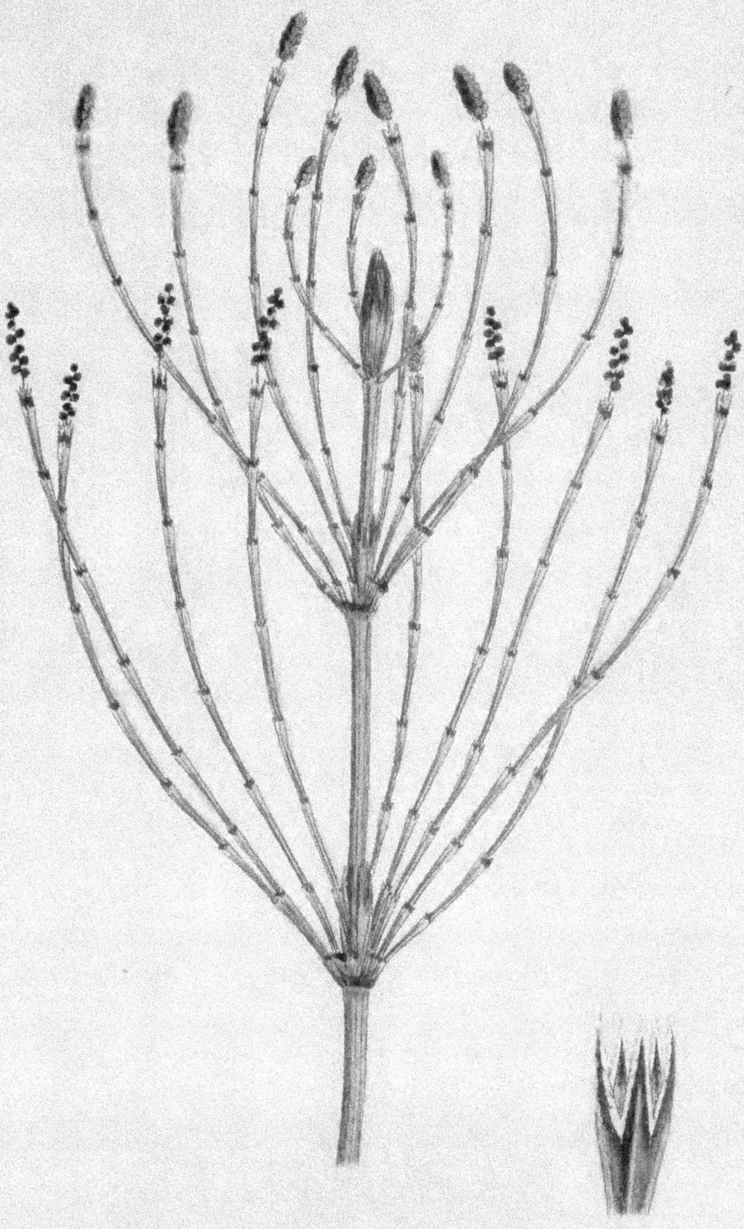

Equisetum palustre var. polystachion

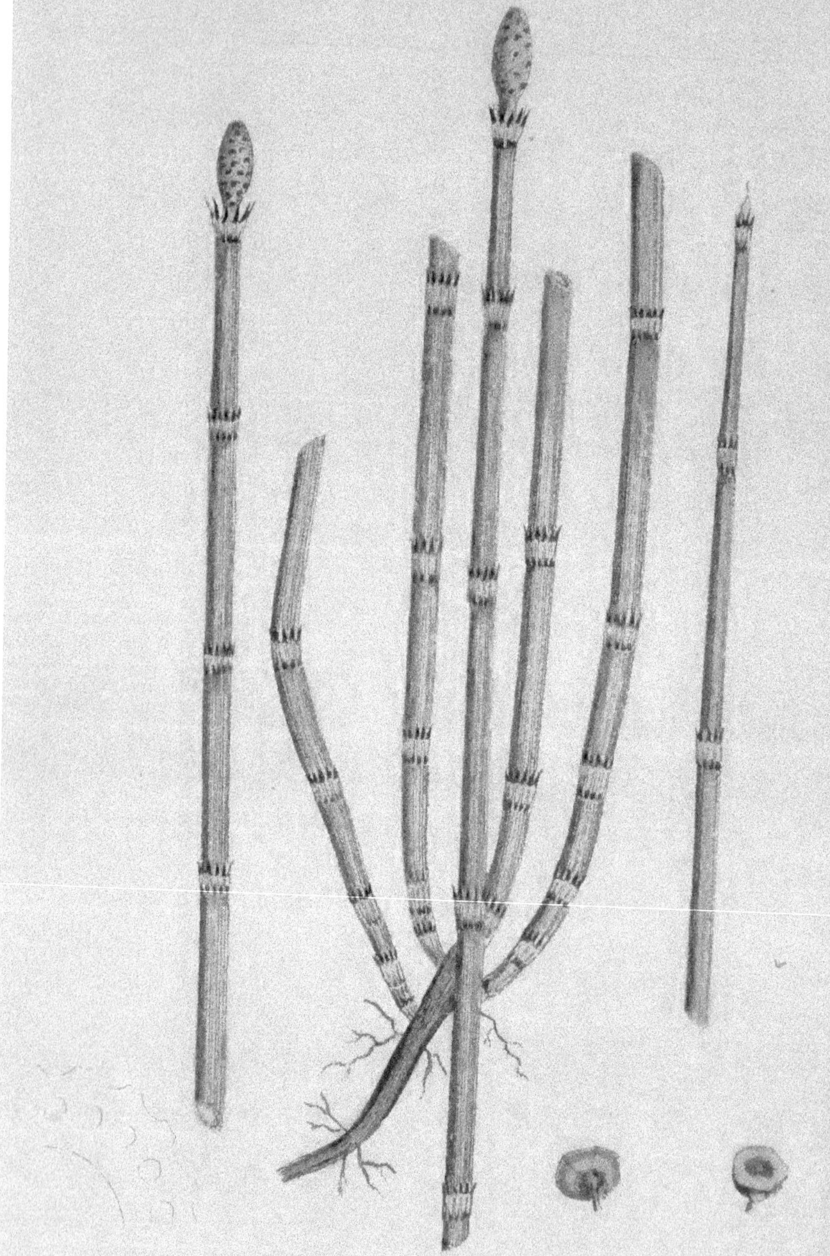

Equisetum hyemale.

Fecit

2. *Nudum*. Stems nearly or quite simple, dwarf. *E. palustre* γ. *nudum*, DeCandolle.

Grows in sandy places on which water accumulates, and on loose sand hills and banks. Found in Scotland, Yorkshire, Lancashire, Devonshire, and Cornwall. Specimens from different localities varied, from six or eight inches to less than two, in the length of the stem, and are otherwise so diversified in character, that a simple figure would be insufficient to convey a general idea of the variety. Mr. Newman, who, in his "History of British Ferns and Allied Plants," ed. 1844, p. 49, has given a figure of a Devonshire specimen, remarks, "Some of the examples are erect, others prostrate; and those which grow on sand-banks have the roots densely fibrous and clothed with minute fibrillæ. The small size, often prostrate habit, branchless stems, sandy habitat and densely clothed roots, have induced many botanists to consider this plant a variety of *E. variegatum* rather than of *E. palustre*; but, after a careful examination, I am unable to find any character whereby to distinguish it from the latter; the root, stem, sheaths and catkins seeming to me nearly identical with those of the usual form of the species." With these observations I concur at present, but only from examination of dried specimens; cultivation of the three may hereafter lead to an opposite opinion, or even to the establishment of this as a distinct species.

3. *Alpinum*. Smaller upper branches abortive. Sheaths with four or five angles and teeth. Hooker, British Flora, p. 451. "Boggy places near springs on the higher parts of the Breadalbane mountains." Perhaps an intermediate form.

It may be grown in the manner recommended for *E. sylvaticum*, and the variety *polystachion* is very ornamental when in fructification.

EQUISETUM HYEMALE. Rough Horsetail. Shave-grass. TAB. VIII.

Stems simple, very rough, with from fourteen to twenty ridges. Sheaths close, with as many dark, slender, subulate, deciduous teeth as ridges.

Equisetum hyemale, *Linnæus*. *E. B.* 915. Generally adopted.

Though rather to be regarded as a local than a common species, this is very widely distributed over the different parts of the kingdom, in England and Wales, in Scotland and Ireland. Its favourite localities are wet woods, bogs, marshes, and the borders of rivulets. In England it is more frequent in the northern and midland counties than in those of the south. The stems, branching from the rhizoma near the surface of the soil, rise to the height of two or three feet, sometimes, but rarely, producing a single lateral branch here and there, but never any of those whorls that so strikingly characterize the species already described; they are of a dark green colour, and rough like a file, owing to the prominence of the double row of sharp siliceous crystals of the ridges: the barren ones become so much attenuated towards the extremity as to lose the naturally erect position and curve over to one side, but the fertile ones are nearly equal in diameter throughout, shorter, and rigidly erect. The sheaths closely invest the stem, and are at first of a similar green colour, but ultimately acquire a pearly whiteness in the middle part, forming very conspicuous bands at intervals of two or three inches throughout its whole length; these bands are rendered more distinct by the base of the sheath having a broad dark or blackish-brown border, and a narrower margin of the same hue formed by the blunt bases of the dark deciduous teeth. The cone is very small, dark-coloured, and terminates in an apiculus. It is matured about the beginning of August. The barren stems usually present rudiments of fructification at the apex.

This is the species chiefly employed for mechanical purposes, on account of its roughness, and its long simple stems are largely imported from Holland under the name of Dutch Rushes, being used for polishing hard woods, ivory and metal by turners and other handicrafts. Some botanists have expressed a doubt respecting the identity of the continental with our indigenous species, but except in its larger size, and consequently more numerous striæ and corresponding fistular cavities in the interior of the stem, no positive character of distinction is traceable. The British plant from Gamlingay Bog, Cambridgeshire, cultivated in my garden for thirty years, frequently rivals the imported "Dutch Rushes" in these respects, the number of ridges and smaller tubes varying from twenty to twenty-eight in the larger stems. Lightfoot informs us that "in Northumberland the dairymaids employ it to scour and clean their milk-pails," a purpose for which the more common *E. arvense* is often used elsewhere. Its medicinal qualities, dependent upon a slight astringency, though formerly extolled, have long been disregarded. Cattle seldom eat it; indeed it is said to occasion the teeth of cows to drop out, and to be injurious to sheep, evils probably due rather to the marshy condition of the land on which it grows than to any deleterious quality of the plant itself, as it has the reputation of being wholesome to horses.

It is easy of cultivation, and as the rhizoma does not extend so rapidly as to become injurious to its neighbours, no confinement is necessary; while the tall dark-green stems with their white band-like sheaths form compact tufts, that contrast agreeably with the feathery fronds of the larger Ferns. Though it grows naturally in

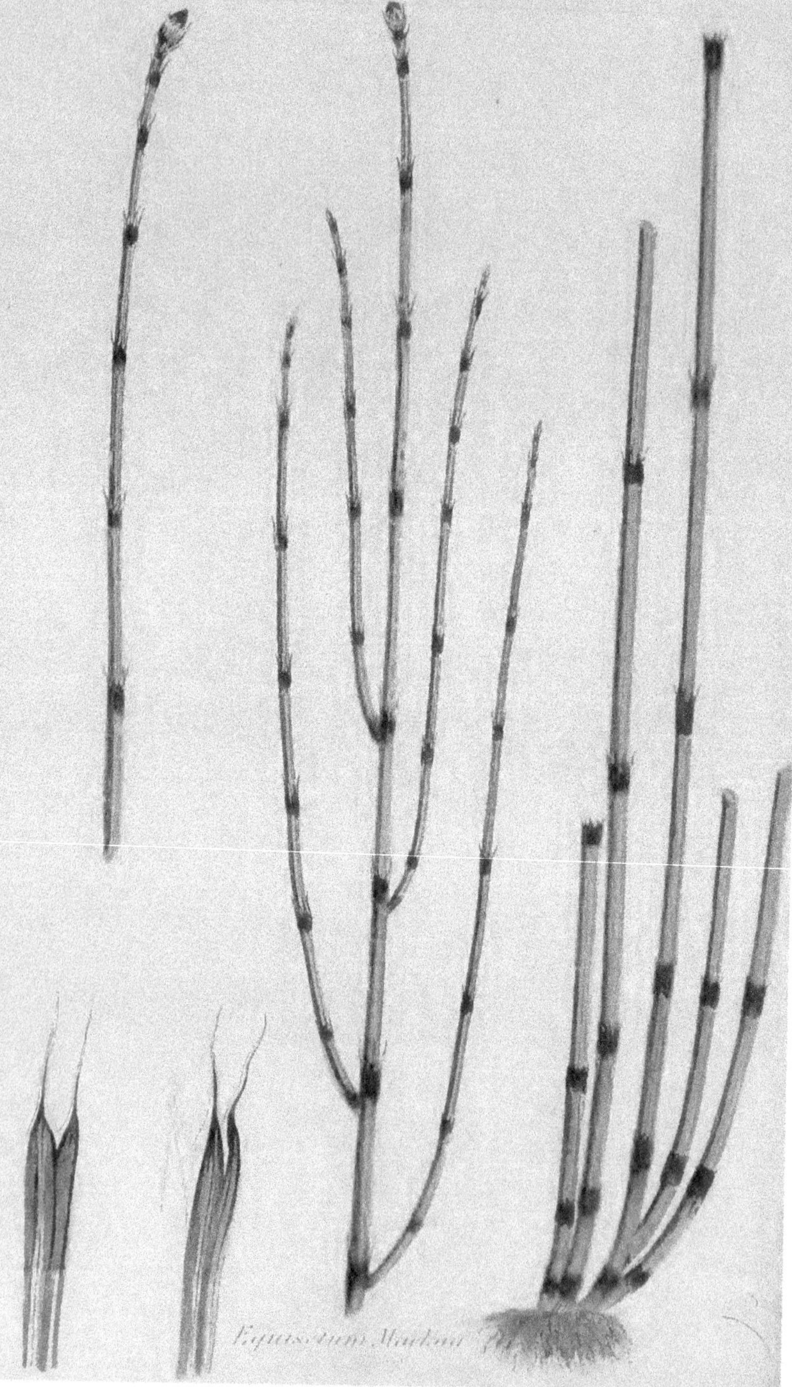

Equisetum Mackaii

wet places, any shaded situation in the garden where the soil is at all retentive of moisture may be selected according to convenience; and being evergreen, and little affected by the severest cold of an English winter, adds greatly to its ornamental value in the shrubbery or Fern plantation.

The claim of the four following to rank as species is very equivocal. If it be admitted, they will constitute, with a few others of exotic growth similarly circumstanced, a group of marked character, of which E. hyemale *may be regarded as the type. Such group will be distinguished from the other plants of the genus by the greater roughness and rigidity of the stems, and their tendency to a simple form of development; by the branches, when present, being produced singly and alternately, and according with the principal stem in structure and appearance, instead of assuming the contracted form and verticillate disposition exhibited by those of their congeners. To these features may be added the comparatively small size of the fructifying cone and its universally apiculate termination.*

Equisetum Mackaii. Mackay's Equisetum. Tab. IX.

Stems erect, simple or slightly branched, very rough, with from eight to twelve ridges. Sheaths close, ultimately wholly black, with long, aristate, somewhat flexuose, persistent teeth.

Equisetum Mackaii, *Newman, Hist. Brit. Ferns,* &c. ed. 1844. 25. *Babington. Moore.* E. elongatum, *Hooker.* Not of *Willdenow.*

A native of mountain glens in Ireland and Scotland. First observed by Mr. Mackay in August 1833, "on moist banks near a waterfall, at the upper end of Colin Glen, Belfast;" since by Mr. Moore and others in many of the glens and ravines of the north of Ireland, and in Scotland. The stems grow erect from the height of one to three or four feet, forming tufts like those of *E. hyemale,* which they resemble in roughness, but are more slender; they are generally simple, but not uniformly so, being frequently branched, especially towards the upper part, as shown in our middle figure. The branches are always solitary, and, although springing like the whorled ones of other species from below a sheath, have rather the character of divisions of the stem itself, and assume the same erect position and indefinite development; occasionally, in very luxuriant specimens, they produce secondary branches, but always in a corresponding manner. The ridges resemble those of the preceding species, except that they are fewer in number. The sheaths are at first of a pale green colour, almost white, terminating above in a black rim, but eventually become wholly black. The teeth are usually persistent; they are black, long, flexuose, and bristle-like, more or less dilated at the base. The cone is small, almost black, and terminates in a small pointed process (apiculus). It matures in August.

Leaving out of consideration the number of ridges and striæ, a feature liable to variation in these plants, depending, as experience demonstrates, upon luxuriance of growth and accidents of season and situation, the distinctive character of *E. Mackaii* rests almost exclusively upon the hue of the sheaths and the form of its teeth-like divisions. What importance may attach to such circumstances, in an order occupying so low a grade on the scale of vegetable organization as that before us, remains to be ascertained. In higher groups, colour, and even leaf-division, hold only a very subordinate value in the separation of species; the former indeed being rarely, if ever, resorted to by the scientific naturalist, while the latter is in many instances so susceptible of modification as to be next to useless.

The slender character of the stems in our plate, so different from those of the stouter *E. hyemale* immediately preceding it, and more especially its branched condition, would appear at first sight to render the previous remarks unnecessary, and the probable identity of the two plants chimerical; but the practical botanist will comprehend readily the association of such apparent extremes by intermediate forms, and the possibility that such may be the case in the present instance. *E. hyemale,* when luxuriant, occasionally branches in this manner at the upper part, while *E. Mackaii* is more commonly seen in the form of the left-hand figure, Plate IX., simple. Differences of this description are of such frequent occurrence as the result of circumstance, that they are utterly valueless in a question of specific correspondence; and in regard to the estimation they deserve in the allotment of the rank of species to varieties in *Equisetaceæ,* I may quote the authority of one of the most industrious and observing naturalists of his time, M. Vaucher of Geneva, who, in his monograph of the order, after remarking on the general habitats of these plants, observes on the contrary that, "we find them occasionally in sandy and dry situations, as, for example, *Equisetum multiforme;* but this species appears to be greatly influenced by the nature of the soil in which it grows, for sometimes it develops only a small number of slender and very short stems, while vegetating in richer ground, we find springing from the main tuft stems so much larger and more copiously branched that they might be supposed to belong to a different species." Similar causes may be implicated in the production of this and the three following British plants, as they have been in many other instances among the higher groups of the vegetable kingdom, leading to an unnecessary multiplication of species, in

Equisetum Wilsoni

Equisetum variegatum

the absence of all the more positive organic conditions of structure upon which alone they ought to be founded.

EQUISETUM WILSONI. Wilson's Equisetum. TAB. X.

Stems erect, simple or slightly branched, nearly smooth, with eight or ten furrows and broad intervening ridges. Sheaths close, concolorous with the internodes, but margined with black at the summit. Teeth short, obtuse.

Equisetum Wilsoni, *Newman, Hist. Brit. Ferns*, &c. ed. 1844, 39, a variety of E. variegatum. *Babington. Moore.*

First noticed by Mr. W. Wilson, growing in water, at Mucruss, Killarney. The stems are erect, often two or three feet high, simple, or occasionally branched, especially towards the lower part, as in our figure, the branches being usually single and alternate, but sometimes opposite; the number of ridges is not to be depended upon, varying in specimens before me from six to twelve, according to the thickness of the stems; but they are remarkable in all on account of their great comparative breadth and flatness, and the slight prominence of the siliceous crystals, which renders the plant much less rough than any of its immediate congeners. The sheaths are scarcely so close as those of *E. hyemale*, being slightly bulging or inflated above the insertion; they resemble the stem in colour, except at the upper margin, which is black where it passes into the bases of the short, broad, bluntly wedge-shaped teeth, the dark hue of which is relieved by a pale membranaceous border. The small, blackish, apiculate cone is characteristic of its near alliance, not with *E. variegatum* only, but with the species of which that may be regarded as a dwarfed and otherwise diminished type.

EQUISETUM VARIEGATUM. Variegated Rough Horsetail. TAB. XI.

Stems decumbent, simple or slightly branched, very rough, with from four to ten ridges. Sheaths slightly enlarged upwards, black, with pale, membranaceous, obtuse teeth, each tipped with a dark deciduous bristle.

Equisetum variegatum, *Willdenow. Weber and Mohr. Smith, E. B.* 1987. *Hooker. Newman, Hist. Brit. Ferns*, &c. ed. 1844, 31. *Moore.* E. variegatum, β. arenarium, *Babington.* E. multiforme, α. variegatum, *Vaucher. Macreight.*

A native of sandy ground, especially on dunes near the sea, on which it often accompanies *Ammophila arundinacea* and other sand binding plants; likewise of mountain valleys among the sand and other debris washed down by torrents. The plant varies very much in size in different habitats; being sometimes almost minute and with stems not more than an inch or an inch and a half in length and nearly prostrate, when it is *E. reptans*, *α*, of Wahlenberg. In its most common and maritime form in this country, as represented on our plate, its habit is rather decumbent and spreading than prostrate, and the stems attain a length of six or eight inches, though they are often nearly buried in the drifting sand, among which the rhizoma branches and extends occasionally to a considerable distance. The stems are very slender compared with those of other species, sometimes almost filiform; they are deeply furrowed and exceedingly rough, equally so indeed as those of *E. hyemale*. The sheaths are rather loose and gradually expanding upwards, where they divide into longish wedge-shaped teeth terminating in a fine bristle, which however soon drops off. The colour of the sheaths varies, frequently on stems from the same root; in general they are black at the lower part and with a black border at the base of the teeth, but sometimes the greater portion is of the same hue as the stem, the blackness being confined to the upper margin, where it generally extends into the middle part of the teeth, and contrasting with their white membranaceous edges, and the ordinary pale green hue of the stems, has obtained for the plant its characteristic specific name, though that of *arenarium*, expressive of its usual habitats, would have been more consistent. The small cone is apiculate, and invested at its base by the widely expanding terminal sheath, a general feature of the group: it matures in August.

The above description applies only to the form represented in this work, or as it is met with growing in sand; any deviation from specific characters as given in others, and particularly those of older date, must be ascribed to the prior association of this with the two preceding and, perhaps, the following one likewise.

The greater value of characters founded upon differences or resemblances in the internal structure of organic bodies, over the superficial ones of colour and outline, is a point universally admitted by naturalists; and it cannot be denied that important evidence of specific identity may be afforded by comparison of the interior organization of the stems of the Equisetums. Mr. Newman in the work above quoted, has, with much good taste and careful drawing, given magnified transverse sections of those of all the British species, and no one who may either contrast these figures of the first seven as they stand in the foregoing arrangement, or, what would be more satisfactory to the practical botanist, examine for himself, could do otherwise than admit their positive distinctness of character; but it is otherwise with the four following. In all of these as in *E. hyemale* a single peripheral series of tubes,

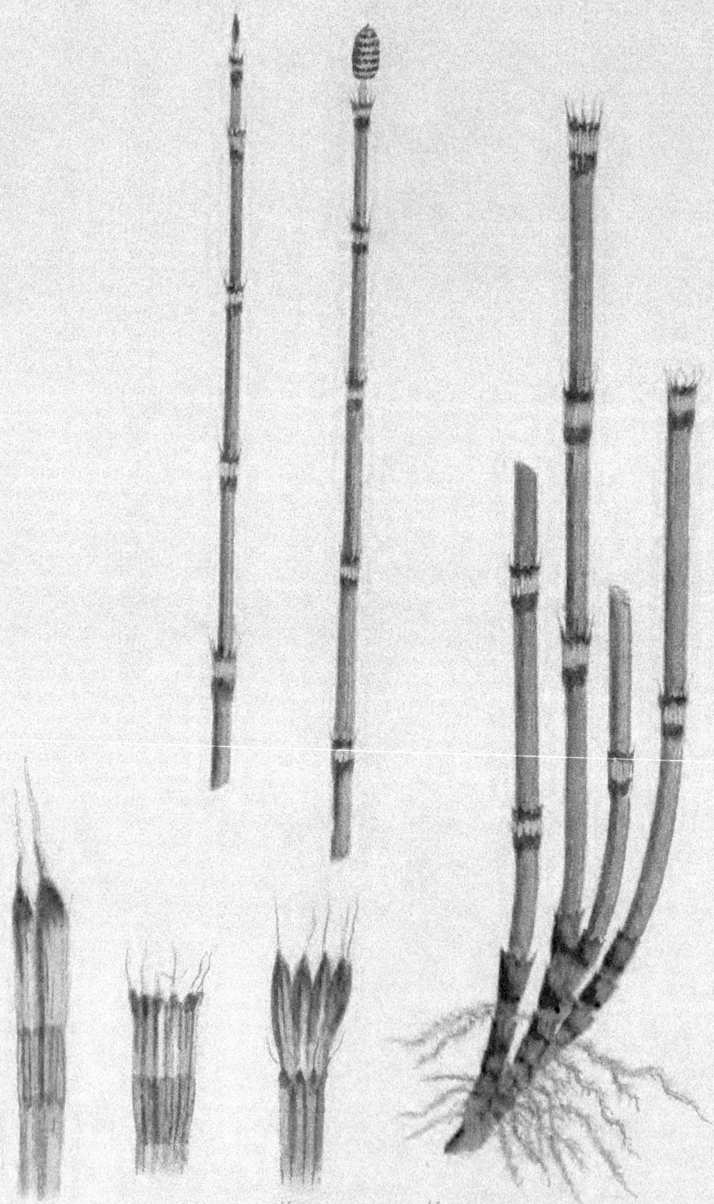

Equisetum Moorei

alternating with the ridges, surrounds the large central one of the internode, differing only in number according to the diameter of the stem, if we except a slight deviation of form expressed in that of *E. variegatum*, a circumstance probably originating from Mr. Newman's drawings having been made from dried objects: examined in the recent state, I have almost uniformly found the smaller tubes of the circumference cylindrical.

It is due to the author of the talented work referred to in these remarks, to state that he is indisposed to the unnecessary multiplication of species, and only yields, in according such rank to some of the non-verticillate forms of Equisetum, in deference to the views of other botanists of deserved reputation.

Equisetum Moorei. Moore's Equisetum. Tab. XII.

Stems erect, simple or slightly branched, rough, with from ten to fourteen ridges. Sheaths slightly enlarged upwards, black at the lower part, pale above; teeth black, obtuse, terminating in long, pale membranaceous subulate awns.

Equisetum Moorei, *Newman, Phytologist.*

The only specimens I have seen of this plant are in the dried state, and, except in the generally variegated hue of the sheaths, they are not distinguishable from those of *E. Mackaii*. In a tuft now before me, kindly forwarded to Mr. Sowerby by Mr. Moore, from Rockfield, Wicklow, Ireland, the longest stems, terminating in fructification, measure three feet. In habit it does not differ from the other upright species or varieties, and it approaches in roughness that last named (see our Tab. IX.); though none of the examples that have come under my notice show any tendency to branch in the manner there represented, in the middle figure, while in the present instance every stem is simple. The number of ridges, depending as it does on luxuriance of growth, is a feature of no value in specific distinction; neither is the proportional roughness, as it is not attended by any different arrangement of the siliceous particles upon which it depends, but only upon their greater or less prominence. The pale brownish hue of the middle part of the sheaths is a striking feature, but one of very equivocal importance, and, though a general one in this plant, the lower sheaths are almost always wholly black, while those of the upper part of the stem are frequently concolorous with it, the teeth excepted.

One circumstance, if correctly stated, is certainly indicative of variation from the ordinary character of the group: it is remarked that it "dies down in winter." Unacquainted with it in the living state, I am unable to testify to this peculiarity, which no observable difference in structure seems to warrant. All of the other immediate allies of *E. hymenale* resemble it in the evergreen habit.

ISOËTACEÆ.

This order consists of a single genus, which has been variously disposed by different botanists. Its structural affinities are not very readily traceable either with Lycopodiaceæ, where it is placed by DeCandolle, and most others who have adopted his arrangement generally, or with Marsileaceæ, to which it was transferred by Bartling and latterly by Dr. Lindley, as well as by myself in Vol. 8 of the second edition of 'English Botany,' 1841. In the present instance, closer comparison of its fructification with those of its supposed allies has induced me to adopt the separation as an order, proposed by the late Professor Burnett, of King's College, London, 'Outlines of Botany,' i. 310,—an allotment apparently warranted by the peculiarity of habit and structure, independently of that of the reproductive organs. By some botanists it is associated with a group of aquatic plants under the title of Hydropterides or Water-Ferns.

ISOËTES. Quill-wort.

Gen. Char. Seeds or sporules contained in membranaceous cases or conceptacles, imbedded in the dilated bases of the leaves. Conceptacles of the inner leaves filled with minute particles forming an impalpable powder: those of the outer containing an indefinite number of rough angular or subspherical granules.

The germination of the granules of the outer leaves has been observed by many botanists, and indeed frequently takes place within the conceptacles; hence their character as seeds, or at least as reproductive bodies, is beyond dispute, but it is otherwise with regard to the powdery particles included in those of the inner ones. It is still a subject of speculation whether these latter be only abortive forms of the true sporules, or whether they fulfil any specific function, as some have supposed, according with that of the pollen in flowering plants. All of the small natural orders, however, occupying in modern botanical arrangements an intermediate position between the higher and lower forms of vegetation, are more or less similarly circumstanced in this respect; some of them have even been at times referred to the Phanerogamous group; while, collectively speaking, the little positive evidence hitherto obtained, together with the frequent occurrence of two distinct forms of the reproductive apparatus among the lower grades of the Cryptogamous series, as the sea-weeds and lichens, militates against the opinion that these forms are other than contingent modifications of

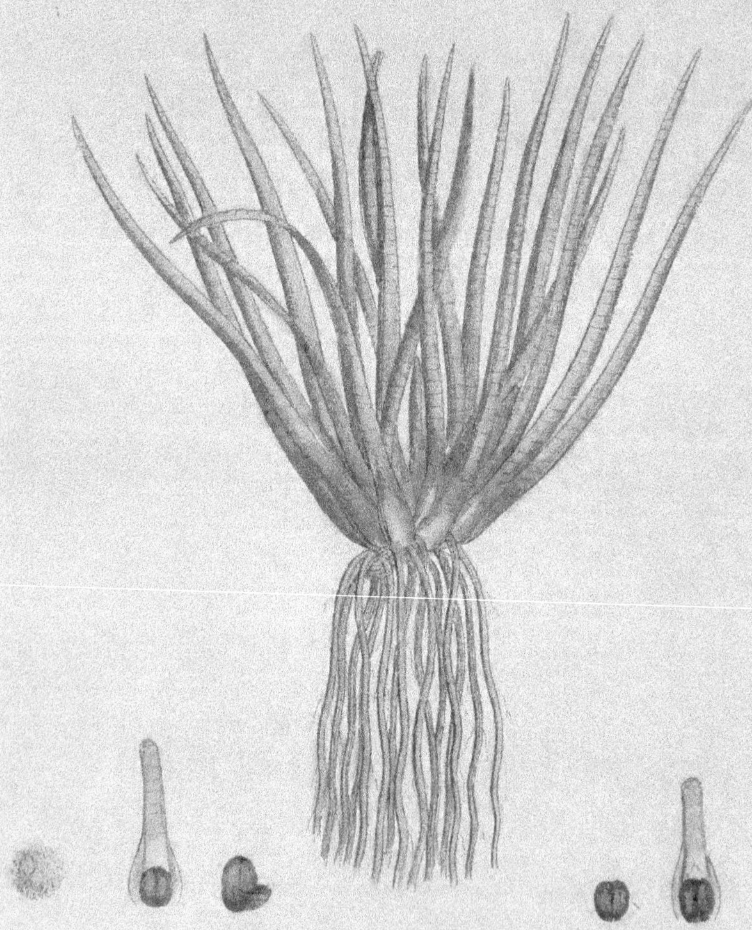

Isoetes lacustris

the same, or, at most, only prefigurations of organs requiring a higher state of structural development for the performance of their relative functions. That such is or is not the case in the genus before us is a point incapable of present decision.

The plant—for the existence of more than one species is doubtful—is aquatic and always grows submerged. It is met with throughout the north of Europe and North America. The generic name is derived from ἴσος, equal, and ἔτος, the year, and was bestowed on it by Linnæus in allusion to the evergreen habit.

Isoëtes lacustris. Lake Quill-wort. Tab. XIII.

Leaves radical, subulate, bluntly quadrangular or semicylindrical; consisting internally of four longitudinal series of angular cells.

Isoëtes lacustris, *Linnæus. E. B.* 1084. *Hooker, Lond.* 131. *Newman, Hist. Brit. Ferns, &c.* ed. 1844, 381.

Always found growing submerged, at the bottom of lakes and other still waters, in alpine districts especially. In many of the clear rocky lakes of the north of England, Wales, Scotland and Ireland it is most abundant, covering them so densely with its grassy-looking foliage as to give them the appearance of submerged meadows. The stem is a kind of cormus or tuber, about the size of a hazel-nut in large plants, fixed by thickish, white, tubular, generally simple, root-fibres. The leaves, growing in a circular, erect, or slightly spreading tuft from the crown of the cormus, are smooth, semi-transparent, and of a somewhat horny texture: their structure is remarkable, and may be described as consisting of four parallel tubes, divided transversely into numerous cells, and very brittle in the direction of their septa, which are visible externally. The fructification is about the size of a small pea, imbedded in the dilated and bulging bases of the leaves, and concealed by them, except on the inner face, where a circular opening displays the membranaceous conceptacle, sufficiently thin and transparent as it approaches maturity to admit of the granules being seen through it; it is in the best state for examination about the end of July.

This plant is liable to variation in different localities as regards both the size and the direction of the leaves, which are usually erect, but sometimes widely spreading, and in the latter case are generally broader, so as to have occasioned some botanists to regard them as different species.

Isoëtes lacustris admits of cultivation in shallow clear water, and increases rapidly, but to insure successful growth the bottom should be covered with sand an inch or two in thickness over the soil, so as to keep the water transparent, which must at the same time be sufficiently deep to avoid freezing throughout. Under these circumstances it may be grown with *Lobelia Dortmanna*, *Pilularia globulifera*, and other plants of similar habit; but a turbid or muddy condition of the water quickly destroys it, probably by excluding the light.

MARSILEACEÆ.

Aquatic, perennial, creeping plants, with alternate erect leaves having a circinate vernation. Fructification axillary, sessile; consisting of oval or spherical coriaceous conceptacles, usually of one form, but containing either individually or respectively two dissimilar forms of reproductive organs. The genera associated in this order are very uncertainly charactered by structural affinity, and correspond chiefly in habit. They are distributed in standing waters over most of the temperate parts of the world. A single species is indigenous to these islands.

PILULARIA. Pill-wort.

GEN. CHAR. Conceptacles solitary, nearly sessile, globose, coriaceous, four-celled, four-valved; each cell containing bodies of two kinds attached to a common receptacle.

The fructification resembles a pill or pepper-corn, hence the name, from the Latin *pilula*, a pill.

The single known species of which this genus consists, occupies a more equivocal position in the vegetable kingdom than *Isoëtes*. The globular conceptacles include numerous small bodies, attached to a membranaceous lining, which, extending from each of the valves, forms the four cells, as shown in the enlarged sectional figure on the right in Tab. XIV. The bodies occupying the upper part of each cavity contain a yellow powder resembling the pollen of a flowering plant; those of the lower part are larger, more turgid, and terminate in a small projecting point, which may be compared to a stigma: of these two forms the upper ones have been supposed to be anthers, the lower pistils; and under this view, the four-valved conceptacle including a mass of inflorescence is usually described as an involucre. Admitting such an explanation of the œconomy of the parts in question to be correct, *Pilularia* is here misplaced: it is a monœcious flowering plant; and experiment on the propagating capabilities of the dissimilar contents of its conceptacles is in favour of this decision. The supposed anthers are inert, while the pistils vegetate, pushing forth first their radicle to fix them to the soil, and afterwards a leaf or cotyledon. In this respect they resemble those of *Zostera* and some other aquatics of low organization, the first especially, the simple inflorescence of

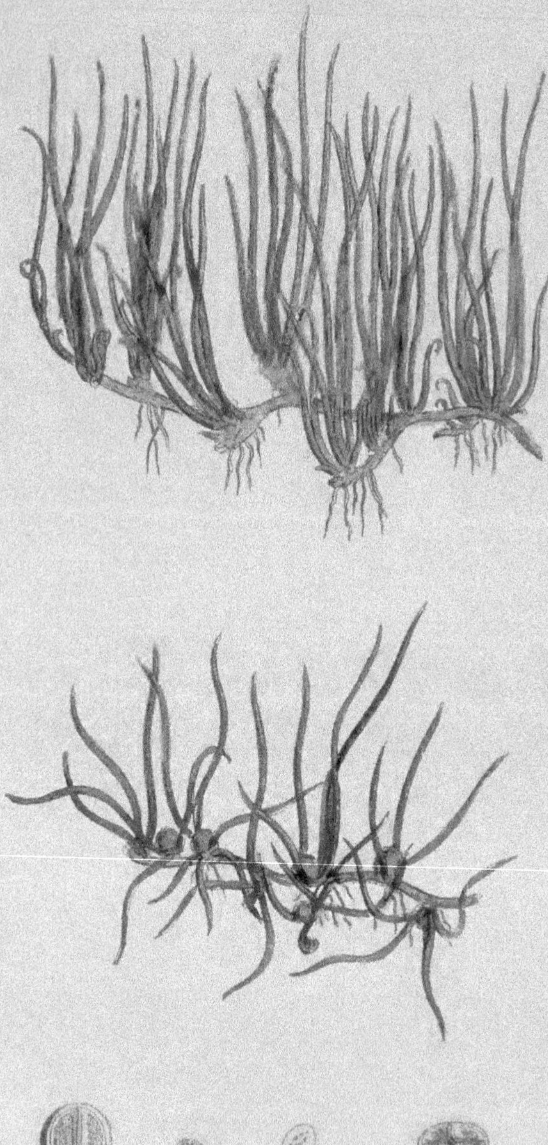

Pilularia globulifera.

which, inclosed in the hollow of its sheathing stems (see Eng. Bot. tab. 467. 2nd ed. tab. 4), approaches that of the plant before us. Still it must be admitted that the subject of vegetable propagation is, in regard to the inferior orders of plants, one of great complication and uncertainty, and that although, in the idea of the general or superficial botanist, a determinate limit may seem to exist between the flowering and flowerless species, such distinction is only the result of the absence of immediate proof that influence, analogous to that of the pollen of the former class, is concerned in maturing the reproductive germs of the latter. Among Ferns, and even among Mosses and Lichens, deviations from the normal character of species are not of unfrequent occurrence, and to an extent that, if it does not confirm their hybrid origin, tends to suggest its probability. The application of the term *Cryptogamous* to all these plants, records the doubt entertained by its author and admitted by his successors, concerning the existence of a difference of such vast importance; and every real step that we make forward in the study of their obscure physiology contributes to expand into universality our belief, that the same grand principle operates to the perpetuity of every existing form of organic being.

The peculiarities of *Pilularia* and the œconomy of its fructification, growth, &c. were made the subject of a valuable essay by M. Bernhard de Jussieu, in the "Mémoires de l'Académie Royale des Sciences, 1739," and more recently by Mr. Valentine, in the 18th volume of the "Transactions of the Linnean Society," both of which are well worthy the study of the physiological botanist; but our space will not admit of extract.

PILULARIA GLOBULIFERA. Pill-wort. TAB. XIV.

Rhizoma slender, elongated, creeping; producing leaves and roots at regular intervals. Conceptacles axillary, nearly sessile on the rhizoma, hairy.

Pilularia globulifera, *Linnæus.* *E. B.* 521. *Hooker, Fl. Lond.* tab. 83. *Newman, Hist. Brit. Ferns,* &c. ed. 1844, 393.

It may be regarded as a local rather than a common plant, but is at the same time widely distributed, and where met with generally most abundant. The long slender rhizoma creeps along the surface of the mud or sand in shallow water about the margins of lakes and pools, and sometimes in places only occasionally overflowed, especially on sandy and gravelly heaths, forming often, by its abundant branching and entanglement, a dense covering over the soil, to the complete exclusion of other plants. Some botanists have remarked that the *Pilularia* is never found in deep water nor in a state of constant submersion, but this is certainly incorrect, as I have met with it in Llyn Ogwen, Llyn Idwel, and in some parts of the Lake of Llanberis, covering the bottom at a depth of between one and two feet, in situations where it could rarely, if ever, be left exposed: under these circumstances the leaves were longer and exceedingly slender, and no fructification appeared to be formed; indeed the latter is only abundantly produced where the plant grows in open and comparatively dry places unfavourable to the more luxuriant development characterized in our upper figure. The leaves are coiled in vernation like those of the Ferns, erect, smooth, and slender, and, under water, even hair-like; in height they vary according to circumstances from one to four or five inches, forming clusters or tufts arising at intervals from the rhizoma opposite to similar tufts of rootlets. In fertile plants the leaves and rootlets are seldom more than three or four at each node, and the former not above one or two inches long; but in barren specimens the tufts of both are crowded and indefinite, and the leaves especially so, as well as more slender and taller. The solitary conceptacles spring from the axils of the leaves, supported by a pedicel so short that at first sight they appear sessile; they are nearly globular, but with a tendency to become conical at the apex, about the size of a small pepper-corn, brown, and hairy. Divided transversely they are seen to be four-celled, and separate in maturity into four equal valves. The upper half of each cell is lined with minute sessile, somewhat elongated or club-shaped, yellowish bodies, the stamens or anthers of Jussieu and others; the lower half is occupied by larger roundish or oblong sessile, one-seeded thecæ or ovaries, crowned with a small blunt projection, which is probably a stigma. The relative number of these bodies varies in different conceptacles, which, appearing in May, become successively matured to the end of autumn.

Our figures will convey a general idea of the barren and fertile states of this very curious plant, only it must be remarked that the leaves vary from the size represented to an almost hair- or bristle-like fineness.

It is easily cultivated on an artificial bog, or in a shallow pan with a mixture of peat soil and sand just covered with water, a situation in which fructification is sometimes abundantly produced, under a moderate exposure to the sun.

LYCOPODIACEÆ.

Perennial plants, resembling Mosses in the arrangement of their foliage and in general aspect, but in no other respect, their structural characteristics being widely different. To Ferns they bear about an equal relation with the rest of the *allies* so called, but are considered more especially to approach them in the structure of their stems, which contain an abundance of the large woody vessels denominated annular ducts. Dr. Lindley, in his 'Vegetable Kingdom,' has remarked, that the larger kinds "seem to imitate Coniferous Gymnogens (the Pine or Fir tribe) in their manner of growth, and in their tendency to collect their spore-cases in cones," and again that they are "intermediate, as it were, between Ferns and Coniferæ on the one hand, and Ferns and Mosses on the other,"—observations that, however imaginative, and consequently not perhaps strictly scientific, their basis, are still valuable as showing the difficulty experienced by even our best systematic botanists in the arrangement of these outlying orders of the vegetable kingdom.

The stems of the Lycopodiaceæ are generally slender and creeping, but occasionally erect, their texture solid and wiry; the creeping ones often extending several feet or even yards in length. The leaves are small, sessile, without veins, in most instances very closely set, and often imbricated. The fructification consists of minute cases or thecæ, sessile in the axils of leaves or bracts, and two kinds are usually met with on the same plant: the one, bivalvular, and containing a powdery substance, the particles of which under a high magnifying power are seen to be globular; the other, three-valved, enclosing a few comparatively large subspherical granules, which are marked with three prominent ridges radiating from one extremity. The relative position of these thecæ, differing chiefly in their contents, is, upon the elongated axis of a *Lycopodium*, similar to that of the conceptacles upon the shortened or rather abortive one of *Isoëtes*,—that is, those the contents of which are powdery occupy the upper part of the axis, corresponding to the centre of the cormus of the latter plant; while the granule-bearing ones are developed below them, or in the situation representing the outer part of the cormus. This circumstance has been noted, as justifying the reference of *Isoëtes* to the order before us, notwithstanding the striking difference of its habit; but it is chiefly important on account of its coincidence with the ordinary disposition of male and female flowers among the higher orders of plants, and thus lending some equivocal support to the opinion of those who consider the upper cases *anthers*, their contained powder *pollen*, while the lower ones are *pistils* and their granules *seeds*: this opinion has, however, been reversed by Link and others, and the whole subject is yet under speculation. That the granules are seeds, or at least sporules, is certain, as their germination has been frequently observed; but we have not yet any positive evidence respecting the functions fulfilled by the powdery particles, which Willdenow states grow likewise. I have tried them several times without success.

The genera of this order are few; three or at most four are capable of being well charactered, and of these the normal one alone contains the few species indigenous to Great Britain.

LYCOPODIUM. Club-Moss.

GEN. CHAR. Fructification either in the axils of the leaves, or contained in erect bracteated spikes. Thecæ one-celled: some two-valved, including minute powdery particles; others three-valved, or rarely four-valved, containing from one to about four nearly spherical rough sporules.

The generic name, from λύκος, a wolf, and ποῦς, a foot, seems to have been founded upon some fanciful resemblance between the branches or spikes of some species and the paw of that animal.

The species, about 200 in number, are very widely distributed, some being adapted to support the extreme cold of lands within the Arctic Circle, and others to vegetate under the corresponding excess of tropical heat; the latter forms are, however, the most abundant. They are all evergreen plants of a rigid habit, usually growing prostrate, and rooting at intervals; their stems clothed throughout with numerous small scale-like leaves, which are either more or less densely imbricated, or spreading in two principal series. These dispositions of the leaves and their minuteness, added to the general form of growth, give to the Lycopodiums very much of the aspect of gigantic mosses; though the internal structure indicates a far higher grade of organization, approaching indeed to that of the flowering plant, while the economy of their fructification is altogether dissimilar.

Those of Europe, and other temperate and cold climates, generally occupy the most exposed situations, growing on open heaths and moors and on the declivities of mountains, but very often in woods and other sheltered places. *Lycopodium alpinum* and *L. Selaginoides* are said to cover extensive tracts of country in Lapland almost to the exclusion of other vegetation, the former especially clothing the sides of the mountains. In the warmer parts of the world and within the torrid zone, the order is almost exclusively confined to moist shady situations, chiefly abounding in the dense humid forests of India, Tropical America, and the islands of the adjoining seas.

Though hitherto little employed in Europe either in medicine or the arts, these plants seem to possess some important properties, which, if the elaboration of active proximate principles affords any standard of organic complexity, would place the Club-mosses higher on the scale than any of the groups among which they are classed by botanists. *Lycopodium rubrum, L. catharticum,* Hooker, is powerfully cathartic, and is administered in Spanish America, suc-

Lycopodium clavatum.

cessfully it is said, for the cure of elephantiasis; its violent action has obtained for it the popular name of *Yatum condenado*, from *Yatum*, great devil, *condenado*, accursed: similar qualities, though less in degree, belong to some of our indigenous species, as well as to others of tropical countries.

Though growing naturally in the most exposed places, the British Lycopodiums are not easy of cultivation in the open ground, especially in the vicinity of London,—a fact due, perhaps, rather to the loose character of the surface soil in which they are planted, and the absence of sufficient moisture in the atmosphere during the principal season of growth, than to any other circumstances: in a close frame or in a shaded greenhouse they may be grown very luxuriantly. All of the exotic species, especially those of warm climates, succeed well as house plants, and, from their trailing habit, are admirably adapted for covering the surface of the soil around the larger species of Ferns.

LYCOPODIUM CLAVATUM. Common Club-Moss. Wolf's-Claw. TAB. XV.

Stem creeping. Leaves scattered, finely serrated, incurved, hair-pointed. Fertile branches erect. Spikes stalked, two or three together; their scales ovate-acuminate, finely toothed.

Lycopodium clavatum, *Linnæus*. *E. B.* 224. Generally adopted.

A native of upland heaths and high pastures in many parts of the kingdom, but most abundant in rocky and mountainous districts. The procumbent, repeatedly branched stems spread in all directions, but on declivities chiefly downward, to the length of many feet or even yards, throwing out strong root-fibres at intervals of a few inches, which fix them firmly to the ground; hence the plant is exceedingly useful on the steep sides of hills and mountains, as it serves to bind the soil and prevent the looser particles from being washed away by the rain and spring torrents. The leaves are crowded, entirely covering the stem, and curving upwards from the latter as it lies along the ground; they are linear-lanceolate, terminating in a white filament, and slightly toothed or serrated on the edges. The fertile branches vary much in height, from three to six or eight inches; they are erect, densely leafy like the others at the lower part, but clothed above only with a few scattered, narrow, pale green or yellowish, closely appressed scales: at the summit each stalk bears from one to three, but usually two, cylindrical spikes of a pale greenish-yellow or sulphur colour and one or two inches long, composed of imbricated bracts, broad at the base but acuminated upwards so as to be somewhat triangular in their general outline; the small, yellowish, kidney-shaped thecæ are developed singly in the axils of these bracts, and ripen towards the end of August, opening transversely to discharge the almost impalpable powder by which the species is propagated.

A decoction of the plant is employed in Poland for the cure of that most horrible of human disorders, the Plica Polonica. The powdery contents of the thecæ are collected in large quantities for sale, under the name of Lycopodium, or Vegetable Sulphur. This powder is highly inflammable, consuming instantaneously and with a slight explosion; hence it has been employed in Germany to produce imitative lightning in the theatres, and very extensively there and elsewhere in the manufacture of fireworks: so repellent is it of moisture, that, if scattered over the surface of water in a basin, a stone may be picked up from the bottom without wetting the hand. It is sold by the druggists in this country, as an absorbing powder to prevent excoriation in young children, and for application to skin wounds; for which purposes it is imported from different parts of northern and eastern Europe, where large quantities of the spikes are collected in the autumn to supply the demand, which is far from inconsiderable.

This species seems to be distributed throughout the northern hemisphere. The elegance of its long trailing and variously branched stems renders it a general favourite, and few plants are equally capable of adaptation to ornamental purposes, especially in the form of wreaths and festoons. Linnæus, in his 'Flora Lapponica,' mentions his having seen the Lapland children with their heads decorated with garlands, formed by so wreathing it that the double spikes projected on all sides, recalling to his mind the idea of the fauns and satyrs of the old mythology; and in some parts of the continent, where it grows commonly, its graceful curvatures are usually conspicuous among the winter decorations of the houses and churches.

To cultivate the Common Club-Moss successfully, it should be removed from the heath with the soil attached to the central or principal root; and in planting, whether in pot or on the ground, especial care is needed to ensure the drainage which in the wild state is always provided, and without which indeed the plant will not subsist, as due observation of its natural habitats will evidence. A poor soil and one incapable of retaining much moisture is no less essential. The manner in which the British Lycopodiums are generally offered for sale by the Fern collectors precludes all but the remotest chance of their after-growth: in the case of the present species, the elongating stems are simply torn from the ground without reference to the root from which they emanate, and the few scattered fibres attached to them, even if perfect, which they are not, would be insufficient for their maintenance; added to which the length of time, often several weeks, that elapses between their

Lycopodium annotinum.

removal and replanting, renders the existence of life rather problematical at the period when the latter occurs, and in most instances we might as reasonably expect the Christmas holly branch, planted in May, to grow, as the *Lycopodium clavatum*, fresh and green as it may appear, from the collector's basket.

LYCOPODIUM ANNOTINUM. Interrupted Club-Moss. TAB. XVI.

Stem creeping: branches ascending. Leaves spreading, obscurely five-rowed, linear-lanceolate, minutely serrated, acutely pointed. Fertile branches erect. Spikes oblong cylindrical, sessile, terminal, solitary.

Lycopodium annotinum, *Linnæus*. *E. B.* 1727. Generally adopted.

The rarest of our indigenous species. The only spot on which it has been found in the southern division of the kingdom is on the side of the Glyder mountain, Carnarvonshire, above Llyn-y-Cwn, where, though formerly abundant, it is now of rare occurrence, if not, indeed, latterly exterminated. In Scotland it is rather widely distributed, though generally at considerable elevation, especially on the Cairngorum and Clova Mountains. The strong, wiry, tough stems do not spread to the same extent as those of *L. clavatum*, though they root at intervals in a similar manner, and the habit of the two is very different: in the present species the leaves spread out and are often even reflexed; the arrangement in five rows is not at first sight very evident, but it gives in recent specimens an angularity to the general outline of the branches especially that can scarcely be overlooked. The fructifying branches present a contraction in the foliage at the base of each annual elongation, giving them a jointed appearance, whence the specific name *annotinum*, literally, marked yearly. This peculiarity, eminently characteristic of the species, originates in the successive annual postponement in developing the spikes of fructification at the summit of the branches in question, each such branch requiring a varying number of years to elapse, apparently from three to seven, previous to its attaining the condition of fertility: this latter condition may occur earlier or later according to circumstances, and I have examined specimens in which a partial development of the spike had taken place at a previous period, but, proving abortive, the branch had elongated above it in the following year, leaving no other remains of the fructifying effort, except a more distinct separation of the two leafy extensions, bearing in the interval a few rounded scales or bracts in lieu of leaves. There can, I think, be little question that the assertion of Sir J. E. Smith, in the 'English Flora,' respecting the proliferous character of the axis of fructification, originated from the observation of similar specimens; he describes the "flowering branches" as "erect, densely leafy, but little subdivided, each terminating in a solitary upright spike, whose scales, being deciduous, seem to leave the branch partly naked; but it afterwards bears proper leaves, except a few diminished ones just under where the spike had been, and produces, in the following season, another spike: hence the jointed or interrupted aspect of the branches." In modifying the description of the species for the second edition of the 'English Botany,' this explanation was retained as plausible; but my acquaintance with the plant rested at the time on a solitary preserved specimen: the after-examination of many both recent and dried examples, exemplifying an economy altogether different to that detailed in the work above quoted, has led to these remarks. The after-extension of an imperfect spike into a leaf-bearing branch in this plant, has its parallels in *Abies nigra* and some other Conifers, in which abortive cones become similarly elongated.

Its geographical range seems to be less limited than its frequency and abundance, and extends through the northern parts of Europe and North America, but with a general tendency to elevated habitats. It is recorded by Linnæus, however, as rare in Swedish Lapland and growing in woods, and similar localities are assigned to it in Canada and in the adjoining states of the American Union.

Lycopodium alpinum. Savin-leaved Club-Moss. Tab. XVII.

Stem creeping: branches ascending, dichotomous, fasciculate. Leaves imbricated, in four rows, oblong lanceolate, keeled, acute, entire, appressed. Spikes sessile, oblong cylindrical, terminal; their scales ovate lanceolate, flat.

Lycopodium alpinum, *Linnæus*. *E. B.* 234. Generally adopted.

Frequent and often very abundant on the mountains and high moorlands of the north of England, Wales, Scotland, and Ireland, but, as the specific name implies, only to be met with in districts of considerable elevation. The stems are exceedingly tough and almost woody, creeping and rooting at intervals like those of the Common Club-Moss, which frequently accompanies and interlaces with it, and which they emulate in length and tenacity. The branches, from two to four or five inches high, spring in tufts from the rooted parts of the stem, dividing repeatedly in a dichotomous manner, all the divisions terminating on, or nearly on, the same level, and thus forming compact shrub-like groups. Both stems and branches are completely clothed with leaves, more or less densely imbricated, in four rows, which, differing in size and form on the alternate sides of the barren branches, give them the ap-

Lycopodium alpinum.

Lycopodium Selago.

pearance of being somewhat flattened in one direction. The leaves are oblong approaching to lanceolate and rather obtuse than pointed, with an indistinct keel or midrib, and destitute of serratures. The fruit-bearing spikes terminate the upper divisions of the older branches, and, owing to the dichotomous character of the latter, are usually in pairs; they are about three-quarters of an inch in length, rather thicker than the branches, and of a paler hue; their scales or bracts are broad at the lower part which covers the theca, but narrower above, terminating somewhat obtusely like the leaves. The general hue is a dull bluish-green, but the spikes are yellowish, especially as they approach maturity about the end of July.

Of the properties of this plant but little is recorded that can be depended upon, except that it communicates a yellow dye to wool. Sir W. J. Hooker, in his 'Journal of a Tour in Iceland,' 1809, remarks upon its employment by the inhabitants of that island to the following effect:—"A vast heap of *Lycopodium alpinum* lying before the priest's house drew my attention, and, on inquiry, I found that it was used for the purpose of giving their *wadmal* (woollen cloth) a yellow dye; which is done by merely boiling the cloth in water, with a quantity of the *Lycopodium* and some leaves of *Vaccinium uliginosum*. The colour imparted by this process, to judge from some cloth shown me, was a pale and pleasant, though not a brilliant yellow." Other species of the genus yield a similar colour, among which is the continental *L. complanatum*, a plant often confounded with the present by the earlier botanists.

The Alpine or Savin-leaved Club-Moss is a very elegant species, well worthy of cultivation, and from my own small experience not more difficult to grow than its more common and more generally distributed congener, *L. clavatum*; but the same uncertainty, arising from the circumstances under which it is usually obtained, attends its introduction.

In geographical distribution, the tendency to elevated habitats appears to be the only limit to its extension in the temperate and colder districts of the northern hemisphere. The distinction between the European plant and the Canadian, *L. sabinæfolium* of Pursh, appears at least very problematical.

Lycopodium Selago. Fir Club-Moss. Tab. XVIII.

Stem short, erect or slightly decumbent: branches fastigiate, pichotomous, level-topped. Leaves densely imbricated, obscurely eight-rowed, very rigid, linear-lanceolate, acuminate, entire. Thecæ in the axils of the leaves.

Lycopodium Selago, *Linnæus*. *E. B.* 233. Generally adopted.

Frequent, and often very abundant, on heaths and barren sandy and stony uplands in most parts of the kingdom, though apparently preferring those which are elevated above the surrounding parts of the country. In mountainous and rocky districts especially, it is one of the most common and generally distributed of our indigenous species, and occupies in many places a greater elevation than any of them, *L. annotinum* perhaps excepted. The plants are like little compact bushes, varying in height, according to the soil or degree of exposure, from two or three inches to a span. When sheltered from the wind the growth is usually rigidly erect, but when exposed to its influence, the weight of the compact tuft in the larger plants occasions them to assume a decumbent position, and sometimes, rooting thus, the prostrate stem acquires a considerable length, and a habit is induced so different to that ordinarily met with, that it might at first sight be regarded as belonging to another species. The stems and branches, repeatedly dichotomous, are closely imbricated with rigid, glossy, linear-lanceolate acuminate leaves, obliquely disposed in eight rows, an arrangement most readily observed by holding the ends of the branches perpendicular to the eye. The fructification is very unlike that of any other British Lycopodium: no spikes are formed, but the thecæ are developed singly in the axils of the ordinary leaves, most abundantly, but by no means exclusively, towards the upper parts of the branches; indeed they are not unfrequently found throughout the plant: their production seems to take place at a certain age, or rather under a certain condition that occurs at periods varying in different individuals, and is associated with a peculiarity, unnoticed by any botanical author since it was referred to by Dillenius as a newly observed fact, in his 'Historia Muscorum,' until Mr. Newman called attention to it by the following passage in the 'History of British Ferns and Allied Plants:'—"On the Welsh mountains I have observed that only a portion of the plants appear to be in a thriving and healthy condition, the larger ones almost invariably being loaded with fructification, and exhibiting symptoms of incipient decay. With the exception of Dillenius, I think no author has noticed this peculiarity; and this learned writer rationally concludes that each plant exists for a definite term and then dies. Whether the term of its existence be biennial, triennial, or longer, I leave for future observers to decide; but I have not the slightest doubt that its existence has a fixed term, as suggested by the great muscologist." The condition of the older fructifying plants alluded to by Mr. Newman, attracted my attention in the Snowdon district many years back, but not being at that time familiar with the celebrated work of Dillenius, I was at a loss to account for a phænomenon which afterwards furnished an undeniable explanation of the fact that specimens removed in the fertile condition uniformly died, while the others survived one, two, or even three years, and then died with the rudiments of fructification in the axils of their leaves. We may therefore, I think, regard *Lycopodium Selago* as a plant of biennial character, which, like others of the same ordinary duration, occasionally survives for a longer period when circumstances postpone the production of the thecæ.

It is frequently viviparous; small leafy buds, that eventually drop off and vegetate, being developed in lieu of thecæ in the axils of some of the upper leaves of the branches. This mode of reproduction is very common, especially at great elevations, and, as in similar circumstances among the Mosses as well as the higher orders of vegetation, seems to be often, but not constantly, attended by non-development of the true seeds or sporules. One of the middle branches on our plate represents two of these buds in the natural position: Mr. Newman has illustrated very fully their structure and œconomy (page 378 of the work above quoted), but an extract would be too long for our pages, and it will be sufficient further to remark that the buds in question afford a very convenient mode of introducing the plant to cultivation, as they quickly root and grow freely under glass. As they are often produced in considerable numbers, it is probable that in certain situations they constitute the principal source of propagation.

The Highlanders and other northern peoples employ this plant, instead of alum, as a mordant to fix their colours in dyeing: with Brazil-wood especially it is said to produce a beautiful and permanent blue; *L. clavatum* and other species are sometimes used with a similar effect. They likewise prepare from it an irritating ointment, and occasionally administer the decoction or infusion internally as an emetic and cathartic: Linnæus refers to a similar use of its emetic quality in Sweden, where it is sold by many of the medicine venders, under the name of *Muscus catharticus*; but he adds, on the authority of Rothmann, that it is violent in its operation, and apt to induce vertigo and convulsions, unless given in very small doses. The same decoction, he informs us, is used by the country people, as a detergent wash to destroy the vermin that infest their swine and cattle.

The specific name *Selago*, according to De Theis, is derived from the Celtic *sel*, sight, and *jach*, salutary, it being once held a valuable remedy in diseases of the eye, for which purpose the ointment is stated to be still employed in the Highlands of Scotland, producing an effect somewhat similar to that prepared from Savin (*Juniperus Sabina*).

The geographical range of the normal form of *Lycopodium Selago* seems to be limited to the Eastern Hemisphere, where it is very common in northern Europe and the adjoining parts of Asia. In

North America, *L. lucidulum* of Pursh, *L. reflexum* of Schkuhr, resembles it very nearly in habit, in the axillary position of the thecæ, in the frequent development of deciduous buds or bulbs, and in the octoserial disposition of the leaves, and, with the exception of the latter being reflexed instead of densely imbricated, I am unable to discover any decisive feature of distinction; the toothed character of the margin is not constant in Canadian specimens and is sometimes present in the European species, the leaves of which, though never so widely divaricated or spreading as those of the American plant, occasionally display, the lower ones especially, a tendency to become reflexed. The moister habitats affected by *L. lucidulum*, "low sphagnous grounds and on the banks of shady rivulets," would be alone sufficient to produce a more important alteration in general character. These remarks apply equally to objections respecting the identity of other species of *Lycopodium* regarded as common to the two hemispheres.

Lycopodium inundatum. Marsh Club-Moss. Tab. XIX.

Stem creeping, short: branches few, simple, short, erect. Leaves scattered, linear, entire, acute, curved upwards. Spikes terminating the short erect branches.

Lycopodium inundatum, *Linnæus. E. B.* 239. Generally adopted.

Occasionally found on moist boggy heaths in different parts of the kingdom, but it is a local rather than a common species, and more frequent in the southern counties of England than elsewhere; in alpine districts especially its occurrence is rare. It seems to have a very slight attachment to the soil, a circumstance that accounts for its preference for places from which the turf has been recently pared off, leaving little or no other vegetation to contend with; in such situations it is frequently so abundant as to cover the dark peaty soil, which is essential to its more luxuriant state of growth, with a verdure of the brightest green. The specific name refers to its preference to spots upon which water accumulates occasionally during the winter rather than to any tendency to aqueous habitats, as it will be generally met with in situations so well drained as to be perfectly dry during the heats of summer, and over a subsoil of sand or gravel. The stem creeps closely pressed to the ground, rooting at intervals by strong fibres that scarcely reach half an inch below the surface; it is very rarely branched, on account of its peculiar habit of dying away annually, leaving only the extreme growing point, from which a new extension takes place the following year; hence a specimen producing two or more prostrate branches during one summer, as is occasionally the case, would, in the succeeding one, form as many distinct plants. The leaves are narrow-

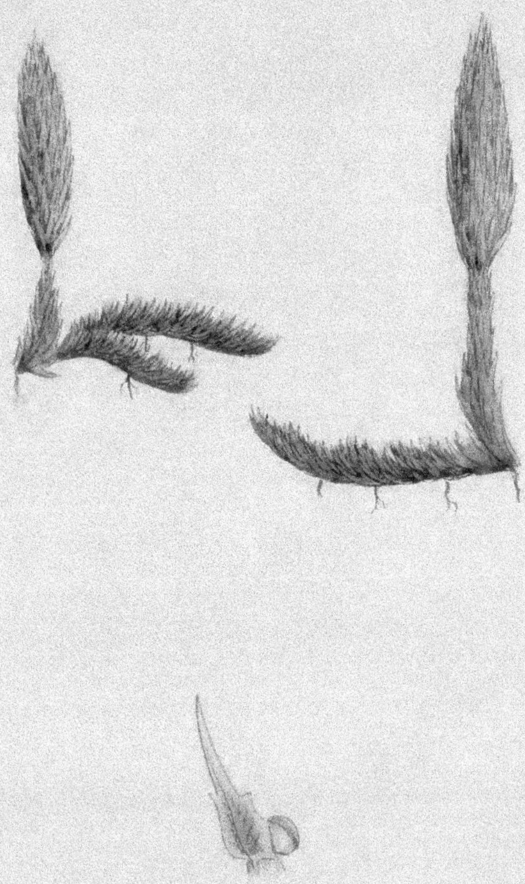

Lycopodium inundatum.

Lycopodium selaginoides.

linear and acute, curving upwards, and of a bright yellowish-green hue. The erect branches described in the above specific character are not always present, especially where the prostrate stem itself becomes branched, their elevation being associated with the production of fruit: they are usually single, from one to three inches in height, and terminate in a solitary spike occupying about half or one-third of their length, whose leaves, bearing the thecæ in their axils, are broader towards the base than those of the stem, and are occasionally furnished with a tooth-like projection on each side. The thecæ are nearly globular, and ripen about the end of August or the beginning of September.

For cultivation, the turf containing the plants should be cut off without interfering with the roots, taking with the mass a sufficient surface to admit of the following annual extension. The failure, which is complained of by most persons, of their efforts to grow this interesting, though not showy species, appears to be owing to want of management in this respect and to the planting in loose soil; the latter error very slight observation of its natural habitats would teach us to avoid, as the ground that bears it always has the appearance of having been beaten and washed, so as to leave no shifting particles upon the surface. Its very short roots are ill adapted to fix it in the artificial compost employed for growing Ferns and many of its more deeply rooting congeners.

Lycopodium Selaginoides. Lesser Alpine Club-Moss. Tab. XX.

Stem creeping, much branched, sinuous. Leaves scattered, lanceolate, ciliato-dentate. Spikes solitary, sessile at the extremity of short erect leafy branches.

Lycopodium Selaginoides, *Linnæus*. *E. B.* 1148. Generally adopted by English botanists. Selagiuella spinulosa, *Koch*.

In boggy ground, on the sides of hills, and especially about rills and waterfalls, in the rocky districts of the north of England, Wales, Scotland, and Ireland, this is not unfrequent. The numerously branched prostrate stems root at intervals like those of the other procumbent species, but appear to take very slight hold of the soil; they are slender, leafy throughout, and spread by their somewhat sinuous branches much in the manner of those of *L. clavatum*; the plant is, however, of comparatively very small size, and otherwise totally different in habit. The leaves are grass-green, shining, lanceolate, and rather spreading; and are remarkable among the species of this genus for their deeply serrated margins, the serratures terminating in fine cilia-like points, whence the English name Prickly Club-Moss, bestowed upon it by some writers. The fructification is developed upon the older branches, two or three of which in the course of the summer become elongated and, at first assuming an ascending position, eventually grow erect, varying from one to three inches in height, according to situation and soil. The extremity of the branch gradually assumes a different character from that which it had in the procumbent state, becoming thicker and club-shaped, with leaves larger and broader at the base, in the axils of which two kinds of thecæ are developed, those toward the upper part of the spike opening with two valves and discharging an impalpable powder, those of the lower part separating with three divisions and discovering three or four large grains nearly the size of poppy seed. This is the only British Lycopodium in which the two forms of the reproductive apparatus mentioned in the generic character are uniformly to be met with; in the others the occurrence of the granule-bearing thecæ is either rare or they are but sparingly distributed; I have found them on three species, *L. clavatum*, *alpinum*, and *Selago*, and close examination of these and others may probably lead to the establishment of the fact that their production is less limited than hitherto supposed: their frequent occurrence in the imported powder is not perhaps a circumstance of importance in the question, as, though chiefly the produce of the Common Club-Moss, we know not what other species may be collected with it in those parts of the continent whence the upply is obtained.

With the exception of the smaller size of the specimens, there does not appear to me to be any essential difference between the Canadian plant under this name and our English one.

I have not had *L. Selaginoides* under cultivation. The only plants that have come under my notice in this part of England were kept under a bell-glass, in which state they had existed two years, but no fertile branches had made their appearance last August, and the specimens had not a healthy aspect.

CHARACEÆ.

These are aquatic plants, and always grow submerged, preferring stagnant to running water, though occasionally met with in slow rivers. They are of annual duration only, and but slightly attached to the muddy bottom of the ditches and pools that are their favourite habitats. Their slender, wiry stems are more or less branched in a dichotomous manner, very brittle, and conspicuously jointed, each articulation being surrounded by a whorl of slender branchlets. In the subgenus *Nitella*, the appearance of the stem is that of a single transparent tube divided transversely at intervals. In *Chara*, properly so called, the central tube, or rather succession of tubular cells, is surrounded by a number of smaller ones; and the whole is generally encrusted by a comparatively thick coating of calcareous matter, carbonate or phosphate of lime, a secretion of the plant itself, and bearing some analogy in its disposition to the siliceous particles in the stems of *Equisetum*, and, according to Sir D. Brewster, exhibiting similar optical phænomena.

The organs of reproduction are of two kinds, axillary to the branchlets and in many instances accompanying each other:—1. *Globules* of a red or orange colour, consisting externally of eight triangular valves, enclosing a mucilaginous fluid, investing spiral filaments, and cells containing minute reddish granules. 2. *Nucules* of an oval form, composed externally of two envelopes, the outer very thin and transparent, the inner formed of five or more spirally twisted filaments, enclosing a cavity containing minute granules which appear eventually to combine into a single seed. The extremities of the spiral filaments often form a crest on the summit of the nucule.

These curious bodies have been variously described by different observers, a circumstance attributable, perhaps, rather to the different periods of incipient or matured growth under which such examinations have been made, than to error in the appreciation of their results. For more detailed accounts of the complicated structures of both *globules* and *nucules*, the reader is referred to the succeeding descriptions of those of *Chara flexilis* and *C. aspera*.

Young plants may be freely raised from the *nucules* of all the species, which, however, certainly partake more of the character of deciduous buds than of seeds; the spiral filaments of the envelope representing a whorl of branchlets. The notion that the *globules* are stamens, or that they fulfil an analogous function, is no longer tenable: the remark by Wallroth of having witnessed their germination, I have myself seen attested by the growth of those of *C. aspera* in several successive years; the plants produced were always clustered, two or more together, and presented a striking contrast to those springing solitarily from the nucules of the same.

The Characeæ are widely distributed, inhabiting stagnant waters, both fresh and salt, in almost every part of the world. The species are all of a dull greenish hue, and generally give out a disagreeable fetid odour. Their œconomical value is to be sought in the ministry of nature, under which, in common with many other aquatic vegetables lower in the scale of organization, they constitute an important series. They tend to maintain a healthy condition of the water in which they grow, and at the same time assist, by their annual development and subsidence, in elevating the bottoms of pools and lakes, until they are brought sufficiently near the surface to be further solidified by the successive vegetation of the numerous species of Rush, Carex, Equisetum, &c.; and subsequently thus aid in forming a soil endued with the essence of fertility, and requiring only modification by the art and industry of man to convert it to his immediate use and benefit. The quantity of calcareous matter elaborated by some of the Charas—so great as to have acquired for them the vulgar name of Stoneworts—is an admirable adaptation for this purpose, like the siliceous deposits, before alluded to, of the Equisetums. The share indeed that such plants have had, even from a distant geological epoch, in increasing the solid surface of our present lands, is evinced by the abundance of their fossil remains in the freshwater strata overlying the chalk in the Isle of Wight, about Paris, and elsewhere. These remains consist both of the stems and nucules, but chiefly the latter, called by Lamarck, *Gyrogonites*, under the impression that they were the shells of a testaceous animal: their identification, together with the important fact, that those of *Chara hispida* abound in the calcareous marls of Forfarshire, while the same species exists profusely in a living state in the lakes that still cover portions of their surface, may be regarded as among the most beautiful and interesting discoveries of modern science. Dr. Lindley remarks that "the fetid effluvium arising from them is regarded as very unhealthy, and one of the sources of the malaria of the Campagna of Rome." The salubrity of this or any corresponding odour is questionable; but whether the atmosphere of that renowned region of sickness and death, or that of our English swamps and fens, would be improved by the absence of plants that subsist upon the impurities of their waters, is doubtful; we expect neither the sweep nor the scavenger to exhale Eau de Cologne, but the value of their services as ministers of cleanliness is not less certain, nor their efforts for the abatement of nuisances less desirable and praiseworthy.

In consequence of the exceeding tenuity of the cellular membrane constituting the organic structure of these plants, and its all but perfect transparency in *Nitella*, as likewise in *Chara* itself, when the calcareous incrustation is removed, the movement of the vital fluid contained in their tubes or cells may be distinctly seen by the assistance of a microscope. The public attention was first directed to this curious phenomenon by Professor Amici of Modena, and similar movements have been since traced in the cells of a variety of other plants, but not in any affording equal facility for examination. The fluid contents of each elongated cell or tube form a rotating current always in the same direction, ascending on the outer side, or on that farthest from the axis of the plant, and descending on the inner, although no partition exists between the two courses, as is evinced by the fact, that of the granules or molecules floating in this fluid, one or more, pursuing a course upward or downward with one side of the current, will be occasionally attracted into the other and forcibly carried away in the opposite direction, It is by the presence of these molecules, which are more opaque than the medium in which they float, that the circulation, or *rotation* as it is technically termed, of the containing fluid is distinguishable: they vary considerably in dimensions, but the largest cannot be distinctly traced with a lens whose focus is more than $\frac{1}{13}$ of an inch, and to follow their movements successfully in the aggregate, the higher powers of the modern achromatic microscope are required. The velocity of the motion has been variously stated as estimated by different observers; but it is dependent upon the time of year, and, more especially, upon the surrounding temperature; below 50° Fahr. the movement is either so slow as to be scarcely perceptible, or it ceases altogether.

The claim of this order of plants to rank among the "Fern Allies," however incongruous that assemblage undoubtedly is, must be considered as more vague and uncertain than that of any of the preceding. Its place in any arrangement has never been satisfactorily determined. Linnæus commenced by placing the genus *Chara* among the flowerless plants of his class *Cryptogamia*; and afterwards, regarding the *globules* as *stamens*, and the *nucules* as *pistils*, removed it to the Phanerogamous or flowering series. Later botanists have been equally divided as to its real affinities, and, after having been successively transferred from one group of aquatic plants to another, and eventually established as a distinct natural order, it still remains an anomaly in botanical classification. In certain points of general structure it approaches that of the Confervoid Algaceæ, but the nature of its reproductive organs is too complicated to admit of its being placed so near the bottom of the structural scale; and, though Dr. Lindley in his "Vegetable Kingdom" has adopted this allotment of Characeæ for convenience sake, he does not fail to point to its other affinities. In the second edition of "English Botany" I placed Characeæ after Equisetaceæ, remarking that there is sufficient resemblance between the nucules of *Chara* and the sporules of *Equisetum*, independent of many peculiarities in mutual habit and organization, to warrant its temporary position as a reduced form of that order. The resemblances in question are very striking, if we set aside the fact that the Charas are destitute of any true vascular or woody tissue—in both orders we shall then have stems interrupted at intervals by articulations, and having the central cavities or internodes encompassed by a series of smaller ones; earthy secretions constituting an integral portion of the organic structure; the absence of true leaves; the whorled branchlets; and, lastly, the reproductive organs so evidently formed by modification of such whorls at the base of an embryo stem, as exemplified in the spirals covering the nucules of *Chara*, and the spirally curved stamen-like processes investing the sporules of *Equisetum*. Critically considered, these analogies may be rather specious than real; but it is to be lamented that a similar objection may apply, and with equal force, to many other items of vegetable classification, founded upon so-called natural affinities which have no firmer foundation than such resemblances.

The globules and nucules being in some species developed upon the same, and in others upon different plants, these latter are described as being *monœcious* or *diœcious*.

CHARA.

GEN. CHAR. The same as that of the Order, of which it is probably the only genus extant.

The name *Chara* is of uncertain derivation; it was applied by the ancients to some aquatic plant with edible roots, memorable as being resorted to, under a scarcity of provisions, by Cæsar's soldiers, during the war in Spain against Pompey. Linnæus adopted it for the genus before us without any reference to its former signification beyond that of corresponding habitat. The species are now usually arranged under two subgenera.

1. NITELLA.

Plants more or less pellucid; not striated; joints simply tubular.

CHARA FLEXILIS. Flaccid Nitella. TAB. XXI.

Plant monœcious. Stems slender, smooth, flexible, pellucid. Branchlets pointed, nearly equally forked, or trifid. Nucules and globules approximate in the forks of the branchlets, ebracteate.

Chara flexilis, *Linnæus. E. B.* 1070. C. nidifica, *some authors.* Nitella flexilis, *Agardh, Syst. Alg. E. B.* ed. 2.

A very weak, slender plant, far from unfrequent in ditches and other stagnant waters. The whorled branchlets are generally forked or trifid at the extremity, but occasionally simple, and sometimes so much divided as to give them a clustered appearance; which latter state has probably occasioned it to be confounded with another species, as *C. nidifica.* The nucules and globules are produced in the forks of the branchlets of the upper whorls, and are, for the most part, unaccompanied by the short bracteal appendages or modification of secondary whorls which characterize those of *C. Smithii* and some others: they are sometimes found side by side, but seem to be most frequently solitary. Mr. Babington describes the nucules as having six striæ, which is perhaps generally the case; but the spirals of these curious organs are too liable

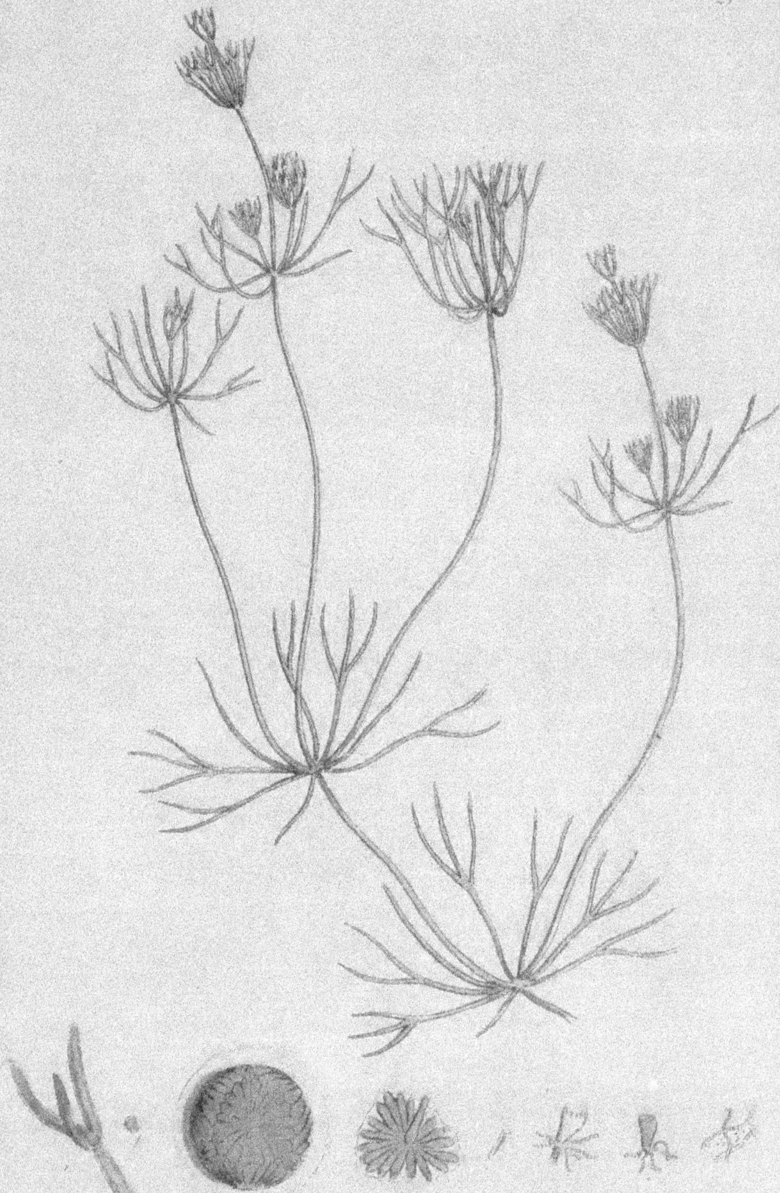

Chara flexilis

to vary in number to be depended upon as features of much value in specific distinction.

The following remarks upon the structure of the globules in this species are extracted from the description given of them by the Rev. M. J. Berkeley, under his notice of *Chara Hedwigii* in E. B. Supp. 2762, and are valuable as conveying a general idea of their complicated development:—

"The globules are not perfectly globose, but slightly obovate, with a very short pedicel: beneath the transparent external membrane, the surface is divided into eight equilateral triangles by one horizontal and two vertical great circles; in the centre of each of these triangles is a subrotund area, from which lines radiate regularly, so as to form obovate oblong cells,—the line which radiates from one triangle running to the middle of the outer boundary of the corresponding cell in the adjacent triangle. The globules are filled with a mass of transparent, colourless, flexuose, confervoid filaments, with articulations about equal in length and breadth; and minute orange spherules, whose diameter is less than that of the filaments, are contained in the radiating cells of the triangles, which are raised on the inner side. These spherules are immersed in gelatine, as the green spherules of the stems are. In the centre of each of the spherical triangles into which the surface is divided, on the under side, arises perpendicularly an orange-coloured cylinder which bears on the top a bell-shaped cup, which is at first orange, being filled with the same granules as the cells, afterwards pellucid and striate or plicate at the margin. At the place where the cup is attached to its pedestal, the confervoid filaments originate.—It appears that the orange matter contained in the radiating cells has access, by means of the hollow pedestal and bell, to the curved filaments. The pedestal is certainly hollow, as, when dry, the orange mass contracts exactly as the colouring matter does in the joint of a *Conferva*." Such appears, with slight variation, to be the general structure of the globules throughout this genus; and that they, as well as the nucules, are modifications of the primary organs of the plant, viz. of the stem and branchlets, will be readily admitted by the attentive examiner; but, beyond this, our knowledge of their relative functions is at present little more than speculative. The globules attain maturity and fall off, generally, long before the nucules, the parts composing them separating more or less at that period: but the fact, that young plants spring from them, at once decides against the supposition that they fulfil the office of anthers.

The structure above described is well illustrated by Mr. Berkeley's magnified figures of the parts mentioned. Figure *a* represents the divided extremity of one of the branchlets bearing a globule; *b*, a globule separated; *c*, the same greatly magnified;

d, one of the triangles seen from within, with its pedestal and radiating cells; *e*, the pedestal when dry; *f*, one of the cups, with a portion of its pedestal and accompanying confervoid filaments; *g*, the same cup and filaments as they appear at an earlier stage, without the pedestal; *h*, the filaments and granules.

Chara syncarpa. Twin-fruited Nitella. Tab. XXII.

Plant diœcious. Stems slender, equal, smooth, flexible, pellucid. Branchlets bluntish, apiculate, nearly equally forked or trifid. Nucules or globules in the forks of the branchlets, ebracteate.

Chara syncarpa, *Thuillier*. *Babington, Man. Brit. Bot.*

The striking difference between this and *C. flexilis*, as shown on our plates, must not be depended upon, as the two forms present every intermediate gradation. I have not found them together, but am informed that they not unfrequently occupy the same waters. The distribution of submerged aquatic plants is at all times a subject difficult to be ascertained, and although that of the present is apparently limited, it is probably not more so than others which are regarded as common. To previous habitats in Sussex, Cambridgeshire, Caernarvonshire and Galway, we may add the pool on Wandsworth Common, Surrey, in which *Stratiotes aloides* abounds, and a ditch in the meadows near Dulwich College, where it grows in company with *Ranunculus pantothrix*, as well as other stagnant waters in the same county. If a distinct species, which is very doubtful, the leading characteristic must be sought in the peculiar bluntness of the branchlets, so dissimilar to those of *C. flexilis*, and their apiculate termination, both of which are exhibited in the magnified views on the right side of our plate. The diœcious disposition of the nucules and globules, though usual, is not constant; they attain their maturity in June.

Chara translucens. Translucent Nitella. Tab. XXIII.

Plant monœcious. Stems thick, equal, smooth, flexible, pellucid. Sterile branchlets spreading, simple, not articulated. Fertile whorls of small bi- or tri-furcate branchlets. Nucules small, oblong, two or three together, just below the bract-like branchlets that surround the solitary terminal globule.

Chara translucens, Persoon. *E. B.* 1855. Nitella translucens, *Agardh, Syst. Alg.* 124. *E. B.* ed. 2. 1467.

Found in deep stagnant water only, and, though widely distributed, far from frequent. The thickness of the stems and branchlets

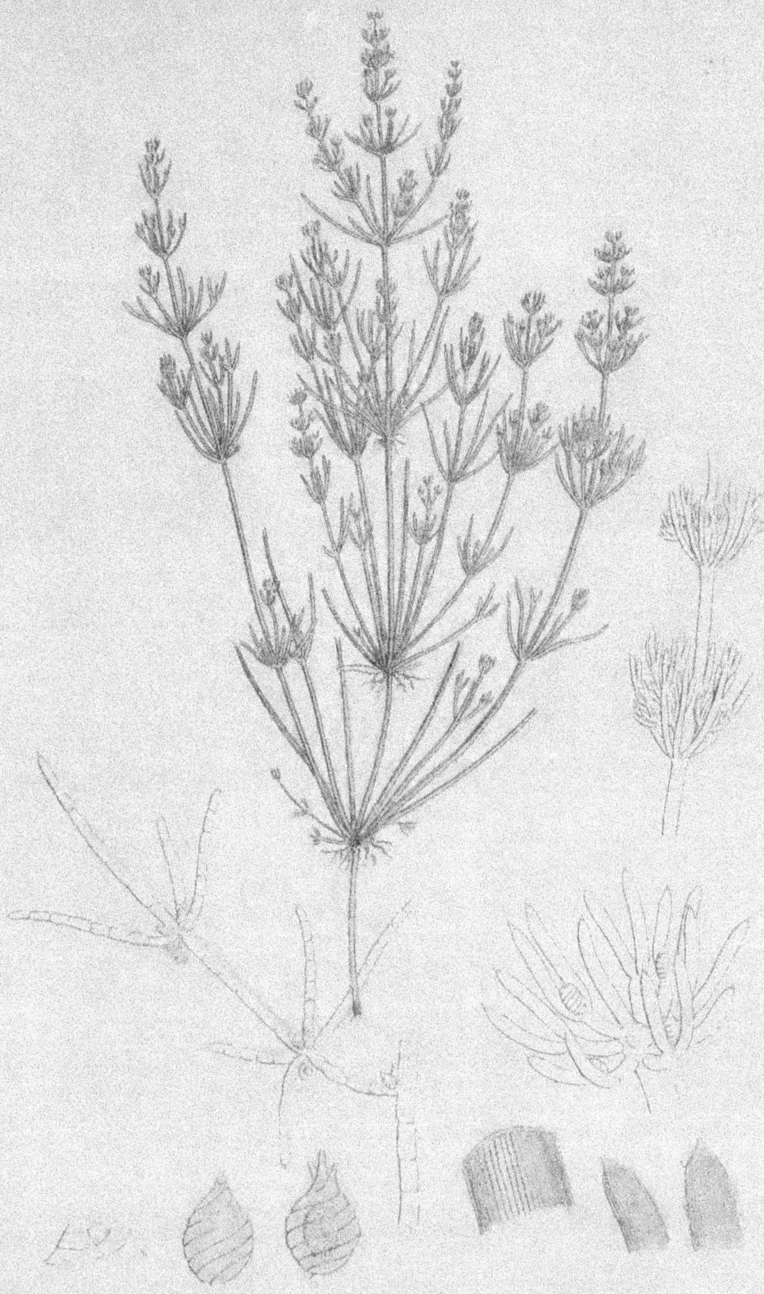

Chara syncarpa

Chara translucens.

Chara gracilis

varies in different situations, but is usually very striking compared with that of the other species of the subgenus *Nitella*. The branchlets of the fertile whorls, being small, closely placed, and tending to an erect position, have the appearance of being capitate. The number of spirals composing the nucules is from five to seven; the relative situation of these organs to the solitary globule is shown in our magnified figure. The whole plant is very smooth and glossy, and the greater size and transparency of its long continuous cells render it the most valuable of all the species for microscopical examination of the rotating fluid. It may be found in fructification from July to September.

CHARA MUCRONATA. Mucronate Nitella.

"Plant monœcious. Stems slender, equal, flexible, transparent. Branchlets strongly mucronate, nearly equally forked or trifid. Nucules and globules together at the forks of the branchlets, without bracts."

Chara mucronata, *Braun*. *Babington, Man. Brit. Bot.*

Found by Mr. Borrer in a marsh-ditch at West Grinstead, Sussex. I have not seen this plant. Mr. Babington describes it as being "rather thick;" the secondary branchlets once or twice forked, and the terminal subdivisions rather shorter than the others. The nucules have four or five spirals, and mature in July.

As a species distinct from *C. translucens*, the above description is not very satisfactory. The apiculate termination of the forks of the fertile branchlets is shown in our figure of the latter plant, and the term *mucronate*, though nearly synonymous, is scarcely applicable to any such appendage to the extremities of the branchlets of this family; the point in question being generally formed by an abortive or contracted cell. The absence of bracts affords a character of greater apparent value, but even this is equivocal, as the organs so called, in other species or varieties, are only modifications of branchlets.

CHARA GRACILIS. Slender Nitella. TAB. XXIV.

Plant monœcious. Stems very slender, equal, smooth, flexible, pellucid. Branchlets in loose whorls, repeatedly divided; terminal segments apiculate, shorter than the others. Nucules and globules produced together, one of each, at the subdivisions of the branchlets, ebracteate.

Chara gracilis, *Smith*. *E. B.* 2140. Nitella gracilis, *Agardh, Syst. Alg.* 125. *E. B.* ed. 2. 1470.

Found by Mr. Borrer in boggy pools in St. Leonard's Forest, Sussex. By others in Llyn Idwel, North Wales, and in Jersey.

There is a peculiarity in the general aspect of this plant, especially when viewed in water, that would induce the observer to regard it as a perfectly distinct species. The comparatively small size, and the almost hair-like tenuity of the whorled barren branchlets, that spread out diverging so much from the stem as often to become deflexed, added to the compact, almost capitate appearance of the fertile ones, render it the most elegant of its kind. It is of a pale green hue, glossy, and almost transparent. The fructification is axillary to the subdivisions of the upper branchlets, and unaccompanied by short bracteal appendages. A single nucule and globule generally grow side by side, but they are often solitary, and sometimes, as observed by Mr. Wilson, to whom we are indebted for its Llyn Idwel habitat, occur on separate plants, thus departing from the monœcious character. The nucules are subglobose, proportionally large, with from four to six spirals, and, with the globules, are perfected in August.

The different size and more complicated division of the branchlets, both exceedingly arbitrary features of distinction, alone separate this from *C. flexilis.*

CHARA TENUISSIMA.

"Plant monœcious. Stems slender, equal, flexible, transparent. Branchlets short, in dense, compact, subglobose whorls, repeatedly divided into from three to seven segments; terminal segments mucronate, longer than the others. Globules and nucules each solitary, but together at the subdivisions of the branchlets without bracts."

Chara tenuissima, *Desvaux. Babington, Man. Brit. Bot.*

Found by Mr. C. C. Babington in peaty ditches in Cambridgeshire. I have only seen this in the dried state, in which it is scarcely possible to trace any material difference between it and *C. gracilis.* It must, however, be admitted, that preserved specimens of these slender aquatics afford little foundation for inquiry into specific distinction. Mr. Babington's description presents some apparently important characteristics at variance with such a conclusion: "Very small and slender. Branchlets very much divided, forming little globose compact masses, which are often much incrusted. Nucules subglobose, with from six to eight striæ, minute, but three times the diameter of the branchlets, and placed outside of them. Globules much larger than the nucules." Fructification matures in July and August.

CHARA SMITHII. Smith's Nitella. TAB. XXV.

Plant diœcious. Stems slender, equal, smooth, flexible, pellucid. Branchlets blunt: those of the primary whorls simple, elon-

Chara Smithii

26

Chara prolifera

gated, sterile; those of the axillary branches numerous, densely crowded, bearing three secondary branchlets (bracts) at the articulation of the terminal joint. Globules stalked, subtended by the three bracts. (Nucules unknown?)

Chara Smithii, *Babington*. C. nidifica, *Smith*. *E. B.* 1703. Nitella nidifica, *E. B.* ed. 2. 1469.

The plant figured in 'English Botany,' Tab. 1703, under the name of *Chara nidifica*, as a native of salt-water ditches in some of the southern and eastern shores of England, is involved in some obscurity: that it is not that so called by some continental botanists, seems probable at least, though not altogether decided. The simple, much elongated branchlets of the primary whorls, and the crowded and divided characters of those bearing the fructification, though sufficient to hold it distinct from *C. flexilis* and its near allies, are equally characteristic of the two following, *C. prolifera* and *C. Borreri*, as is likewise the presence of the three bracts, so called. The stalked condition of the globules may or may not be constant, but as it occasionally occurs in others where that curious organ is generally sessile, it can assuredly not be regarded of much importance in the present instance.

The figure and description refer to specimens found by Mr. Borrer in a ditch at Lancing, Sussex.

Chara prolifera. Proliferous Nitella. Tab. XXVI.

Plant monœcious. Stems slender, equal, flexible, pellucid. Branchlets blunt: those of the primary whorls simple, elongated, sterile, usually of three or four joints; those of the axillary branches numerous, densely crowded, bearing three secondary branchlets (bracts) at the articulation of the terminal joint. Globules sessile, accompanied by one or more nucules, subtended by the three bracts.

Chara prolifera, *Braun*. *Babington, Man. Brit. Bot.*

First noticed by Mr. Borrer, growing in ditches, at Cley, Norfolk, in 1806, and afterwards in Hayling Island, Hants, in May 1853. The following is his description of it in the latter habitat:— "The plants grow erect in dense clusters, a few inches high. Root of very slender, colourless, transparent fibres, with whorled finer fibres at the knots. Stems at about an inch from the base beset with a whorl of longish, blunt, pointed, barren branchlets, and divided into several primary branches, similarly whorled with branchlets, from the axils of which again grow short branches, and much crowded, shorter whorled branchlets. These last are curved upward and inward a little above the base, and at the point of curvature produce, on the upper side, a cluster of sessile globules and nucules intermixed, subtended by three, sometimes four, bracts shorter than the continuation of the branchlet; one of which bracts diverges at right angles from the under side of the branchlet, while the others are curved upward, clasping the fructification. Clusters of nucules are sometimes produced at the base of the branchlets likewise."

Mr. Borrer observes that the incrusted state of all his specimens was such as to render the three or four joints existing in each of the whorled branchlets with difficulty discernible, and this is not an uncommon circumstance with other species or varieties of *Nitella*, though apparently dependent in a great degree upon the character of the water in which they vegetate.

Chara Borreri. Borrer's Nitella.

"Plant monœcious. Stems slender, equal, flexible, pellucid. Branchlets strongly mucronate: those of the primary whorls simple, sterile, long, jointed; others on axillary branches, many densely crowded, bearing three short and one long bract at their first and sometimes second joining. Globules stalked or sessile, in company with several nucules, and subtended by the three shorter bracts."

Chara Borreri, *Babington, Man. Brit. Bot.* C. nidifica, *Borrer, E. B. Supp.* 2762, note.

The indefatigable botanist whose name this plant bears, found it in a marsh-ditch at Henfield, Sussex, about seven miles from the sea in a direct line, but occasionally affected by the tide, in July 1827. At the time, he seems to have regarded it as identical with that since named *C. prolifera,* found by him at Cley, in 1806, differing only in being of a larger size. Mr. Babington, while bestowing upon it the rank of a species, remarks upon its near resemblance to both the latter and *C. Smithii,* "but larger;" the "one long bract," in his specific description, above quoted, according with our terminal joint in those of the plants in question. The inconstancy in the development of the globules, either stalked or sessile, reduces its distinctive character to one simple feature, viz. the termination of the blunt branchlets in an apiculus.

Chara polysperma. Many-seeded Nitella.

"Plant monœcious. Stems slender, equal, flexible, transparent. Barren and fertile branchlets of the primary whorls once or twice unequally branched, middle branch longest: branchlets of axillary branches many, densely crowded, much subdivided into short joints, mostly finely pointed. Nucules and globules placed at the joinings of the branchlets between the lateral rays."

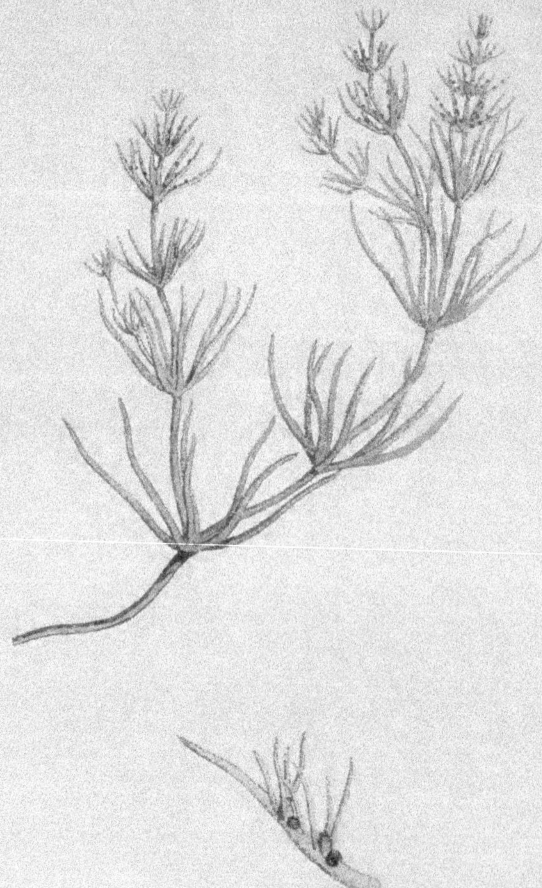

Chara vulgaris.

Chara polysperma, *Braun.* *Babington, Man. Brit. Bot.*

Found in running water, near Bury St. Edmunds, and Cambridge. Mr. Babington remarks that this species is distinguished from the three preceding by the absence of true bracts. Wanting recent specimens, his farther description is here adopted :—

"Small. Branches with two or three ascending branchlets, often again branched at their first joining; often, but not always, there is a simple branchlet beneath, and at right angles to the main branch at that point. Globules stalked, directed downwards. Nucules clustered, sessile, directed upwards."

There is much in the general aspect of this plant in favour of its claim to be considered a distinct species, which is more than can be said of many of the preceding. It is, indeed, the only one of those unfigured in our work, of which I regret that the incapability of obtaining living specimens at the required time, prevented us from illustrating by careful drawing and *bonâ-fide* description.

2. CHARA.

Plants more or less opaque, generally brittle; striated; joints compound, the central tube being surrounded by smaller ones, except toward the termination of the branches and branchlets.

Chara crinita. Bearded Chara.

"Plant diœcious. Stems slender, coarsely striated, thickly beset with setaceous spreading clustered spines. Branchlets abbreviated. Bracts whorled, slender, equal. Nucules narrowly oblong, shorter than the bracts."

Chara crinita, *Wallroth.* *Ann. Bot.* tab. 3. *Babington, Man. Brit. Bot.*

A native of stagnant brackish pools. Discovered by the Rev. W. L. P. Garnons, in Burdoch Pool, Falmouth, Cornwall. Stems erect, slender, smoothish, and rather flexible, slightly branched, pale green; coated with as many tubes as there are branchlets in each whorl. Whorls of eight or ten short branchlets, each of seven joints, with six bracts at each articulation. Nucules solitary, with about twelve spirals and a prominent crown.

I do not find either the number of spirals, or the prominence of the nucule crown formed by their extremities, at all constant in the present or in other species of this subgenus.

Chara vulgaris. Common Chara. Tab. XXVII.

Plant monœcious. Stems opaque, scabrous, brittle, obscurely striated. Whorled branchlets slender subulate: the fertile ones with many clusters of short ramuli or bracts on the upper or inner side, each numbering about four, two or more of which are much longer than the single nucule and globule which they accompany.

Chara vulgaris, *Linnæus?* *Agardh, Syst. Alg.* 128. *E. B.* 336.
Chara fœtida, *Braun.*

Common in ponds, ditches, and slow streams. The whole plant is of a yellowish or reddish-green hue, and usually so much incrusted as to render its structure very obscure. The stems vary with the depth of the water from a few inches to a foot in length; the apparently simple branchlets being about the length of the joints from the articulations of which they proceed. The upper whorls only are fertile. The nucules present twelve or thirteen spirals, and are terminated generally, but not always, by a short crown. In most instances, a single nucule and a single globule accompany each other in each little tuft of the bracts so called: they may be found throughout the summer.

It is generally spoken of as being the most fœtid of the British species of *Chara*, but this character seems much dependent upon the condition of the water in which it vegetates.

Chara hispida. Bristly Chara. Tab. XXVIII.

Plant monœcious. Stems opaque, thickened upwards, brittle, striated, bristly or spinulose. Branchlets elongate; the fertile ones especially with many whorls of short ramuli or bracts, the innermost of which are longer than the solitary nucule and globule they accompany.

Chara hispida, *Linnæus.* *Agardh, Syst. Alg.* 128. *E. B.* 463.

Not uncommon in ditches and turf-pools. The earthy incrustation is often so dense as to give the plant the appearance of a petrifaction, though in some habitats it is nearly wanting. The surface of the stems is minutely tuberculate, and more or less deeply and spirally grooved, in consequence of the arrangement of the small outer tubes. The bristles or spines vary in abundance in different localities. The branchlets are simple, subulate, pointed toward the extremity, and composed of about seven joints, with a whorl of from four to seven short bracts at each articulation. The ovate nucules occupy singly, with a globule, the upper side of the whorl of bracts, those to which they are axillary being longer than the others. The odour is very fœtid.

Chara tomentosa. Tomentose Chara.

Plants "diœcious? Stems thickened upwards, spirally sulcate, rough, brittle, with scattered obtuse papillæ. Branchlets incurved.

28

Chara hispida

Chara aspera

Bracts unilateral, ovate-oblong, mucronate-acute. Nucule shorter than the bract on each side of it, longer than the three in front."

Chara tomentosa, *Linnæus. Babington, Man. Brit. Bot.* C. latifolia, *Willdenow. Hooker, Icon.* 532.

Found in Belvidere Lake, Westmeath, Ireland. "Opake, whitish-green. Stems covered with minute tubercles; papillæ distinct, rather whorled, short, blunt on the prominent primary tubes." I am unacquainted with this species.

Chara aspera. Rough Chara. Tab. XXIX.

Plants diœcious. Stems very slender, nearly flexible, finely striated, beset with scattered, spreading or deflexed bristles. Branchlets of the whorls short, subulate; the fertile ones with numerous whorls of short slender ramuli or bracts, the two innermost of which are longer than the others, and accompany the solitary globule or nucule.

Chara aspera, *Willdenow. E. B. Supp.* 2738. *Agardh, Syst. Alg.* 130.

Not unfrequent in bog-pits and other stagnant waters in the North of England, in Wales, and Scotland. Stems one or two feet in length, varying with the depth of water, densely crowded; beset with slender, acute, straight, spreading or deflexed bristles, which seem to be scattered without order, or perhaps very irregularly whorled. At the base of each whorl of branchlets is a row of long appressed bristles, connected in pairs, of which one points upwards and the other downwards. Between the outer tubes and the central one, in both the stems and branches, is a green cellular substance, arranged in lines alternating with the striæ, and separated, or broken transversely at intervals, giving them a spotted appearance. The branchlets, from six to nine in a whorl, consist of about seven joints, each bearing at its articulation five or six slender spine-like bracts. I have never met with nucules and globules on the same plant, and they are uniformly solitary. The spirals of the former are about twelve or thirteen, and terminate in a rather prominent crown. The smaller magnified figures on our plate illustrate the structure of the globules, which does not materially differ from that already described under *C. flexilis*. Mr. Wilson, who discovered this species in Anglesea, and from whose specimens the figure in the E. B. Supp. was drawn, observed, that a coloured column, continuous with the short pedicel of the globule, extends to its centre, whence are given off the pedicels of the eight triangular facets that form the surface.

I have had this species under cultivation in a glass jar for several years, and, although no nucules appeared at any time upon it, young plants were copiously produced every spring.

Chara Hedwigii. Hedwig's Chara. Tab. XXX.

Plant monœcious. Stems opaque, smooth, slender, equal, somewhat brittle, striated. Branchlets elongated; the fertile ones with many whorls of short ramuli or bracts, of which the longest are shorter than the nucules. Nucules ovate.

Chara Hedwigii, *Agardh, Syst. Alg.* 129. *E. B. Supp.* 2762. Chara fragilis, *Babington, Man. Brit. Bot.*

Forms dense masses in stagnant water. Stems from six inches to a foot in length, slender, rather brittle; sometimes partially incrusted, but generally clear and of a bright green colour. Each joint appears, as shown in our magnified figure, to be divided about the middle, in consequence of the smaller surrounding tubes being articulated midway, as well as at the divisions of the central one. The branchlets consist of about eight joints, the three or four lower ones each bearing on the upper side an ovate nucule, much larger than the accompanying globules beneath it, supported by four slender bristle-like bracts, generally shorter than itself, while two or more, either rudimentary or very small ones, complete the whorl.

Chara pulchella. Beautiful Chara. Tab. XXXI.

Plant monœcious. Stems smooth, slender, equal, flexible, striated. Fertile branches with many tufts of short ramuli or bracts, of which the longest are about the length of the nucules. Nucules oblong.

Chara pulchella, *Wallroth. Borrer in E. B. Supp.* 2824. C. fragilis, *Babington.*

Found by Mr. Borrer in Sussex. Chiefly distinguished from *C. Hedwigii* by its flexible stems, and the oblong rather than ovate form of the nucules. The bracts are not so distinctly whorled. In publishing the figure, we are desirous of directing attention to these circumstances, not with a view of establishing it as a species, although its claim to be regarded as such is fully equal to that of some of the preceding, but to mark more strongly the very slender foundation upon which such distinctions are occasionally based. Mr. Babington is doubtless correct, in referring *C. Hedwigii* and *C. pulchella* of the English Botany to the same type; but, admitting this, the question must occur to every careful student in vegetable morphology, whether the sixteen or more acknowledged British species may not be capable of condensation, the greater number being mere accidental varieties of four or five primary forms.

Chara Hedwigii

Chara fragilis

INDEX.

Synonyms and names incidentally mentioned are printed in italics.

	Page	Tab.
Chara	36	
Chara	47	
aspera	49	29
Bearded	47	
Beautiful	50	31
Borreri	46	
Bristly	48	28
Common	47	27
crinita	47	
flexilis	40	21
fœtida	48	
fragilis	50	
gracilis	43	24
Hedwigii	50	30
hispida	48	28
latifolia	49	
mucronata	43	
nidifica	40	
nidifica	45	
nidifica	46	
polysperma	46	
prolifera	45	26
pulchella	50	
Rough	49	29
Smithii	44	25
syncarpa	42	22
tenuissima	44	
tomentosa	48	
translucens	42	23
vulgaris	47	27
Characeæ	36	
Club-Moss	26	
Club-Moss, Alpine	30	17
Common	27	15
Fir	31	18
Interrupted	29	16
Lesser Alpine	35	20
Marsh	34	19
Prickly	35	20
Dutch Rushes	14	
Equisetaceæ	3	
Equisetum	3	
Equisetum *alpinum*	13	
arenarium	17	11
arvense	5	1
Drummondii	6	2
elongatum	15	9
fluviatile	7	3
fluviatile	10	5
hyemale	13	8
limosum	10	5
Mackaii	15	9
Moorei	19	12
multiforme	16	
multiforme	17	11
nudum	13	
palustre	11	
palustre	12	6
polystachion	12	7
reptans	18	
sylvaticum	9	4
Telmateia	7	3
umbrosum	6	2
variegatum	17	11
Wilsoni	17	10
Ferns, Water	20	
Gyrogonites	38	
Horsetail	3	
Horsetail, Blunt-topped	6	2
Corn	5	1
Field	5	
Great	7	3
Mackay's	15	9
Marsh	12	6
Moore's	19	12
Rough	13	8
Smooth	10	5
Variegated	17	11
Wilson's	17	10
Wood	9	4

	Page	Tab.
Hydropterides	20	
Isoëtaceæ	20	
Isoëtes	20	
Isoëtes lacustris	21	13
Lycopodiaceæ	24	
Lycopodium	26	
Lycopodium alpinum	30	17
annotinum	29	16
catharticum	26	
clavatum	27	15
complanatum	31	
inundatum	34	19
lucidulum	34	
reflexum	34	
rubrum	26	
sabinæfolium	31	
Selaginoides	35	
Selago	31	18
Marsileaceæ	22	
Muscus catharticus	33	
Nitella	40	
Nitella, Borrer's	46	
Flaccid	40	21
Nitella *flexilis*	40	21
gracilis	43	
Many-seeded	46	
Mucronate	43	
nidifica	45	
prolifera	45	26
Slender	43	24
Smith's	44	25
translucens	42	
Translucent	42	23
Twin-fruited	42	
Pillwort	22	
Pilularia	22	
Pilularia globulifera	23	14
Quillwort	20	
Quillwort, Lake	21	13
Selaginella spinulosa	35	20
Shave-Grass	4	
Stoneworts	38	
Vegetable Sulphur	28	
Water Ferns	20	
Yatum condenado	27	

CPSIA information can be obtained
at www.ICGtesting.com
Printed in the USA
LVHW101237230223
740172LV00006B/500

9 783382 304140